# REVELATION

## A NOVEL

## MATT KUNZ

REVELATION
Copyright 2022 Matt Kunz

Twitter: @MattKunz59
www.facebook.com/mattkunzauthor
www.mattkunzwrites.com

This work is licensed under a Creative Common Attribution-Noncommercial-No Derivative Works 3.0 Unported License.

**Attribution** – You must attribute the work in the manner specified by the author or licensor (but not in any way that suggests that they endorse you or your use of the work).
**Noncommercial** – You may not use this work for commercial purposes.
**No Derivative Works** – You may not alter, transform, or build upon this work.

Inquiries about additional permissions should be directed to matt@mattkunzwrites.com

Print ISBN 978-0-9976298-7-3
Library of Congress Control Number – 2022902239
Author Photo: Matt Kunz of Milton, GA
Cover Design: Matt Kunz w/ www.canva.com
Bible Quotes are from: New American Bible for Catholics

Copyright © 2022 by Matt Kunz. All rights reserved. This book or any portion thereof may not be reproduced or used in any manner whatsoever without the express written permission of the publisher except for the use of brief quotations in a book review.

This book is a work of fiction. Any references to historical events, real people, or real places are used fictitiously. Other names, characters, places, and events are products of the author's imagination, and any resemblances to actual events or places or persons, living or dead, are entirely coincidental.

Much of this story takes place within the fabulous Red Rock Canyon National Conservation Area outside of Las Vegas, NV. For the sake of the story, I have altered certain aspects and taken a few liberties with some real places and certain political entities which are covered under the First Amendment of the United States Constitution. Thank you in advance for understanding an author's creative license.

# DEDICATION

*To Aunt Lindy.*
*This one isn't cozy.*

Genesis 3:15

"I will put enmity between you and the woman, and between your offspring and hers; He will strike at your head, while you strike at his heel."

Revelation 12:7

Then war broke out in heaven; Michael and his angels battled against the dragon. The dragon and its angels fought back, but they did not prevail and there was no longer any place for them in heaven.

# CHAPTER 1

The dragon vowed to escape, and then he'd become a god. Deep in the earth, he paced. Sulfur filled the air like soup. Darkness covered the dungeon except for the soft glow from the scriptures that covered his cell. A burst of flames escaped between his scales and lit the walls, casting a reflection off a pool of water, water that seeped through the rocks from the underground lake. It cast shadows behind large boulders, creating silhouettes that danced like devils.

The words of the holy scriptures adorned the walls and the floor and the boulders. Wherever he went, their light glowed in a soft blue. He seethed as he paced, his claws puncturing the rock with each step. His jaw flexed with rage. His tail scarred the walls like soldiers scourging a prisoner. His large claws dug through the rock floor, crushing the stone as he imagined the mortal damage he would do.

If only he could escape.

Lights shone in the distance. Two of the Almighty's guards stood at the gate.

The dragon's pupils closed. Even at this distance, the light burned his eyes. Rage filled his chest. He spread his two large

# REVELATION

wings. He hissed, and he paced again, crunching rock, breaking the Word of God. The words reappeared on the pebbles, blue against the darkness.

He remained in the shadows. His yellow eyes shone like the eyes of a viper deep in the darkness.

The distant lights grew bright. A messenger arrived, a third angel, whose illumination added to the guards.

The dragon snapped his jaws. He swung his tail, and he gashed the wall. He picked up his hand, and he clawed the wall, slicing it with his razor-sharp nails. His inner flames burned. He threw fire from his mouth. It tore into a nearby boulder, which melted into magma.

The messenger brought news. He had to get near the light to hear the news. He crushed rock in his dragon claws. He snarled, squinted, and moved toward the light.

He crawled through the shadows toward the gate. He passed large boulders, trying to stay in the shadows.

Galamiel stood on the left, and Joran stood on the right. Their white and blue radiance made it hard for the dragon to see. They had not altered their form as he had, but they stood in the image of God, the same form as man. Their feathery wings folded behind them.

Galamiel's skin was white; Joran's dark. Their eyes grew stern as he approached. Their hands clasped their swords, swords that had cut and pierced him when he attempted to escape through the gate. They held shields made from Heaven's indestructible metal of light. The shield faces reflected a perfect image of Calvary and the Son hanging from His cross. The images appeared as though one was there watching it happen.

The dragon found the nearest large boulder. He pressed his body against the wall, and the shadows covered him.

"Natar," Galamiel said. "It's good to see you. It's been a long time."

"Galamiel. Joran," Natar said. "I bring instructions."

Natar was a Seraphim, his light was bright. But what was he doing here? Natar had not been at the gate in almost three thousand years. Something happened on the surface.

Natar had come when God's people had rejected Him: first during the Flood, second during the Assyrian invasion of Israel, third when the Babylonians took the remaining tribe of Judah. In each instance, man's hearts had left God.

Was it happening again? And if so, what did that mean? Could the dragon escape? Could he wage war on the earth? Could he corrupt a man, establish a nation, and become a god?

Natar handed Galamiel a scroll. It glowed with the radiance of gold.

"We're at that point," Natar said.

"We are?" Joran said.

Galamiel opened the scroll and read it. He frowned. "This is from Michael?"

The dragon raged at the name of Michael. On his shoulder, above his wing, was his missing scale. The fiery membrane was all that remained from the place Michael had pierced him.

"The Almighty respects the wishes of His people," Natar said.

"Are you sure?" asked Joran?

"The Lord always makes a plan."

The dragon hissed. "What is His plan?"

# REVELATION

"Coming out of the shadows, are you Fury?" said Galamiel. Joran unsheathed his sword and held it up. It glowed and shimmered with images of Heaven.

"The shadows contain power," Fury responded. "Victory is won in the shadows."

"Then why will you not face the light?"

"You would have nothing if not the light."

"Would you like to see Calvary again? Perhaps the passing years have dulled your memory."

Fury clenched his jaw and ground his teeth. He picked up a rock and crushed it with his large hands. How foolish were they to give honor to men? Immortals owed nothing to creatures. His clawed fingers twitched with rage. The flames heated his gut. "The End is not here yet. Many souls will join us."

A few seconds passed without a response from the angels. Fury's face slid into an insincere smile. Flames flickered out of his mouth. The Count was all that mattered.

"So what is the news?" Fury asked.

"We have been instructed with orders from the Almighty. You are not to know."

"You told me throughout the ages," Fury said. "You told me when Abraham's descendants were imprisoned in Egypt. You told me when they were sent to Babylon. You told me when they were burned in Germany. Why will you not tell me now?"

Joran said, "The victory is ours."

"Victory is in the eye of the pursuer."

"Enough," Galamiel said, "or you will face the blades again."

Fury laughed. "You know I will heal. And you will not send me to Oblivion, for I am already here."

There was silence. Fury regarded it as a debate won.

"I must return," said Natar. "You have your orders."

"We will obey," said Galamiel.

The shadows on the walls grew as the Seraphim's light moved down the tunnel. Fury peeked around the rock. "What is different? Why will you not tell me the orders? Is there a worry in the Lord's plan?"

Galamiel unsheathed his sword. Joran raised the tip of his blade. The images of Heaven hinted to Fury at the lost treasure of the Rebellion. The two angels spread their wings as they prepared for battle.

Fury laughed. Flames sputtered from between his teeth. "If you will not tell me, then that means there is victory above. What is it? Have the people lost their faith?"

Galamiel pointed his sword. "Go back into the shadows. Your light disappeared at your choosing, and it will never return."

"I have made my choice. I will not honor the creatures. You are weak, and without the Almighty, you are nothing."

"Nor you," said Joran. "You forget that. You have rejected the glory of God."

"I reject it every moment of eternity," Fury said. He laughed again. Then he retreated to the dungeon rear and hid among the shadows.

Fury paced in the darkness. What did they mean? Something at the surface was different. Fury's powers remained limited. He could not read minds, even the minds of the creatures, but he inferred excellent guesses from the mannerisms of others. The guards were not good at deception, as they relied on truth. So when they hid something, they hinted at weakness.

# REVELATION

Fury hissed. Small flames escaped from between his scales. *Is this the moment?* Any weakness was a time to attack. He knew this from the Beginning. Though the guards had their swords, any hesitation by them and he would strike them with his claws, slice them with his tail, puncture them with his bite, and burn them with his flames. He would send them to Heaven, where they'd remain useless in battle until the End.

The sulfur filled his being. Flames grew hotter from inside his chest, and smoke seeped between his scales. He spread his wings. They glowed hot, casting a red glow along the deep walls of his dungeon and dulling the blue light of the scriptures. He had been locked here since the Rebellion. He had an opening. He had to act now.

Fury disappeared. His spirit flew back to the entrance. He hid behind his boulder and re-assumed his dragon shape. He wanted to surprise Galamiel and Joran.

He clenched his hands. He coated his scales to hide the fire in his belly. He prepared himself for the swords, those swords that projected Heaven and had sliced him and scarred him over the years.

He took a moment of silence, waiting, listening.

He attacked. He launched his eternal flames at the guards and whipped his tail at the spot where they stood. He expected their swords to flash and their shields to project Calvary in their defense.

His flames melted rock. His tail smashed a boulder. His claws grasped at the sulfur in the air.

The guards were gone.

He waited.

"Where are you?" he screamed. He wanted revenge. The guards deserved to pay. He wanted to watch them writhe in agony for the many thousands of years they locked him in the dungeon.

There was no answer.

"Where are you!"

Again, no reply.

His voice echoed along the walls, bouncing over the scriptures.

In front of him was the tunnel, dark and sloping upward. Michael had sent him down that tunnel during the Rebellion. The tunnel was open before him.

Was it a trap? Was he released?

He took a step beyond the gate.

Nothing.

No swords. No light.

He took another step.

He waited.

Nothing.

He took a third step. He spread his wings.

Nothing.

He lifted his head high. His chest glowed red. Fire escaped through his scales. He launched his flames. Rocks liquified into red magma.

He was free.

He roared. The sound rumbled through the cave. The ceilings cracked. The walls opened up. Boulders rolled out of their locations. He roared again, this time so loud he wanted the mortal creatures to fear his coming. The earth shook as the dragon moved forward, bringing ruin with him.

# CHAPTER 2

She approached the jutting rock. It angled like a sash on the stone wall. Above it, a fountain poured clear, clean water. As Susan Mercer neared the fountain, she saw how refreshing the water was.

She stepped over a stone and moved closer.

The water came from a small "t" rock formation on a stone wall. It poured pure and clear. She wanted to put her hands in the cool water, to feel it as it covered her palms and ran between her fingers.

The earth shook under her feet. The canyon walls rocked back and forth, sending rocks that fell from their places.

Susan stumbled to keep her balance, placing her hands on the walls.

A channel of hot flames spread between her and the walls, like a canopy around her, blocking her from the fountain. The flames grew higher, reaching the heights of the cliffs.

She screamed. Heat scorched her face. All around her, the canyon burned with fire.

The fountain, it seemed, was the only place untouched by it.

She heard the woman's voice. "Seek the fountain," she said.

"Where?" Susan yelled. "I can't find it!" The floor jolted her off her feet. The fire threatened to consume her.

The woman said again, "Seek the fountain-"

"Where? Where!"

Everything burned, and shook–.

Susan opened her eyes and sat upright, gasping for air. She placed her hand on her chest.

Her t-shirt was wet. Her black hair stuck to the sweat on her forehead.

Her jewelry made a faint clicking sound in its place on her dresser. The pictures on her walls clattered. The blinds on her window tapped against the glass.

The room was moving.

Was she sick?

Her bed moved from side to side. She grabbed the edge of the mattress.

"Earthquake?" she said. She sat still, clutching the mattress.

Earthquakes in Las Vegas were rare. She hoped this one would remain small and end soon.

After a few moments, the blinds ceased tapping the glass, and her jewelry stopped clicking. She listened for any sign of the earthquake. She heard a passing car on the street outside her apartment window.

It was over. She tried to remember her dream-

Beep-Beep-Beep-Beep!

Beep-Beep-Beep-Beep!

She jumped and let out a small yell. She hit the snooze button.

# REVELATION

The time was 5:30 a.m.

She heard the sound of several beads slide over the edge of her nightstand and land with a soft thud on the carpet.

"Oh no!" She turned on the lamp, revealing a painted red lampstand mixed with white Native American hieroglyphics. There was a picture of her and her parents in the mountains of Arizona.

She threw off the warm red bedspread and fell to the carpet floor. She crawled on her hands and knees.

The cold hit her skin under her t-shirt and gave her goosebumps on her legs. She picked up what had fallen, her Rosary, a linked set of fifty-nine pink and white beads roped together in a loop, ending with a small crucifix. It was a gift from her grandmother.

"I'm sorry," she said. She held the Rosary in her hands. She closed her fingers over it, kissed the cross, and set it back on the stand. She sat on the bed. The cold air hit her skin, and she folded her arms.

The dream haunted her, the same dream over and over again. She tried not to think about it.

She got up and turned on the small television. The screen was fuzzy. She had canceled her cable when she lost her job at the law firm, so she relied on small antennas to get local reception. The earthquake must have messed with the antennas. She moved them until she was satisfied with the picture.

The local news was on. A reporter discussed a vote at the Clark County Commissioners meeting.

They did not discuss the earthquake.

She took off her clothes and went into the shower.

She thought about the dream. Why was she having the same dream over and over again? What was the fountain? Who was the woman? Why did it always end in fire?

*Should I try again?*

"No," she said aloud. "I have to go to work."

*But it's a message. You know that.*

"No," she said again. "No. That's why they fired me!" She climbed out of the shower and wrapped her towel around her. In the mirror, her dark hair fell around her high cheekbones, a trait of her Navajo heritage. She shook her head. "I've explored all the canyons. I found nothing."

*Have you?*

Susan hit her forehead with the palm of her hand. "No. No. No!" She saw her reflection in the bathroom mirror. "I'm not losing another job."

She threw off her towel and then went to her closet. She pulled down her black pants and her McDonald's uniform shirt. She put them on and frowned at the mirror.

"I'm rebuilding," she said as she adjusted her name tag. The news on the TV still had not mentioned the earthquake.

Maybe she had imagined it.

Maybe she had imagined the whole dream.

Maybe she was going insane. *Is this what happens to people before they become clinical?*

"I'm not going insane," she said. "I'll get back on my feet."

*Seek the fountain.*

Susan put on her McDonald's hat. She caught her frown one more time as she looked in the mirror.

# REVELATION

She threw on her coat and picked up her keys. Unopened letters lay on the counter. She did not want to see her bills, bills she could not pay.

She grabbed her cell phone. There were messages left overnight, no doubt creditors trying to reach her. Before opening the door, she paused, closed her eyes, and prayed. "Mary, I need to rebuild. I have bills to pay. I've lost so much already."

She opened her eyes. The TV newscaster's voice was still in the bedroom. She'd leave the TV on to scare away any would-be burglars. If they cut off her electricity, so be it. She waited for Mary's answer, a thought that wasn't her own, to tell her it was alright, to go to work and rebuild her life, to hope for a husband and a home and children–.

"...and, guess what, Las Vegas. Many of you woke up to an earthquake this morning," said the newscaster.

So, there was an earthquake. Maybe I'm not going crazy, she thought.

She closed her apartment door behind her and went down the stairs. The pre-dawn Las Vegas air had a chill, brought on by a southern wind. Folding her arms, she hurried down the stairs to her rusty Saturn. The door creaked as she opened it. She shut the door, turned the ignition, and put her hands on the steering wheel. The check engine light was still on while the engine chugged.

*Seek the fountain.*

"I'm going to work. I'm going to work," Susan said. The sun brightened the sky, and its rays hit the streaked windows and the stucco walls of the apartment complex.

*Seek the fountain!*

Susan struck the steering wheel with her hands. "What do you want from me? I can't do it again. You're ruining me. Get out of my head!"

A man came through the stairwell. She hadn't seen him before, as new tenants were in and out of her complex all the time. Susan blushed, embarrassed. "I'm going crazy," she said.

She let herself calm down. She reached in her pocket and pulled out her pink and white Rosary. "Please," she said. "I've tried. I have nothing left. If I go, I'll lose everything."

The engine hummed.

Susan dropped her head and closed her eyes. She had already searched the canyons of Red Rock, the mountains, cliffs, and canyons west of Las Vegas.

She had searched them all, all except one - Ice Box Canyon. The first time she had the dream, she thought nothing of it. But it came again.

And again.

And again.

After the fifth time, Susan decided Mary, the mother of Jesus, was trying to speak to her. Maybe it was a figurative message, like "find the fountain of my love," or something like that. Susan went to Mass and learned to say Rosaries. She prayed and tried to be a better person, follow the Ten Commandments, and love her neighbor. Susan felt satisfied.

The dream kept coming.

One morning, the dream was so strong, Susan woke in a panic. She had been a teacher at a public elementary school then, so she called in absent. She had to interpret the dream.

# REVELATION

She drove to Red Rock, her best guess as to where the dream was leading her. She hiked up one of the canyons to seek the fountain.

She found nothing.

When she returned, she went back to school. In the middle of class, one of her students asked her why she was absent. Enamored by the dream, Susan shared the details with her class.

Word got back to the administration. The administration determined she had violated the Separation of Church and State by forcing religion upon her students, and she was terminated.

Susan hit the want-ads and found a job working the front office in a law firm. She enjoyed the stories and the challenges the legal profession provided, and she thought she'd go to law school one day.

The dream seemed to go away, but a month later, it returned.

Susan ignored it. She focused on her work, but the combination of sleepless nights and the stress of the firm took its toll.

Like before, the dream came to her one night, and she couldn't ignore it anymore. She gave in. She called in sick and explored Red Rock. Again, she did not find a fountain. When she arrived home that evening, she found an angry voice mail on her phone. It was a managing partner. She had forgotten to mail a deposition to the courts, and it cost the firm a trial. The partner fired her in the voice message. She was out of work.

The dream kept coming.

In between odd jobs, trying to make ends meet, she explored the canyons of Red Rock. She had purchased a map from the visitor's center, "X"-ing them off one at a time as she searched for the fountain. There was one left - Ice Box Canyon.

Her job at McDonald's awaited.

Frustrated, Susan released the steering wheel and slammed it with her fists. The car horn honked. "Why, Jesus, do I have to do this?" Her cell phone lay in her cup holder. She clenched her teeth. She reached down, picked up the phone, and dialed the number. She put the phone to her ear and heard the ringing.

"I'm losing it," Susan said.

More ringing.

"Please don't pick up. Please don't pick. Please don't... - *she picked up* - uh...hi Jenny...yes, good morning... Yes, it is early. Hey Jenny, I'm sorry but I won't be coming in to work... yes. I know... yes, but I can't make it today... Jenny? Can I make it up... yes. I know... I'm sorry... yes... okay. Good bye." She hung up the phone. She listened to the engine for a few seconds before she turned it off.

Her Rosary beads rested in the passenger seat. "There'd better be a Heaven," she said. She climbed out of her car, took off her hat, and returned to her apartment.

# CHAPTER 3

Lee Tommen poured his coffee. He picked up envelopes and magazines on the kitchen counter, inspecting underneath them. "Where's my lucky pen?".

"In the drawer." Joan sat on the sofa in the den, sipping her coffee.

Lee grumbled. He opened the drawer, found his lucky pen, and put it in his shirt uniform pocket next to his checklist that he wrote last night.

"Honey, come watch this." Joan rested in her blue bathrobe. The flat-screen television above the fireplace showed a map of Clark County. A news reporter said, "…and the earthquake measured a 3.1 on the Richter scale. The amazing thing is geologists are telling us the epicenter was right under metro Las Vegas."

The TV switched to two reporters sitting behind their desk. "No one has confirmed if we have any fault lines under Las Vegas Boulevard, have they?" asked the second reporter.

"No, but sometimes these things happen. The earth is a vibrant organism. Even though we don't always feel it, the ground below us is constantly moving."

"Isn't that interesting?" said Joan.

Lee poured his coffee, keeping it black. "We've had earthquakes before." He paced inside the kitchen, holding his coffee cup.

Jenn's hair dryer buzzed upstairs.

"Isn't she done yet?" Lee said.

"You know girls." Joan watched as Lee moved back and forth. The news showed a map on the TV. "I know we've had some tremors before, but this one seemed stronger."

Lee sipped his coffee, and it burned his upper lip.

"You alright?" Joan asked.

"Yeah." Lee focused upstairs.

"Will we have any aftershocks?"

"People in California deal with this sort of thing all the time. It's no big deal." He blew on his coffee before he took another sip.

The hair dryer stopped. Lee moved toward the stairs.

Joan frowned. "You're still upset about last night?"

"She should have been home on time."

"Go easy on her."

"She's testing me, Joan. She's testing us."

The TV reporter asked, "Will we get any aftershocks?"

"While geologists can't say for certain, they believe this was a rare occurrence and we shouldn't have anything else to worry about," the other reporter said.

"There's your answer," Lee said, pointing at the TV.

Joan said, "Just don't be too harsh on her."

Jenn walked down the stairs. She had given up on the hair dryer and pulled her blond hair into a ponytail. She had her pink backpack flung over her right shoulder.

# REVELATION

"Young lady, we need to talk about last night," Lee said.

Jenn rolled her eyes. "Good morning, Dad."

"Now tell me. Why did you come home late?"

"I don't know, Dad. I tried-"

Joan interjected, "Honey, did you feel that earthquake this morning?"

"There was an earthquake?"

"Did you sleep through it?"

Lee said, "Joan, I'm trying to have a conversation here."

Jenn asked, "There was really an earthquake?"

"Yes, there was," Lee said. "Now, why were you late?"

"Dad, we were just having fun. Rachel's dog was chasing tennis balls. I guess we lost track of time."

"That's no excuse."

"Can we get a dog?"

"We've already had that discussion."

"But Dad-"

"No." Lee crossed his arms.

Jenn turned away. "Always the same."

"Now don't get smart with me."

"Dad, I have to go to school." She poured some coffee and cream into her Yeti. She sipped, then she grabbed a strip of bacon and took a bite.

Lee could not believe his teenage daughter was drinking coffee. What was next, cocaine! "I'm going to have to ground you for the next week," Lee said.

Jenn swallowed hard. "No, you can't!"

"I'm your father, and I can do what I want."

"I made plans to go camping at Lake Mead next weekend. Rachel's bringing her dog!"

"Well, you should have thought about that while you were throwing tennis balls."

"I'm not a little girl, Dad."

"You have no idea what's out there." He set his coffee mug hard on the counter. The cup thudded and coffee spilled out leaving dark streaks that ran down the cup and brown droplets on the counter.

Jenn said, "Mom, Dad's being unreasonable."

Joan held her coffee cup in her hand. "This isn't the time to discuss this."

Lee said, "There's consequences for our actions, and she has to learn to obey the rules."

Jenn picked up her backpack and thermos. "I'm off to school."

"We'll talk about this later, young lady."

She slammed the side door as she went to her car.

Joan leaned back on her sofa. She took a sip of her coffee as the news continued on the TV. "Well, that went well."

"She has to learn," Lee said.

"She just turned seventeen. She's learned to drive. She wants to explore. She's finding out who she is."

"Being late isn't part of that. She has to show restraint."

"Lee…"

"And she's not going camping next weekend."

"Now don't be too hard on her," Joan said. "She was seven minutes late. It could have been a lot worse."

# REVELATION

Lee picked up his coffee again. "I'm a first responder. If I'm seven minutes late, someone dies."

Joan got up from the sofa and walked to Lee. "Here. Have some bacon."

"I don't feel like it."

She put her arms around him and kissed him on the cheek. Lee's face softened. Joan said, "You know, I've always said I like a man in a uniform. But when you wear yours, you're all business."

"I worry about her."

"I know you do." Joan squeezed him.

Lee hugged her back. "I see a lot of things in my line of work, and I don't know what I'd do if I ever lost one of you."

"It's not easy being a fireman's wife, either, you know."

"Captain," he said.

"New Captain," she said. "First shift. You nervous?"

Lee relented and took a strip of bacon. "I guess so. I want to do a good job. The guys are depending on me."

"I know. That's a lot of responsibility."

Jenn's car backed out of the driveway. She had to correct it as she almost hit the mailbox. Lee grimaced in anticipation. Jenn drove slowly down the quiet subdivision street. "Some leader I am. I can't even lead my own daughter."

Joan smiled. "You'll figure it out." She tapped the pen in Lee's shirt pocket. "You bring that lucky pen home after your shift, you hear?"

"Every day I do it's a good day." Lee kissed Joan and released her. He ate his bacon and put down his coffee cup. He reached down for his pack and headed out the door. "I'll see you after my shift." He blew her a kiss. "Call me if you need me."

"My hero," Joan said.

Joan had put a comfortable living room together. She appeared graceful as she returned to clean the kitchen. Marrying her was his best decision, he thought.

Joan said, "Wear your coat. It's going to be cold and windy today."

Lee grabbed his fireman coat out of the closet.

"Watch out for any earthquakes," Joan said.

"Yeah," Lee said. He shut the door behind him and walked to his car in the cold morning air.

# CHAPTER 4

Fury left a trail of red light. He sped through the tunnel. He left the dark behind him as he fled his dungeon buried deep within the earth.

He flew for miles, following the tunnel in an elevated slope. Rocks, stone, magma, and sulfur passed him.

The tunnel turned upward. He sped up it like a rocket and ran into a stone ceiling. He remembered this entrance, having passed through here thousands of years ago during the Rebellion, thrown here by the Archangel Michael.

Fury remembered that moment, as he remembered it every day. God revealed his plan of Creation to the angels. God revealed that he would become a man, be born of a woman, and how all the angels would bow down to these creatures called man. Fury declared he would bow to no creature. Spirits were superior. Oh, the insult to suggest an angel should bow to a woman whose flesh was mortal!

He would have none of it. That is why he, and a third of the angels, rebelled. They would not concede. They would not bow low to creatures less powerful, less magnificent, less enlightened. Less, period!

Fury remembered the battle. The war was vicious, with angels of light and angels turned demons fighting for supremacy over Heaven. He remembered slicing several angels in two, whose immortal spirits streaked upward into Heaven, where they would remain until they healed.

His co-rebels fought hard. He remembered how several were struck down, their spirits leaving red streaks as they fell through the void to the planet in the distance, the place God called Earth.

Fury had fought as his name implied. God had made him a force, an Archangel like Michael. Having chosen his side with the Rebels, Fury used his tail to strike at lesser angels, his jaws to tear off their wings, his claws to pierce their torsos.

Fury dominated the angels until Michael, his pointed sword and shield ready, attacked from above.

Fury had not seen him coming until the last moment, Michael's sword glinting with the power of God's light, his wings spread for battle, his eyes golden, his soul bent on winning. His sword pierced Fury through the spine between the wings above the shoulder. Fury had felt pain everywhere. His spirit became a red light, and he fell to Earth in a crimson streak where he traveled through the void, toward Earth, and into this tunnel. Here, he was locked in the dungeon, his scale missing where Michael's sword had pierced him.

In the dungeon, he had healed - and waited.

Blue writing adorned the stone and faced him from the ceiling. It said, "Ten Commandments." Then the line below it read, "I am the Lord thy God. Thou shalt have no other gods before me."

Fury swiped his claws at the writing, gashing it.

# REVELATION

"I will be that god before you," he said. "I will be the god of men!"

Fury took his large claw and slashed the stone down the center. He tore into all the commandments, scratching through them.

He would replace the commandments with new ones that removed man's free will. In Heaven, God might rule. But here, on Earth, he would rule. Here, he would be a god.

Fury worked his plan in his mind. He had not seen a man, for the Rebellion had happened before the Sixth Day. He had heard of man's technology when the guards received the news, but he knew not their strengths. They were creatures. They were mortal. Their souls would be judged upon their demise. They would know fear, whereas he, an immortal spirit, would never know fear. He knew rage. He knew power. And he knew that he, in his spirit, could rule a man; yes, even possess him. He would do that. He would become a god. He would make a priest and a king to rule humanity, and he, Fury, would be the god of man on Earth until the end of time.

Creation did not bind his spirit. He could move through the thickest stone if he so chose.

Yet this was not just a stone. God formed this dungeon in the Beginning. He designed it to lock him inside. Fury could not pass through the seal. No, he would have to break it.

His head displayed red scales. His eyes turned bright yellow, and red horns grew above his brow.

He stretched his neck.

His white teeth surrounded his serpentine tongue.

His body pressed against the tunnel walls.

His forearms grew muscular, and his hindquarters filled with power. His tail whipped from side to side, as spikes protruded from his spine. His wings bent along his back as the tunnel walls pressed against him. He was now in full physical form. If a cowardly man were near, he would see the dragon and die of fright.

Gravity took hold. When Fury felt it, he laughed. Gravity was a weak law created by God. The Almighty would not even let man, whom he loved so much, fly! Yet, he expected the angels to bow to man.

Ha!

Fury breathed in the sulfur and filled his lungs. His ribs expanded against the walls of the tunnel. His large scaly wings spread against the sides. His rear haunches dug into the walls.

His tail pressed against a cleft in the tunnel. His head reared back, he leaned forward with his front muscular forearms. He slammed his full weight and shoulders into the stone. The walls caved in around him.

They will cave, he thought. Creation is weak!

The stone seal cracked, splitting the written commandments. Gravity dropped shards into the blackness of the tunnel.

He pressed again.

The seal broke into several pieces. He struck at the seal with his powerful claws, and it split into large chunks.

He pushed with his giant hands.

The seal went up into the air. Light shone through the chunks, penetrating the darkness. Dust floated within the soft beams of light, spinning and circling with the influx of air.

He pressed and tore at the seal.

# REVELATION

More rocks gave way and fell with the power of gravity.

His wings flexed. His haunches pushed.

The seal broke apart into many chunks. He pressed harder with his body. A small piece fell past him, down through the sulfur-filled air to the dark bottom of the tunnel. A rumble echoed when the chunk crashed down below.

Fury grabbed the large remaining piece with his hands, wrapping his claws around it. He pushed one last time. The stone lifted into the light. He shoved it, and it rolled down the slope of a mountain. It collided with a large boulder and shattered. The sound of the collision echoed between the mountain peaks. A flock of birds flew into the sky, spreading in all directions and awakening the quiet of the morning.

After thousands of years in captivity, Fury was free. The early sun shined its rays on the mountain crests. He felt its warmth. He remembered when God had formed the sun, saying the words "Let there be light." The angels, already created, had seen God's plan unfold. The sun had great power, yet its powers were less than that of the weakest angel.

Fury huffed at the sun. If he wanted, he could rush into it, stir up the gasses, and destroy the Earth.

Yet that would be too easy, and too many men would reach Heaven upon their demise. No, he wanted to rule, to corrupt, to ruin souls. He would have to exert his power here, on the surface of the Earth. He would have to become feared. He would have to be worshiped.

To the east, a sunbeam reflected off an item in the distance. He did not need to squint, as his eyes were not affected by this light. Was that metal flying through the air?

He laughed.

It was! Man had built a device from the minerals in the ground and learned to fly. Fury clenched his teeth. Man had so little power. Yet God had withheld so much from them due to Adam's sin.

Below the flying machine, there were more glints. Towers stood tall, also made of minerals. A great city spread across the valley. It had multiple buildings. Amidst the buildings, more machines carried men and women from place to place. Houses filled the valley. Activity bustled as the sun climbed higher in the east.

He saw their souls. They were not bright white and blue, with the light of holiness, as the angels were. Most were gray or black, the souls of indifference. Some were red, and those seemed to congregate together. Without the brightness of blue and white, the light that came from prayer, and a connection to God, the city would fall to corruption.

These red souls, he thought, would begin his rise to power. One of them, redder and blacker than the others, would become his priest.

He studied the mountain ridge where he rested. A snow-covered peak lay to his north. To his west was a desert valley, with miles of wasteland and uninhabitable mountains. To his south was another mountain, and a black path that looked like a road, and several metallic machines reflected the light from the sun. Nature surrounded him: rock, desert, sky, air. A few distant stars shone with the approaching sun.

He knew not man's capability of defense. Being immortal, he had time. He would study. He would learn. He would find man's weaknesses. He would do his planning where he stood. Yes, he would begin here.

The wind blew from the south. The wind was cold, but it did not affect him. He took in a deep breath, and he smelled the ocean, the desert, the smog, the cities, the ozone, and all the elements in the atmosphere. The sky was too blue. There was no threat to the people in the valley.

He would change all that.

Fury's pupils slanted. His horns above his brow grew redder. He stretched his head and his neck high toward the sky. He raised himself onto his hindquarters and clawed at the cold wind.

The wind whipped around the contours of his body. It whistled around his scales and the spines that protruded from his back.

He spread his wings. They first turned yellow and then glowed a red aura. If anyone were paying attention from the city, miles away, they would have seen him, a small red shadow stretching his great wings atop the mountain crest. Power went out of him.

Then he stopped. He lowered his wings and stood on all fours.

The red aura went away. His pupils went back to normal. His eyes were like long reptilian slants inside golden retinas.

Now, he waited.

He wanted time to study man. He wanted to know man's strengths, his weaknesses, his wants, and his sins. By the time the storm arrived, he would know how to control man's hope, how to put fear into his mind, and how to ruin his soul.

He watched, waiting for his power to work.

The southern wind picked up speed. The temperature dropped several degrees.

The blue sky remained blue.

Far away over the distant mountains, a cloud appeared. It was small and dark. It spun like a tiny hurricane as it grew larger. The wind pushed it in his direction. It expanded, from west to east, slowly but ever-growing larger.

In a short while, it would arrive, ready to serve his purpose.

# CHAPTER 5

Lee honked his horn. The driver had pulled in front of him, and he swerved. "Everyone's acting funny," he said. He glared at the other driver, who returned the gesture, then turned away when he recognized Lee's fireman uniform. If there was any benefit to being a fireman, it was that people had a hard time being a jerk to you.

Of course, there was always the exception.

Lee turned right onto Flamingo Rd. In another mile, he'd cross Las Vegas Boulevard where he'd pass Bally's, the Bellagio, and Caesar's Palace.

Bally's was on his left. It hadn't always been called that. Decades ago, it was the MGM Grand Hotel and Casino. In 1980 one of the restaurants in the casino caught fire, and the sprinklers didn't work. The posh decorations went up in flames, and the fire spread at an incredible rate of several feet per second. The plastic burned at a temperature multiple times higher than that of many erupting volcanoes. Eighty-five people died, and over seven hundred were injured in what was the second-worst hotel fire in America.

He imagined what it was like for those people that tried to escape, who were scared. How the firemen rushed to save them, but couldn't rescue all those lives.

He shook his head back to the road. Perhaps the earthquake had him on edge.

Perhaps it had everyone on edge.

Traffic seemed odd. It was heavier than normal. Slower. He didn't see any accidents. Few people crossed the roads, except for the few jaywalkers, which was normal.

The sun was behind him, leaving bright rays that shone into the eyes of oncoming drivers. They drove as they always did, but something was different.

He turned on the radio. The local jockeys were discussing the morning's earthquake, and how odd it was that the epicenter was right under the city.

A caller chimed in: "Is Hoover Dam in danger?" he said.

"No," said one of the DJs. "But that would be awful if it cracked."

"How would they fix it?"

"With today's government spending, no telling what they'd do."

Lee chuckled. Politicians had no idea what they were doing. They campaigned, promised a bunch of stuff, but in the end, they had no idea how to execute it. Eventually, things went back to normal, and nothing happened until the next person campaigned, promising things they couldn't do.

Another car pulled in front of him. Lee swerved, this time hard. He was so surprised he forgot to honk his horn. The driver was a man oblivious to him.

# REVELATION

"The earthquake's got everyone nuts," he said.

"I'll tell you what," the DJ said. "Waking up to my bed shaking hadn't happened since I was in college."

"Did you just admit that on the air?" said the other DJ.

"Hey, I studied," he replied. "I just picked the wrong major."

Laughter.

Lee didn't find it funny. He wanted to laugh, but he had to focus. Today was the first day of his first shift as Captain of Fire Station 53, a new outpost on the western edge of town. He wanted to be a good leader. He had applied for other captain positions in the past, always being passed up because he needed more experience in some form or fashion.

He had come into being a fireman later in life. He had been in accounting, but something told him he needed more. Not that accountants weren't important – they were – but being in an office all day dragged on him, and he caught himself looking out his window to see what was going on outside. He worked out each evening to get the frustration out of his system. He didn't want to come home to Joan and Jenn being out of sorts.

The day Lee told Joan about his desire to join the Fire Department, she encouraged him. How he loved that woman. He had been so nervous to tell her, but when she agreed, he wanted nothing other than to make her proud.

Lee had applied to the Clark County Fire Department, which had agreed to hire him. They put him through the training. It was a pay cut, but he and Joan made it work. And when he came home, even though the hours took some getting used to, Joan commented on how he was smiling much more.

It took some years before he received a promotion. His salary wasn't enough, and he worried about Jenn's college, so he had done all the steps to get the training necessary for advancement. Test after test after test he took and rejection after rejection after rejection returned to him with each application. "You need more of this, or you haven't done enough of that," they would say.

But when this outpost came open, Chief Sawvel called him. "Here's your chance," he said.

It wasn't the post Lee wanted, but he wouldn't say no. He took the job as soon as they offered it.

And today was the first day.

He had a few reports for the day shift. Juan Carasco was an energetic fireman in his mid-twenties who liked the excitement and seemed almost overeager. He bragged about how hot his girlfriend was during downtimes, but it was more for show than it was for ego.

There was also Nate Silverton, a new recruit out of school and who had finished his training. Lee thought it best to train a new kid quickly and, if the kid advanced and was promoted, that would bode well for his own career.

And there was Rob Joyner, a loyal fireman and a friend who Lee brought to Station 53 upon his promotion. Lee appreciated having someone else with some seniority. Rob set the tone.

The traffic stopped.

"What now?" he said.

Drivers slowed down. Cars put on their brakes. A white box truck pulled in front of him, and he couldn't see the problem. As the traffic inched forward the truck moved, allowing him to see. A

# REVELATION

car was on the side of the road. An older lady with gray hair stood on the sidewalk. She kicked a tire. She seemed upset.

From Lee's angle, the lady's rear passenger tire was flat. She had no idea what to do.

"Sawvel's going to have to wait," Lee said. He turned on his emergency lights and nudged his car to the right.

# CHAPTER 6

Amy covered herself as she sat up. A gust of wind blew against the tent. The tent wall pushed inward as cold seeped in and hit her skin. Her back ached from sleeping on the desert floor. A thin padded mat had cushioned her as she slept in their sleeping bag. Ricki and Tahoe were outside the tent. She smelled smoke. "Making breakfast?" she said.

"You're up!" Ricki was attempting to cook oatmeal in his mess kit pot. "Hungry?"

"Yeah." She exposed herself before she found her t-shirt. She caught Ricki stealing a glance through the tent door. She blushed. Boys, she thought.

Tahoe walked up to her. He was a black, gray, and brown Australian Shepherd and wore a red body harness. Mornings like this, Tahoe would bounce around, excited for the day's adventure. He didn't do that this morning, though. His body stood, studying the northwest mountains.

"Hey, boy." She patted his head.

Tahoe acknowledged her, then walked away and pointed his ears at the mountains.

REVELATION

The mountains stood majestic to the west. Across the desert stood the world-renowned cliffs of Red Rock Canyon. She didn't *see* anything peculiar.

Odd, she thought. What's gotten into Tahoe?

Ricki poured some oatmeal into a paper cup and stuck a plastic spoon in it. He brought it to her. "Here."

"Thanks."

"Breakfast of champions."

"I see that." The oatmeal needed sugar, but she didn't complain. No matter what Ricki did, even if he made a mistake, he was going places, and she was determined to be by his side. "Why are you up so early?" she said.

"Something woke me up," he said. "Did you feel the ground shake last night?"

Amy blushed.

Ricki shook his head. "No, I don't mean that. I thought I felt an earthquake."

"You did?"

"Maybe." He fixed his oatmeal and stirred it with his plastic spoon.

"I didn't feel an earthquake. But I had some weird dreams."

"Hmmm," Ricki said. "Tahoe's been acting strange all morning." Ricki squinted from the rising sun. His breath hung in the cold air. He sat next to the small fire he had built. He set down his oatmeal and put his hands in his coat pockets to keep warm.

Amy said, "Do you still want to go?"

"Of course. That's what I do. I make a plan, and I do it."

Amy climbed out of her sleeping bag and put some long johns over her t-shirt. Then she buttoned a flannel shirt over her torso before pulling on her pair of blue jeans. She put on her coat.

She shivered. Why was it still so cold?

She wrapped the sleeping bag over her coat around her shoulders like a blanket. She stepped out of the two-person pop-up tent. Her breath clouded in the morning air. Her hair blew in the southern wind. Tahoe kept his ears pointed to the tall rock cliffs along the mountain range.

"Tahoe. Are you alright?"

Tahoe acknowledged her, licked his lips, then pointed his head back to the mountains.

"See. That's what I'm talking about," said Ricki. He stood up and moved toward the tent.

"What's he looking at?"

"I don't know. But maybe we'll find out."

Amy swallowed a spoonful of oatmeal. "What do you mean?"

"Our hike today. It's in that direction."

Amy shuddered. "Does he know where we're going?"

Ricki took down the tent. He bent the tent poles and tied them together. "Doubt it."

Amy had enjoyed her adventures with Ricki. His nature photographs had grown his blog and podcast followers enough so that he was able to make money through print sales and affiliations. He hadn't earned much, but he told her the bank account was growing. Part of the fun was that he lived for adventure. Her dad said he was trying to escape the realities of the world, that she should ditch him the first chance she got.

## REVELATION

She told her dad she'd follow Ricki anywhere. She hadn't spoken to her father since.

"Maybe we should take pictures somewhere else today? You know, explore a different canyon and then come back here tomorrow," Amy said.

Ricki stuffed the tent in the pack. He loaded it into the back of his blue Subaru Outback, a used car he said he had bought from his photography teacher in San Diego. "No, it's a beautiful morning, and the light's perfect. It'll shine into the canyon and we'll see all kinds of colors. Besides, my followers have told me they can't wait to see my post on this tonight."

"Maybe we can surprise them," Amy said. "Don't your followers like surprises?"

"Sometimes yes. Mostly no." Ricki put out the fire. He poured some coffee into two cups and handed one to Amy. "Today, we go to Ice Box Canyon. I have several threads from people saying they're excited to see our photos. Tomorrow we're doing the La Madre Springs. And Thursday we're going to do the red rocks themselves, sort of as a grand finale. We have to stay on schedule. I've got people in Europe wanting to see my next three blogs. Let's stick to the plan."

Amy noticed Tahoe hadn't moved. The Australian Shepherd's ears remained attentive, his head cocked to the left as if he were listening for something. He didn't appear excited as was usual the morning of a hike. Rather, he appeared concerned, like something was wrong.

"Are we going to take Tahoe?" she said.

"Of course. He's the star of the show. If he's not in the photos, it'll be a wasted trip."

Amy sipped her coffee.

Ricki finished breaking down the campsite. He loaded the remaining items into the Subaru. "Amy, would you get Tahoe and bring him into the car?"

Amy set her coffee cup down. She walked over to Tahoe. She knelt beside him and put her arm over him while keeping the sleeping bag over her shoulders.

He licked her once, but then pointed his ears at the mountains, listening to whatever was across the desert.

"What is it, boy?" she said.

Tahoe whined.

She brushed his fur. The cold air lingered on his smooth coat.

She studied the desert; Joshua trees, sagebrush, and sand. Lots and lots of sand. It was not the soft sand, like at the California beaches, but a rocky sand, the kind that hid rattlesnakes and scorpions.

In the distance was Red Rock National Conservation Area, where giant protruding cliffs reached 3,000 feet high, standing like a testament to millions of years of erosion. Between the cliffs and where she stood, there was the hard desert.

And thorns.

Everything had thorns. The trees had thorns. The sagebrush had thorns. The reptiles had thorns. The bugs had thorns, like those pesky scorpions. The rocks had jagged edges that scratched and scraped you. Even the giant rock cliffs jutted out of the ground like enormous thorns, the result of an ancient geologic process. The more Amy tagged along with Ricki, the more she appreciated all the natural landscapes. But the thorns she could do without.

Tahoe flinched.

# REVELATION

She grabbed his collar. The sleeping bag slipped off her shoulders and the cold wind hit her neck.

Tahoe moved like he wanted to run away from the cliffs. He jerked his collar, but Amy held on.

"Calm down, boy." She put Tahoe's leash on his harness.

Tahoe tugged at the leash.

"What has gotten into you?" Amy said.

"Everything alright?" Ricki asked.

"He's nervous about something."

"He'll be alright. Just get him in the car."

Amy opened the back door and coerced Tahoe to climb inside. His tongue dripped with saliva as he panted. His eyes were wide.

"It'll be alright," Amy said. She patted him on the head, and she shut the door.

Strange, she thought. Tahoe loved car rides, but not this morning. Something bothered him. She grabbed her sleeping bag off the desert floor and brushed the dirt off it. She stuffed it in the bag and put it in the back of the Outback. She picked up her coffee and climbed into the passenger seat.

"Here we go," Ricki said as he sat down beside her. He turned the ignition, and they drove onto the dirt road and left the campsite. A few bumps later, they found pavement. Tahoe watched the mountains as they turned north to Red Rock National Conservation Area.

Amy studied the cliffs through the windshield. *What does Tahoe know?*

# CHAPTER 7

Susan wore jeans, a flannel shirt, tennis shoes, and a warm coat. She squinted at the morning sun. She turned the key in her ignition. The Saturn engine whirred, but wouldn't start.

"Oh, what are you doing?" she said. She tried again with the same result. She checked the gas gauge. Full. She filled it up yesterday with the little money she had left. "Come on. You worked earlier!"

Her neighbor, Joe from 2C, came from the apartment stairwell and stared at her as she worked the ignition. Joe frightened her, though he never gave her a cause. He was a card dealer at one of the hotels in town, or so he said. His roommate, Roger, said he was only a bartender, but was "moving up the totem pole," or so Joe told him. Joe's dark complexion wasn't what bothered her, it was something else. Maybe it was the circles under his eyes. For a man in his late twenties, he looked like he was nearing fifty.

Her chin dipped down as if she could hide. Her "Our Lady of Guadalupe" prayer card stared back at her from her passenger cup holder. Her Rosary hung on her rearview mirror.

Joe passed her like she wasn't even there.

# REVELATION

She tried the ignition again. "Come on, Mary, if you want me to go…"

The engine rumbled. Susan pressed her palm to her heart. "Thank you," she said. She counted the contents on her passenger seat: one bottle of water, one pre-paid cell phone, and her second Rosary. The first one she kept in her pocket. She was not a hiker. She had bought her coat and shoes at Goodwill. Would they hold up on a hike at Red Rock? Maybe, so long as it didn't rain.

She remembered the woman's voice. It was calm and gentle. If the flames hadn't scared her so much at the end of her dreams, she'd want to sleep and never wake up. But they always ended like a nightmare, waking her up screaming and sweating.

The woman told her to go, to find the fountain. How many times had she gone to Red Rock? Several. Her trips ended in blisters, rolled ankles, and disappointments. She had yet to find the fountain.

Last night's dream seemed more intense than the others, more urgent. The fire seemed more threatening. Its heat burned the hairs upon her skin.

Tat! Tat! Tat!

Susan gasped and raised her hands in self-defense. Joe?

Through the window, she heard a voice. "Hey Susan. You okay?"

It was her neighbor, Roger, Joe's roommate..

"Roger, please don't sneak up on me again." Roger was a young guy, right out of school. The hard knocks of life had not yet affected his pleasant demeanor. She had spoken to him a few times in the hallway.

Roger made the motion to roll down her window.

She pressed the window button and the glass dropped a few inches.

Roger said, "Sorry. You just looked anxious. I see you got your car started. Is it running okay?"

"She's hanging in there,"

"You going to work?"

Susan's cheeks flushed. "Not today."

Roger put his hands in his coat pocket. "Okay. Well, if you're around tonight, Joe and I are going to have a get together to watch the Knights. I don't know if you're into hockey, but you're welcome to come join us."

Susan felt a warm sensation. Was he asking her out? Roger seemed nice, but how'd he get a roommate like Joe? "I don't know," she said.

"Oh, come on. It'll be fun."

She closed her eyes.

Roger's apartment was a few paces from her front door, and it was nice to get an invitation. Maybe she read Joe wrong. Maybe he was tired, and that's why he had the dark circles. Maybe she imagined things.

Maybe she should get out more.

Maybe she should get back to living.

She remembered her mission. If this trip ended like all the others, uneventful, then she'd forget the dreams and the woman's voice, and she would never visit Red Rock again. This would be it - her "Last Hurrah". The sooner she got up there and nothing happened, the better.

REVELATION

"Tell you what. I have to run out of town for a bit, but I don't want to be long. I'll be back, and if I'm back before the game starts, I'll knock on your door."

Roger took his hand out of his pocket and gave a thumbs up. "Awesome. It'll be fun. You like wine?"

"Sure," Susan said.

"Red or white?"

"Surprise me." She waved goodbye and backed out of the car space. Her engine made a funny sound, and her exhaust launched white mist into the cool air.

Roger waved.

Susan put her hands on her head, embarrassed by her car's hiccups. She pulled out of the lot, turned onto the side streets that took her north, and soon she was driving her Saturn on 215 and headed West, leaving a trail of white exhaust.

While on the interstate, she prayed, but it was more like talking. She talked to God, Jesus, and Mary, but Mary mostly. She begged for the dreams to end, to get back to a normal life. She took I-215 past the airport and Las Vegas Boulevard.

Several hotels stood tall against the blue sky. The Luxor was built like an Egyptian pyramid, and the Tropicana was adorned with palm trees like a tropical paradise. Blocking her view was the new Abo Hotel and Casino, a tall and wide hotel with kangaroo, boomerang, and koala bear decorations scattered across the property and the hotel building. The entire entertainment venue glittered in the morning sun.

Abo was slang for Aboriginal, and the owners liked the idea of an Australian themed venue in Las Vegas. At its proposal, many mocked the Australian idea, saying it was too 1980s, that

Crocodile Dundee had had his day. When the building opened, however, it gained acclaim. A steady flock of American tourists flew to Las Vegas and enjoyed the Abo atmosphere, rather than made the 13-hour flight to the continent of Australia.

Susan passed the hotels and made a sign of the cross. The Protestants called Las Vegas "Sin City", and Las Vegas Boulevard was the focal point of that designation. She wanted to believe it was just tourism, that people could have fun and not be impure. She didn't want to judge. As her dreams grew more intense, though, she found herself judging more and more.

She focused on the road. She crossed I-15. The mountains, red and purple, stood tall in the morning sun.

Her check engine light came on. Blood rushed into her face. "Oh, now what's going on?" Her gas gauge was full. She listened to the engine. Cars whizzed past her as she stayed the speed limit. The engine sounded okay. "Come on, girl. You can make it. You can make it."

A noise caused her to jerk on the steering wheel. A nearby driver laid on his horn as Susan corrected into her lane.

The noise came again, but it wasn't the engine. It was her phone sitting next to her. She picked it up.

It was her boss.

"Not now," she said. She held the phone to her ear, trying to remember if that was now illegal in Nevada or not. She slouched, hoping no policeman would see her phone in her ear.

"Hi, Jenny," Susan said in her happy voice. "No, I'm not at home…Yes, I'm driving…okay…but…I promise I'll be there tomorrow…I just had something personal…I'm taking today

## REVELATION

without pay, aren't I...okay, I'll turn in my uniform tomorrow...same to you."

Susan shut off the phone. She held her stomach and bent forward. God, she hated getting fired, no matter the job. But she had no options. Her rent was due, she was on her last tank of gas, and her car was about to fill a junkyard. She focused on the mountains. This would be her last time. No more dreams. No more of the woman's voice. No more fountains. No more earthquakes. No more fire. This was it.

She approached the exit for W Charleston Blvd. She took the ramp and turned west.

The mountains shone with red and brown peaks mixed with blue and black shadows. The cliff faces shone in the morning sun.

Strange clouds were forming above the mountains.

Mixed between the peaks were dark shadows.

Maybe the fountain existed. One more place to look, she thought.

If only a money tree grew out of the fountain so she could pay her rent.

# CHAPTER 8

Lee Tommen arrived at Fire Station 53. It was 7:30 a.m., thirty minutes before his shift. Juan's car sat in the parking lot. Lee swore. Juan Carasco had beaten him there. Helping the old lady had delayed Lee, but Juan would give him a hard time nonetheless.

He reached up to his pocket and felt his lucky pen and the edges of his folded checklist. Still there, he thought. *Don't let me down today.*

He got out of the car.

The B shift was finishing their 48 hours.

His C shift was beginning in a few minutes.

As he approached the building, he inspected the structure. It was still new, with no decorations adorning it as often adorned fire stations. There was a sign: Fire Station 53, Clark County Fire Department.

He went into the front door of the small, nondescript building.

The TV was on, showing the local news. The volume was soft. They were discussing the earthquake. The picture showed a map of Las Vegas, and several concentric circles pinpointed an epicenter west of Las Vegas Boulevard, under Blue Diamond Rd.

The B Shift crew moved to and fro as they finished their procedures to make the hand-off to C Shift. Sanchez walked by with a file in his hand.

"Hey Sanchez. Is Captain Nash in there?" Lee said.

"Yes sir. He's waiting for you."

Lee moved toward the main office.

Juan hurried by and intercepted him. "Hey Cap. You're late!"

"Oh, hush," Lee said.

Juan chuckled before he passed through the hallway that led to the hangar.

Lee shook his head and smiled before he stepped into the small side office. He remained standing while B Shift Captain Bill Nash sat behind the new desk. Nash stood up and rubbed the dark skin under his eyes.

Lee noticed the walls were bare. "Hadn't had time to decorate, huh?"

"No. We had five calls last night. And the last two days have been hectic. Kind of surprising. Then this earthquake shook things up. We've gotten all kinds of calls since then."

"Like what?"

"Wackos, mostly. Lots of people think it's the Second Coming, but mostly people burned themselves with spilled coffee."

"Anything big?"

"We assisted Station 47 on a call in Summerlin. And L.V.P.D. had us check on an overheated engine up on 159 at 3:00 am."

"Did the car catch fire?"

"Almost. We called in a water truck just in time."

Nash had papers on the desk. There was writing on the top page, but Nash hadn't had time to complete it. Nash said, "You ready for the inspection?"

Lee reached in his pocket and felt his lucky pen and the folded paper with today's checklist. "I think so," Lee said.

"Wish I could help you more," Nash said. "The guys are finishing their end-of-shift responsibilities. I'll get these reports done. Hopefully we won't get another call in the next five minutes."

"Need help?" Lee said.

Nash sat back at the desk. "No. We've got it."

"Roger that." Lee left the small room and went to the main quarters. Sanchez and Bomar had finished cleaning their equipment. A young man was standing with them, listening to them and asking them questions.

"O'Reilly," Lee said. "Where's your equipment?"

The young man hurried to Lee. "Hi, Captain. I put everything next to the truck. It's packed and ready to load in my riding area."

"We have an inspection today. Make sure you go over your checklist twice, and add anything to it that needs adding."

"Yes sir!"

Lee said, "Where's Joyner?"

Bomar stood up, lifting his self-contained breathing apparatus, more often referred to as "S.C.B.A." "Hadn't seen him yet, Captain."

Lee checked his watch. Twenty minutes until the shift changes. Sawvel would arrive at any time. "Darn it! Not today."

# REVELATION

Juan stepped into the main room, his pride on arriving first showing on his face. "Hey Captain, I have a surprise for you."

Lee's cheeks flushed. "Carasco, I don't need any surprises on an inspection day."

Juan insisted, "Trust me, Cap. It's the icing on the cake."

"What cake?"

Lee followed Juan through the door and into the hangar. The Skeeter fire truck sat empty in the middle, its hood raised. Juan's hands had the residue of engine grease on them. "Something wrong with the truck?" Lee said.

"A Shift told B Shift it was fine, but we don't want to take chances. I thought it best to check."

"This had better not be the surprise."

Juan hinted for Lee to turn around.

"What the hell is that?" Lee said.

"Dog bed, Captain."

"What for?"

"You've seen Backdraft, haven't you? I thought a dog would be good for us."

Lee clenched his jaw before he spoke. "No dogs."

"But Cap'n-"

"No dogs. They get in the way." He pointed at the bed. "Get that thing out of here before Chief Sawvel shows up. And what else do you have to do to the truck?"

Juan rubbed his hands together. "The truck's okay. It needs some new parts, but it'll hold up until we get a new one in the budget."

"Don't hold your breath on that."

"Captain," Nate said. He stood in the doorway, holding the door open. "Joyner's here."

"Thank God," Lee said. He thought he heard coughing. "Where is he?"

"He's sitting down, sir. He doesn't look good."

Lee followed Nate into the living area.

Joyner sat, his head hunched over. His body shook as he coughed.

"Jimminy, Joyner. You look like hell."

Joyner said, "I'll be alright Cap'n." He held back a cough. He looked run down.

Marco stood next to Lee. "Looks like you'll be a man down, Captain."

Joyner said, "I took some Sudafed and some Mucinex. I'll be alright."

Lee rubbed the back of his neck. The last thing he needed was for his crew to come down with the flu, or whatever it was Joyner was carrying. "I'm going to make the call. Joyner, take a sick day. Two if you need it."

"But, Captain-"

"Don't 'but' me. Last thing I need is a dead hero under my watch. This is an order. We have an inspection in a few minutes and I don't want you here getting our Battalion Chief sick. Go home."

"But-"

"Right now, Joyner."

Joyner coughed. "Yes sir." He wobbled to a standing position, coughed again, and walked out the door.

# REVELATION

Lee, Nate, Marco, Sanchez, and Bomar backed away, hinting that they did not want to catch Joyner's cold.

Nash had come out of the office. "By the way, we got a package yesterday." He motioned to the closet. "Not sure what it is, but it looks pretty big." He pulled out a large Amazon box and set it on the table. "We were going to get to it, but the calls kept coming in."

Nate said, "Sir, may I?"

Lee nodded.

Nate pulled out his knife and opened the package. Another box was inside. A picture on the box showed something like a cross between models of an Airwolf helicopter and a Star Wars X-wing fighter.

"What the hell is that?" Lee said.

Nate's grin showed his excitement. "It's a drone. And a good one at that."

"What for?"

"Emergencies." Nate rolled the drone box, examining the pictures. Then he put the box back down on the table and cut it open. "It has a long flight time, and it can travel up to five miles."

"Who the hell ordered it?" Lee said.

Nate said, "I did, sir."

"Kid's right out of college and he wastes no time ordering toys."

Nate pulled the drone out of the package. "I figured since we're covering so much space, it could come in handy."

Nash shrugged. "Council couldn't put enough money in the budget to get us a new truck, but they jumped at something nobody knows how to use."

"I had to use one in training, sir. It'll be good for us to have. Did the batteries come?"

"There were a few other boxes that came with it. They're in the closet," Nash said.

Nate hooked up the battery to the charger. He went to the closet and pulled out the other boxes."

Lee said, "Sawvel should be here any minute. Keep that stuff in there. We don't need this place cluttered during our inspection."

"Yes sir." Nate put the drone back in the box and put it in the closet with the other batteries, but he left the main one sitting out to receive its charge.

"Reports are done," Nash said. "You need anything from me before we go?"

"I've got it under control," Lee said.

Juan came through the hangar door. He wiped his hands with a blue towel. His black radio strap hung over his left shoulder. "Captain, Battalion Chief Sawvel just pulled up."

"Thanks, Carasco. O'Reilly, get your radio strap on and stand in line for roll call."

Nate did as Lee instructed. Juan walked over to Nate, and the two of them stood side by side as Battalion Chief Sawvel came through the door, wearing his Battalion uniform. His gray hair and mustache made him look distinguished. His assistant, Danielle Stewart, followed him, carrying a clipboard.

Lee stood next to Juan. He and his team aligned perfectly.

"Hello, Men." Sawvel said.

"Hello, Chief. We're ready."

"Have you done roll call, yet?"

Lee's voice rose a little. "Just about to, sir."

# REVELATION

"Where's your fourth?"

"We sent him home, sir. He was sick. He argued and wanted to stay, but we figured we'd call in for someone else."

Nash handed Danielle the folder. "Here's the reports, sir. Do you need anything more from my crew?"

"I heard you had a busy night. I never knew the edges of town could be so busy," Sawvel said.

"Council knew what they were doing when they added this station, sir. One week in and it's already getting its use."

Sawvel scanned Lee, Juan, and Nate up and down. "At ease, men."

Lee and his men relaxed. Lee said, "We're all set, sir. B Shift hadn't had much time to fix the place up. But we'll make it efficient if we get any downtime."

"I know you will, Captain." He walked over to the drone battery charging on the desk. "What's this?"

Nate said, "It's a battery, sir. It came with the drone that was delivered yesterday."

"That's right," Sawvel said. "I remember signing off on that. Nothing wrong with a little ingenuity, right Captain?"

Nate had an "I thought so" smirk on his face.

Lee lowered his voice. "That's right, sir."

"How's the truck?" Sawvel said.

Juan stepped forward. "I checked it this morning, sir. It has all its parts, and they seem to be working. It'll need some consistent maintenance, but it'll do until a new truck gets approved in the budget."

Sawvel didn't answer. He took some circular steps and studied the walls. Danielle held her clipboard to her chest, expecting instructions.

Lee waited. There was an uncomfortable silence as he tried to predict Sawvel's next question.

"Nothing out of the unexpected," Sawvel said. "Captain, could you join me in there for a moment?"

"Yes sir," Lee said. He followed Sawvel into the small office. Juan gave Lee a thumbs up before Lee shut the door.

"Captain," Sawvel said. "Congrats again on your promotion."

"Thank you, sir."

Sawvel crossed his arms, and leaned against the desk. Lee stood tall, remaining formal.

"Captain, you're the right man for this post. I hope you're not disappointed I couldn't put you at one of the bigger stations."

"I'm happy to be here," Lee said.

"You know, County Commissioners created this station as an afterthought. It's more to protect their own rear ends than it is anybody else's."

"What do you mean?" Lee asked.

"The Commission had the funds to build another park. But the news kept covering all the danger at Red Rock. Too many tourists without a clue getting into trouble. The more the news covered it, the more the Commission had to do something. So they did. They pulled resources from Station 48. But you probably knew that."

"I had a feeling something like that was happening during the interview process."

## REVELATION

"Station 53 is just an outpost," Sawvel continued. "You know your job here isn't fire protection so much as it is EMS."

"I do, sir."

"Does your crew know that?"

"Yes sir."

"They won't be disappointed?"

"No sir. We take our jobs seriously."

Sawvel relaxed his arms. "I know that. Lee, I'm going to be less formal here. You and Carasco worked for me all those years at Station 15 before I was promoted to Battalion Chief. I always admired your commitment to detail. Your being late to the game made you work that much harder. You wanted to prove yourself."

Lee's shoulders dropped a little. "Sir, I wasted a lot of my life in corporate. I have much to make up for."

"I know you feel that way," Sawvel said. "And I'm glad. But I want to let you know something. There's going to be an opening for a Captain position at Station 15 in a half dozen months. If you do a good job here, I'd like you to interview for the job."

"Who's leaving?"

"Captain Waters. He's got family issues going on in California. Oh, he's not saying anything right now, and he won't even hint about it. But I know human nature pretty well. I won't be surprised if he gives me his notice by August."

"I'm sorry to hear that," Lee said. He remembered his argument with Jenn, and he regretted how he had left it.

Sawvel said, "He'll do what he'll do. In the meantime, do a good job here, and it could leave the door open for you."

"My team and I are ready, sir. We're going to be perfect in everything we do."

"Sometimes perfection isn't enough, Lee. Remember that."

The office was bare. His mind listed all the incomplete items that he still had to finish. He remembered the checklist in his pocket. "Do you still want to see the rest of the building?"

Sawvel stood. "No, Captain. I just wanted to talk to you privately. It's a new facility, and there's going to be some time before you'll have everything operational and efficient. I know you'll get there soon. We'll do a more formal inspection in a couple weeks." Sawvel stood straight, passed Lee, and put his hand on the doorknob. He pulled the door open an inch, but then he stopped and shut the door. He slowed his speech. "Oh, one more thing."

"Yes sir."

"I know you're eager to do a good job. Just remember you can't control everything that happens out there."

"Sir, it's my job. That's why we do our training."

"Training can't cover everything. If I could give you one last piece of advice, expect the unexpected."

Lee kept his mouth shut.

Sawvel nodded, then he opened the door and walked into the main room. He shook hands with Juan and Nate, wishing them well and thanking them for their commitment. Danielle followed behind Sawvel with her pen to her clipboard. She looked disappointed that she hadn't written much on it during their visit.

"Captain," Sawvel said. He reached out his hand.

Lee said, "Thank you, sir."

Sawvel acknowledged his assistant for the first time since he had arrived. "Danielle, do me a favor. Call HR and see who can help here. I'm sure we can find someone who wants to work some OT."

Danielle said, "Yes sir. I'll get right on it." She seemed excited to have something to do.

As Sawvel headed for the door, he stopped. "Remember what I said." He gave Lee a salute, and he and Danielle exited through the front door.

"Everything alright?" Juan said.

"Yeah. Everything's good. He wanted to wish us well."

"Why the secret meeting?"

"He didn't want all the things he said about you to go to your head."

"I knew he liked me."

Nate stood quietly, not sure what he should say.

"Great," Lee said. He tapped Nate on the shoulder. "I've done it now. You and I are going to hear Juan brag about himself for the next forty-eight hours."

"That's right," Juan said. "Think positively, I always say!"

"Captain, who's going to replace Joyner while we're here?" Nate asked.

Lee pushed his shoulders back. "No telling. The Chief will handle that, though. In the meantime, everything must be in order. Get your gear ready."

Nate and Juan busied themselves with their preparations. It was good to see their enthusiasm for the job. Lee didn't want to lose that. The new Station 53 outpost had received several emergency calls during the short time it had been operational. He expected those calls to continue, perhaps increase. They may have to hire some new help as Las Vegas developers built homes further west. His promotion to Station 53 was a substantial opportunity. It would lead to greater things. All he needed to do was prove he could lead.

He reached up and touched his lucky pen. Yes, it was still in his shirt pocket.

Lee left the office and went into the hangar.

The dog bed was gone. Juan had moved it.

The Skeeter sat facing the hangar door. It was a used four-passenger firetruck the department had bought from Boulder City. It wasn't a typical large water truck, but a rigged vehicle that handled small emergencies. It contained several compartments in the rear for mid-sized emergency equipment. It had a small ladder, but if they needed a tall one, or water hose, they'd call Dispatch for a water truck.

Lee opened a rear compartment and removed his S.C.B.A. He checked it over and put it back in the compartment. He grabbed his black and red search and rescue backpack and checked its contents: first aid kit, ropes, climbing gear, four water bottles, compass, scissors, pocket knife, map of Red Rock, and all his required tools. Everything was there. He sat his pack next to the others.

Lee checked another compartment. The EMS board was in its place. He opened the side compartment where Juan and Nate kept the search and rescue packs. It was empty. "What are they doing?" Lee said.

He went around the Skeeter. Juan's and Nate's packs sat along the wall, ready to be picked up at a moment's notice. "There they are."

## REVELATION

As he passed the rear truck window, he noticed something. "What the-?" He opened the back door, and he pulled out the dog bed.

Lee walked into the living area, carrying the dog bed. "Hey, Carasco." Lee lifted it for Juan to see. "Really?"

"Just following orders," Juan said. "I had to think quick."

Lee stuffed the dog bed in the closet and shut the door. "And what have you got there?"

Juan held two devices, large orange pistols. "Flare guns, Cap'n."

"Geez, Carasco. Aren't you overdoing it?"

Juan just grinned. "You never know."

The clock read eight thirty-five. The bright desert sun came through the windows. Nate brought the drone out of the closet and continued to work on it.

Juan looked over his shoulder. "Is the battery charged?"

"Close," Nate said.

The local news was on the television, and the reporters again discussed the earthquake. They made a big deal about the epicenter being under the city. "Dang reporters are going to have the whole city nervous about aftershocks," Lee said.

"Aftershocks?" Juan said.

"Don't you start, too."

"I'm serious."

"Earthquakes come from California. Aftershocks tend to remain there."

Nate clicked the final pieces of the drone together. "That's it. Captain, should we go outside and try it?"

"Not right now. We have the normal checklist to finish."

"I'll put it in the truck." Nate unlocked the charged battery and set up the charge for a new one. He then picked up the drone and carried it to the hangar.

"He's a good kid," Juan said.

"He's green. He doesn't know what he doesn't know."

"His training scores were high. Will he make it under duress?"

"He'd better."

A call came in over the radios. "Dispatch, calling 53. You have an emergency at the Red Rock Scenic Loop, Mile 3 past the visitor center, over."

"Roger," Lee said, and he rushed through the hall into the hangar.

"Already?" Juan said. He jumped up and followed.

"It's going to be one of those days."

Lee grabbed his pack and climbed into the Skeeter driver's seat. Juan and Nate threw their search and rescue packs into their compartment. Juan opened the hangar door and jumped into the side of the truck. Nate climbed into the back seat.

Lee reached into his pocket and touched his lucky pen. It was still there.

The checklist would have to wait.

Lee started the engine. He turned on the siren as the truck hit the asphalt, and the three-man crew sped onto Route 159 westward toward Red Rock.

# CHAPTER 9

The blue Subaru Outback pulled through the gate at Red Rock National Conservation Area. The Visitor's Center was to their left, but they stayed straight, following the 13-Mile Loop. Large red mounds were on Amy's right. From her position, they seemed like bright red sand dunes; but up close they were huge, like giant mini-mountains on Mars rounded with some mysterious geologic force.

As they followed the road, Amy studied the terrain. They approached a sign: "Calico Hills North". An empty large white Chevy Silverado sat in the parking lot.

"Somebody beat us," she said.

"First time for everything," Ricki said.

Amy laughed. She liked Ricki's confidence. She was sure he'd be successful. Since they met at the coffee shop in San Diego, she imagined a life with him, one full of adventure and travel and passion and romance.

She had graduated from college, and she was ready to take on the world. Her dad had told her to get a desk job and begin earning money, but she rebelled. She couldn't be locked inside a building all day. She had to get outside. When she met Ricki, he gave her that chance.

So far, she was right. Here she was, driving around the country, camping in the wilderness, and helping build a business. The money was coming, he said. Slowly, but coming. Her dad said they'd never make it. What did her dad know, anyway? Things were different in his day. You had to be smarter now, and more flexible. Free.

Being tied down meant extinction. She was going to live. No way she'd become extinct!

After several winding miles, the large rock mountains grew near. The cliff faces reached 3,000 feet up. The morning sun reflected the red, purple, tan, and brown hues. Amy imagined she'd see a rock climber dangling from a rope a thousand feet up.

Tahoe pawed at the door.

"You alright, boy?" Amy said.

"Burros," Ricki said.

"Where?"

"Down there." Ricki pointed to his left. A herd of twelve gray burrows had mixed in with some Joshua trees. They stayed close together, their tails to the sun, their ears up, their eyes toward the high cliffs.

Tahoe's ears were up. He ignored the burros. Instead, he faced the cliffs. His eyes studied the canyons. Something about his intensity made the hairs on Amy's neck stand up.

"He's fine." Ricki said as he pulled into the parking lot. A sign said "Ice Box Canyon", and an arrow pointed to the trail entrance. Their Subaru Outback was the only car in the parking lot.

# REVELATION

"It's not the burros," Amy said. "It's something else."

"I said he's fine." Ricki grabbed his yellow North Face X-Pac fanny pack, carrying his camera, phone, sandwich, trail mix, and a bottle of water.

Surprised at his change of tone, Amy raised her eyebrows. "Okay," she said.

While Tahoe remained in the back seat, Amy opened her door and grabbed her Vans Ward Color Block fanny pack, a multi-pack splattered with all the colors of the rainbow. Her hair blew as a southern gust of wind whipped past her. The brown stems of the desert sagebrush blew with each gust of wind. Dark clouds hovered over the edge of the cliff peaks. They appeared to swirl.

"Make sure you pack your poncho," Ricki said. "Looks like some clouds are coming."

"Will there be a storm?" Amy folded her arms.

"It'll be fine. This is about a two hour hike. We'll be in and back in the car in no time."

Despite her layers under her coat, Amy shivered. The wind had a chill in it that went through her.

"It's too cold," Amy said.

"Shouldn't be much wind once we're in the canyon," Ricki said.

The wind stung Amy's face. It seemed dangerous, but Ricki had experience, and this was an adventure. She imagined this evening she would tell stories about today to her online friends while she sipped her Corona.

She filled her rainbow fanny pack with her water, phone, and trail mix. She found her small poncho in the back of the Subaru and stuffed it in her pack. Then she wrapped the colorful pack around her waist. It lumped over her many layers of clothes.

Tahoe walked up to Amy, his mouth open and his tongue out.

Ricki said, "You can handle him, can't you?"

The plan was to keep Tahoe off the leash as they hiked. Tahoe's exploring made for great photos which often brought enthusiastic comments from online followers. Amy liked watching Tahoe navigate the trail, sometimes veering left or right to check out a rabbit hole, but staying on the smooth path of the premade trail.

Sometimes other hikers brought their dogs. While their dogs misbehaved, Tahoe stayed cool, never unfriendly, but always wary. He warned others that he was there to protect his pack. It worked. In all their hikes, no person or dog attacked her or Ricki. Amy felt safe so long as Tahoe was with them.

Tahoe was different today, though. As he stood in the Subaru's rear seat, his eyes remained focused on the canyon.

"I can handle him," Amy said. She opened the door.

Tahoe slowly climbed out of the vehicle. His nails clicked on the pavement. The wind blew his dark fur. He stepped a few paces, but his eyes and his ears remained fixed on the canyon.

"Aren't you excited, boy?"

Tahoe whined. His tongue dripped saliva while he panted.

"I'm going to put a leash on him," Amy said.

"Why?" Ricki fiddled with his camera.

"He's not himself."

"No," Ricki said. "We'll need the shots."

"But-"

# REVELATION

"Look, bring the leash if you want to. But keep it off. We'll use it if we have to."

Amy frowned. She rolled Tahoe's leash, put it in her pack, and twisted the full rainbow-colored pack around her waist. She forced a smile and gave Ricki a thumbs-up.

"Why do you have that stupid colored pack, anyway?" Ricki said.

"It photographs well."

"Trust me. They're not looking at your pack."

Amy huffed. The wind whipped her hair.

Tahoe walked up to Amy. Was he scared?

"Okay, let's get going," Ricki said. He held up his camera and took pictures. Then he stepped to the trail entrance.

Amy said, "Tahoe's nervous. He doesn't want to go."

Ricki didn't stop. His feet crunched on the sand. Over the wind, he raised his voice. "We need him for the photographs."

Amy said, "Come on, boy. We have to support him."

Tahoe groaned.

Amy took several steps to the trailhead, her feet connecting with the pavement.

Tahoe stood where he was, next to the car.

"Come on, boy."

Tahoe shifted, not leaving the Subaru.

Amy squatted. Her hands motioned for Tahoe to follow her. The pitch in her voice rose as she said, "Come on, boy. Come on."

Tahoe shifted again, but then he put his front paw forward and walked to Amy. She rubbed him on the head. "That's a good boy." Amy rose and stepped onto the trail. Dirt crunched under her feet. Ricki was already fifty yards ahead of them, taking pictures.

She followed the trail, watching the rocks as the wind blew in her face. She was layered, but still cold from the wind. Tahoe followed behind her, which was strange because he was often out in front.

Dark clouds formed over the mountains. A rumble echoed in the distance.

Tahoe stopped.

*Why is he acting so strange?* She went back and grabbed Tahoe's red body harness. Tahoe pulled, wanting to go back to the car.

She yelled down to Ricki. "He doesn't want to go!"

Ricki yelled back, "Figure it out. I need the pictures!"

"Hold on, boy," Amy said. Tahoe panted. She twisted her pack around her waist. With one hand, she unzipped it and she took out his leash. She hooked it to Tahoe's body harness. "This will be a first." She stood up and walked.

Tahoe tugged, trying to go back to the car.

She pulled harder.

Tahoe put his head down and followed her, his eyes wide.

As she hiked, the cold hit her face. It felt sharp on her skin. Her ears stung.

The sagebrush and the Joshua tree needles vibrated in the wind.

She jogged to catch Ricki. He had gained a good lead; the weather must have made him impatient.

Tahoe wasn't much help. She pulled on the leash and dragged him. The harness shifted to his shoulders. He stiffened his front legs. His tongue panted harder.

"Come on!" Amy said.

# REVELATION

Tahoe surrendered and followed.

Ricki stopped and waited for them near the canyon entrance. The wind wasn't as bad next to the giant cliff walls. They must shield the wind, she thought.

"I've already taken about thirty good shots. But we need to get to the back. I'm going to need you to get him off the leash."

A rumble of thunder echoed above the canyon walls. Tahoe jumped, jerking on the leash. Amy fell but managed to hang onto the leash.

She waited for Ricki to help her up.

He did not offer help. "If we get a shot of Tahoe up on that rock-"

"Ricki." Amy stood up. Tahoe tugged again at her before she brushed the dirt off her jeans.

"What?"

"He doesn't want to go."

A gust of wind hit them. Ricki's and Amy's hair blew in their faces. "We're going," Ricki said.

"Then you take him," Amy said. "He's acting crazy."

"Look," Ricki said. "Do you want to be a part of this business? Or are you just trying to freeload?"

A rush of fear ran through Amy's abdomen. Ricki hadn't ever talked to her that way. In her panic, she sucked in air, but she couldn't find the words to answer him.

Ricki said, "I'm going to need your help. If you can't handle Tahoe, then we're done."

Tahoe pulled the leash taught.

Amy jerked the leash back. Her face turned red. "Behave!"

Tahoe tugged again. Amy pointed her finger at Tahoe and tugged the leash. She pulled the leash forward and walked with Tahoe ahead of Ricki to the Ice Box Canyon entrance.

"That's good," Ricki said.

"Shut up," Amy said.

She pulled Tahoe up the trail, she was sick that she slept with Ricki last night. How would she get home? She hoped she wasn't pregnant.

She mumbled, "Maybe Dad was right."

# CHAPTER 10

The red Skeeter fire truck sped up Route 159 and turned right into Red Rock Canyon Conservation Area.

"Not many cars today," Nate said.

"Yeah," Juan said, "But I don't like the look of those clouds."

To the left, the first sign of a storm covered the peaks of the mountains. They were dark and thick, not the kind you'd see over the desert, but more the kind you might see at the front of a tornado.

Lee said, "It's one injured hiker. Not too far back. I imagine this won't take long."

They drove through the main gate, waving at the security guard as they passed. "Where is it?" Lee said.

"Calico Hills," said Juan.

"North?"

"Yeah." They continued rounding the Red Rock Scenic Loop until they saw the signs for Calico Hills North. The parking lot was empty except for one white Chevy Silverado. "Theirs?"

"Probably," Lee said. He parked the Skeeter and jumped out. "Let's get our board."

"Got it, Cap'n" Juan said.

The wind hit Lee, and he shuddered. He had his jacket on, but was surprised he was cold.

Nate said, "Wind is crazy!"

"Come on," Lee said. He hurried down the trail. Juan and Nate followed, Juan carrying the orange EMS board.

When they reached the bottom of the hill, there wasn't anybody around.

"You sure they're here?" Nate said.

"Let me check," Lee said. He lifted his hand and yelled toward the Red Rocks. From above, the rocks didn't appear all that menacing. From ground level, though, they appeared like mountains on a Star Trek planet. "Hello!" Lee hollered.

His voice echoed between the rocks.

"The wind may be drowning your voice," Juan said.

Nate stayed silent, listening.

The wind whistled between the giant boulders.

"Captain," Nate said. "Want me to get the drone?"

"You and your toy drone," Lee said.

"I don't hear anything."

"Shhh!"

The wind paused for a moment.

Lee shouted again. "Hello!"

There was a faint woman's voice coming from behind to the east.

"I hear someone," Juan said.

"Let's go."

The three men hurried down the trail toward the voice. They went around a giant red boulder. Two women were on the ground, one was kneeling. The other sat, one leg straightened in front of

# REVELATION

her, the other bent and broken above the ankle. Her eyes were red and tears covered her face.

"Lee rushed to the women. "Hello. I'm Captain Lee Tommen. Looks like you've got a bad one here."

"It hurts like hell," the lady said.

"I bet it does. Looks bad, too."

Nate noticed the ankle and his face turned green. He ducked behind the boulder. They heard heaving.

"Sorry about that," Lee said. "He's new."

The women chuckled, a welcome respite from the accident.

"You been out here long?" Juan said. He laid the board down next to the hurt woman.

"No," said the kneeling woman.

"What happened?" Juan smiled like Bradley Cooper. It was his way of deflecting the situation and keeping the women at ease.

"We were trying to get a morning hike in," the kneeling woman said.

"It's my fault," said the hurt woman. "I wanted to see if I could climb the rock, and I slipped, my foot got caught, and I fell but my foot wanted to stay."

"Anything else hurt?"

"Head is throbbing," she said, "And I twisted my back."

Nate came back around the rock, his face a little less green. "Sorry Captain," Nate said.

"There's our hero," Lee said. He worked a splint around the woman's broken leg.

"Is it a compound?"

"No. Skin's not broken. I don't know how it's not, but it's not."

What can I do?" Nate said.

"Hold tight." Lee fixed the splint.

The wind blew. The sun disappeared, and a shadow covered them.

The kneeling lady stood.

Lee finished working the splint.

Juan said, "Ready Cap'n?"

"I am." The woman's eyes were red. "Ma'am, we need to lift you on this board. I've got your leg splinted pretty good, but this may cause some pain. Does any other part of you hurt?"

"My head and my back."

"Okay. Can you lie down?"

"Yeah."

"I'll get behind you and help." Lee moved around the woman and used his hands to prop the woman's neck. Juan moved under her back and helped her to the ground.

She winced.

"What hurts?" Lee asked. "Your head, neck, or back?"

"No. It's my leg," she said.

"Okay. That's good. I'll take that."

"It hurts," the woman said, wincing.

"I know," Lee said.

Lee helped her lay fully on the ground, then he said to his team, "Juan, Nate, get on either side of her. We're going to get her on this board. I'll hold her head just in case."

"Yes sir," Juan said. He gave his Bradley Cooper smile to the woman and winked.

She laughed, then winced.

# REVELATION

"Okay, on three." Lee nodded to the two. "One, two, three-" They lifted the hurt woman onto the board and set her down. Juan then took the straps and tied her down so she was stable.

Lee stood, and the wind blew into his face. He checked his lucky pen. It was still there. "Okay, gentlemen, let's get these ladies up the hill and back to the car."

"We're so glad you came," said the other woman. "I'm so sorry I didn't know what to do."

"Just basic first aid, ma'am." Lee said.

Juan and Nate carried the hurt woman up the trail, their boots crunching the sand as they went. Lee and the other woman followed. "Do you guys do first aid courses?"

"CPR."

"I'll sign up for that."

"Glad to have you."

They returned to the parking lot.

Dark, swirling clouds covered the western mountains.

The wind penetrated Lee's coat, and though he was glad he was working up a sweat to get his body heat-activated against the cold, the thought of the Skeeter's warm air appealed to him. He hoped this was the last of their problems at Red Rock, and they could work closer to the metro area.

When they arrived at the vehicles, Juan and Nate laid the woman down on the ground. They untied her straps.

"Thank you." The woman sat up again. She was getting used to her leg splint. "Can you help me in our truck?"

"Ma'am, you've got a bad fracture. In this weather, you could go into shock, and soon. You need to get to a hospital."

The two women looked at each other. "I've got a friend at Summerlin Hospital," the other woman said. "I can take her."

"Should we call an ambulance?" Juan said.

Lee said, "We don't have any room in the Skeeter. I'd advise an ambulance, but it might take some time before they get here."

"Sir, the radio's been going heavy today."

"Must be the earthquake. It has the whole town edgy."

"If you'll help me into the truck-" the woman said.

"Cap'n?" Juan said..

Lee nodded.

"Okay," Juan said. He helped the woman. She clenched her teeth, but he managed to get her sitting in the passenger side of the truck. When she sat down, she said, "Thank you."

The other woman said, "I'll drive her. You all have done so much already."

The hurt woman said, "I'm sorry you had to come all this way because of me."

"No problem, ma'am," Lee said. "Let's try not to make this a habit."

The women laughed. Then they shut the doors. As the Chevy's engine started and the truck pulled forward, the women waved goodbye.

Nate waved back.

Juan winked and gave his Bradley Cooper grin.

"Will you stop doing that?" Lee said.

"What?"

"You know."

"But the women like it. Makes them calm."

"I'll be more calm when we're out of this wind."

# REVELATION

"I heard that!"

Juan put the board back in its compartment, and the men climbed into the Skeeter. Lee turned on the engine and ran the heater while he rubbed his hands. He studied the rock cliff formations to their west.

The dark clouds covered the tops of the mountains.

Lee didn't like the looks of them.

# CHAPTER 11

Amy, Ricki, and Tahoe had reached the back of Ice Box Canyon about an hour after they left the vehicle. Amy was tired from everything; the hiking, the cold, the wind, Ricki's sudden change in personality, and Tahoe's rebelliousness. As if the swirling dark clouds overhead weren't scary enough, a strange odor was in the air.

"What's that smell?" Amy said. The odor filled her nostrils, and it was unlike anything she had ever smelled before.

Tahoe pulled hard.

"Stupid dog!" Amy gripped Tahoe's leash.

Tahoe panted, his tongue flicking saliva onto the rocky trail. He must have smelled it, too. She tried to get him to drink from the creek, but the dog ignored it, and every time the leash had some slack he jerked the leash to run back down the canyon trail toward the car.

Amy's shoulders and elbows grew sore from pulling on Tahoe's leash. Will he ever stop?

Ricki did not mention the smell. He had taken photos up the trail, but few were of Tahoe. They were scenic shots, the sunlight coming from the east, casting shadows and lights along the red and tan cliffs.

"You're worthless," Ricki said. "I can't photograph you."

Jerk, she thought. But she had to play along. "Can't you get pics of Tahoe?"

"Not if you can't control him."

Amy clenched her jaw. She thought of letting go of the leash and watching Tahoe run back to the car. Maybe I'll follow, she thought. "Why'd we come all this way if we'd only take pictures of rocks?"

Ricki ignored her.

There was the smell again. "What is that?" Amy said.

"It's sulfur," he answered.

"What's sulfur?"

"Comes from volcanic activity. Strange to smell it up here."

Amy looked around. The large cliffs of Ice Box Canyon enclosed them except for the way they had come. She wished she saw a blue sky, but dark clouds moved above the edges of the cliffs. Were they in a caldera, in the middle of a volcano? The thought of it unnerved her.

Tahoe jerked the leash again, but Amy held on. A sharp pain ran through her elbow.

Ricki glared at her. "Don't hurt Tahoe. Otherwise, you're paying his vet bill."

Amy's eyes flashed. Put on an act, she thought. He has the keys to the car. As soon as we get back, I'm having him drive me back to Vegas, and I'm calling Dad and he'll drive up from San Diego to get me.

She tied Tahoe's leash around a small tree stump. Tahoe pulled the leash, trying to free himself from the tree.

She rubbed her sore elbow. Then she sat down on a rock. Though she wanted to leave, she reminded herself to play it cool.

She took off her rainbow-colored fanny pack and set it next to her on the rocks. She pulled out her sandwich. She took a sip from her bottled water.

She decided to change the subject. "Have you taken all your pictures?"

"Let Tahoe off the leash. I need to at least get one or two with him in it."

"That's not a good idea."

"It's not your decision," Ricki said.

"He'll run."

"I need the shots."

Amy had grown attached to the dog. But Tahoe was Ricki's. "Fine," she said. She reached down to untie Tahoe's leash. She felt bad for the dog, but she was ready to be done with this whole enterprise.

Tahoe jerked the leash, tripping Amy. She fell onto the rock floor, bruising her knees and elbows. The leash escaped her grasp, and Tahoe took off, sprinting toward the northern wall. She watched as he paced under the cliff shadows, dragging the leash and searching for the trail to get back to the car.

Amy held her knee. She didn't see blood, but it stung. A part of her hoped Ricki would ask if she was alright.

"Now look what you've done," Ricki said.

# REVELATION

"You jerk!" Amy said. "How did I ever let you get me to this god forsaken place?" She stood up. "Your dog has the right idea. I'm out of here!" She stood up.

The sulfur smell grew stronger.

Ricki laughed. "You're not going anywhere. I've got the keys, remember."

Amy stomped several feet away. She forgot to watch her step and she stumbled as she navigated the uneven large rock surface. She shouted, "I'm through with you!"

"Whatever."

She limped ten feet down the trail. "I'll hitchhike home!" she said.

"It's okay," he said. "You weren't that good in bed anyway."

Amy threw her arms up. The wind howled above them, while the dark clouds circled the top of the canyon walls. More shadows appeared overhead.

She bent over. Her knee throbbed; her elbow hurt.

Tahoe ran off.

Would she be able to hitchhike back? She was shaking, but she told herself to calm down. Be smart, she thought. He was her ride. He held her captive.

"So, how much money are you making in this business, anyway?"

Ricki was sitting on the rock, munching on a sandwich.

He swallowed and said, "That's none of your business."

"No, it is. If I'm working with you, that is my business. I want my cut. How much are you making?"

"There's no cut. I pay for lodging, food, and water. That was the deal."

"How much are you making?"

"I've told you. Money is coming in."

"How much?"

Ricki stood up. "Look, I've got over a thousand followers. We get a download every day."

"How much?"

Ricki's eyes grew red. He put his hands in his pockets. "Go get my dog," he said.

"You aren't making anything, are you?"

"Go get my dog!"

"How did you even buy that car of yours from your professor?"

Ricki said nothing.

"Oh, my god. You didn't buy it." Amy threw a rock at him, but missed. "Did you steal it?"

"I don't have to take this," Ricki said. He bent down, snatched his pack off the rock, and flung it over his shoulder.

Amy spun around. She yelled at the clouds, her back to Ricki. "You're a car thief! Does that make me an accomplice?"

She heard a noise behind her and felt a cold gust of wind, but she paid it no attention. Her rage grew. She didn't want to look at Ricki. As she faced the other way, she said, "You know what, I'm going back. I don't care if I have to walk to California, I'm going home!"

Ricki didn't answer. Was he ignoring her?

A heat warmed her skin. Sulfur poured into her nostrils. The smell upset her stomach.

So much went wrong, her choices, her relationships.

# REVELATION

Enough. She would do things right from now on. She would listen to her dad.

For one last moment, though, she would let Ricki have it.

She turned around.

Ricki was gone. His half-eaten sandwich was on the stone trail.

Her rainbow fanny pack was resting on the rock where she left it.

Dark red puddles and splattered red dots covered the gray rocks.

*Where's Ricki?*

A shadow towered over her. A large scaly head and hot orange flames poured out between the sharpest teeth she had ever seen. Two yellow eyes grew brighter as leathery wings extended, blocking her view of the swirling storm clouds.

The head struck like a cobra; teeth and flames lunged at her.

As she screamed she had two thoughts; she hoped Tahoe would make it out, and she should have listened to her father.

Then she felt pain, and everything went dark.

# CHAPTER 12

Susan's Saturn pulled into the Ice Box Canyon parking lot. The lot was empty except for a dark blue older model Subaru Outback. It was still morning, so the person or people who drove that car were not too far ahead up the trail.

She chose a parking space facing the mountains and turned off the car engine.

The wind hit the car broadside. She noticed the sagebrush and the Joshua tree needles bending in the cold wind. Dark clouds rolled over the mountains, giving her a dreadful feeling.

Something was wrong. Often her excursions were hot and sunny, as was often the case in the Las Vegas valley. Not today. Today, she had her dream. There was the earthquake, and the weather had turned ugly.

Her sneakers weren't meant for cold.

She grabbed her coat. It wasn't a bad coat, but not made for this type of hiking. She was not prepared, and she knew it. She hit her forehead with her palm. "Stupid!"

In the passenger seat lay her bottle of water and her Rosary beads. Maybe she should say a Rosary before she goes?

# REVELATION

She sat in the parking lot for several minutes. She put the Rosary into her left coat pocket, but she didn't let it go. She let the beads rub between her fingers. It gave her comfort.

The wind howled outside her car windows. The clouds swirled.

"I can't do this," she said.

A rumble echoed from the west. No lightning, as far as she could tell. But there was a rumble.

"That's it. I have to do this another time." She turned her key in the ignition.

The car wouldn't start.

She tried it again, and the engine wouldn't turn over.

"Come on!" She tried a third time.

Nothing.

She brought both her hands up over her forehead and slammed the steering wheel. "Come on. Come on. Come on!" She put her hands back down, her palms ached.

The wind howled.

Without her engine running, she had no heater. The air inside the cabin grew cooler.

The Rosary was in her pocket, and she grabbed it again. She sensed pangs of guilt for losing her cool. "But what do I do? Why do I keep having these dreams?"

She sat in the car. She was stuck. She needed help - but from whom?

She remembered seeing the small red truck as she had passed the red rocks just after the Visitor Center. The side looked like it had an official logo, like a fire and rescue party.

Should she call for help? She didn't know who to call. What would she say? Hi. I had a dream, and I need help looking for a fountain before the fire gets me? Why? Because some strange woman's voice told me to. Crazy!

She sat in her car, watching the clouds roll over the mountain. What if someone drove by? Should she wave them down? Would the fire and rescue people drive this way?

How would she get them to help? She could tell them her car wouldn't start, which was true, but that wouldn't convince them to hike the trail with her. No, she didn't need a mechanic. She needed help getting into and out of the canyon.

The blue Subaru sat in the lot. Who's car was that? The car was an older model. Probably someone who went hiking a lot. The license plate said they were from California.

Maybe they didn't know their way. Perhaps they got lost. It could be easy to assume that they were in danger since the weather changed.

That's it. She knew what she had to do. She had only done this once before, and she never wanted to have to do it again.

She picked up her cell phone. She held it in her right hand and waited a few minutes. She felt the Rosary in her coat pocket. "Forgive me," she said. She turned on her phone and dialed 911.

A woman answered on the other end.

"I want to report a missing person," Susan said.

The woman who answered asked for details.

"Ice Box Canyon parking lot, on the Red Rock Scenic Loop."

REVELATION

Susan breathed as she spoke. Deep in her mind, someone may be in trouble. Maybe I'm not lying, she thought. Maybe what I'm saying is true.

Then again, maybe the missing person will be me?

# CHAPTER 13

Lee drove the Skeeter out of the parking lot. The 13-mile loop would take them around the edges of the mountains, but being an emergency vehicle, they didn't have time for that. He turned the Skeeter left to head past the Visitor Center, planning to return via Route 159 toward Vegas and Station 53.

The mountain peaks had disappeared inside dark clouds. Something bothered him about them. He couldn't say what it was. Something bad was in the area.

Something dangerous. It made the hairs on his neck stiffen.

He studied the rocks. The dark swirling clouds over the westward cliffs did not help. The landscape was becoming covered in shadows.

Strange day, he thought. First, he had his argument with Jenn. Then Joyner got sick leaving him a man down. He was edgy, but everybody was.

And it all began with the earthquake. Was that causing all the angst?

He knew he had to take care of his men. Juan Carasco had a reputation of having a big heart, but sometimes he overdid things.

# REVELATION

It was his personality. Lee had studied his men's profiles when he took the position. Lee figured he'd have to keep Juan grounded.

Nate was young. Though book smart, he didn't have the practical common sense one acquires through experience. Lee liked the idea of molding a young fireman, watching him have success through the years, and feeling he had a part in it. He didn't like the thought of a mistake happening, costing someone an injury, or worse, a life.

But something bothered him.

Juan was looking behind the Skeeter in the passenger rearview mirror. Nate had his focus low, scanning his cell phone.

"What of those clouds?" Lee asked Juan.

"Don't like them," he said. "I'm glad we're going back."

"Me too." Lee waved at the entry gate guard as they passed.

As the Skeeter reached 159, Lee turned it left and hit the gas. Vegas was straight ahead. The morning sun sent welcome rays through the dashboard.

Then a gust of wind hit the Skeeter, and Lee had to control the steering wheel.

"Woa!" Juan said.

"Was that wind?" Nate said.

"Big gust," Lee said. The weather was making him nervous, but it wasn't just the weather. There was something else. What was it? He couldn't figure out what was bothering him.

"I'm okay going back to town," Nate said. "Storm's getting to me."

His words caught Lee off guard. Was Nate nervous, too?

Their radios blared a call from Dispatch. "Fifty-three we have a missing person call at Red Rock. Can you investigate? Over."

Lee dropped his chin. "Of all things. Day's not over, boys." He held up the radio. "We can do it, unless you have someone west of us. Over."

"Negative. Police are answering a call for a wreck on 215 with L.V.F.R. 47 and C.C.F.R. 28. You're the only ones west of there. Over."

Lee lowered the radio, looking at his team. "What do you think?"

"Dispatch hates us," Juan said.

Nate remained silent.

Lee remembered his shirt pocket. Though his coat was on, his lucky pen was still in its place. Lee swore. "Looks like we're going back." He picked up the radio. "We'll be there. Where exactly?"

"Scenic Loop. Ice Box Canyon."

"Back the way we came," Juan said.

Lee nodded, then he raised the radio to his lips. "Heading that way, Dispatch," he said. "Over."

"That's a few miles around the loop."

"Hang on," Lee said. He stopped the car, turned it around, and headed back west along 159. Another gust of wind hit them, and the storm above the western mountains swirled over the peaks.

Lee drove the Skeeter around the scenic loop. They passed Calico Hills North again. The red rocks appeared darker as the storm clouds filled the sky and blocked out the sun. The sagebrush moved with stiff jerks as the wind skimmed over the top of them. The blowing wind rammed the side of the Skeeter, pushing it off course. The engine whirred. The entire ride unsettled him.

"Captain, look at that."

# REVELATION

Lee raised his head. "What?"

"Over there." Nate pointed between Lee and Juan across the desert.

Lee raised his eyes. "I'm not seeing it."

"Look 10 o'clock. The silver backs."

Juan said, "Oh, I see them."

"I'm keeping my eyes on the road. What are you pointing at?" Sure enough, Lee noticed half a dozen silver backs about a mile in the distance. "Burros?"

"They sure are," Juan said. "They're booking it, too."

Lee swerved the truck as it rounded a curve.

"Captain, you want me to drive?" Juan said.

"Knock it off."

Lee slowed the Skeeter The burros were at least a mile away. They left a trail of dust behind them that blew in the wind.

"Captain," Nate said. "I've been out here before, but I have to say I've never seen burros move like that. Usually they just stand around."

Juan said, "Is it the storm?"

The truck rounded another curve, and the burros came into clear focus through the front window.

"Not sure," Nate said. "Looks like they're running from something."

Lee said, "They're headed toward the visitor center. Man, they are moving fast."

The Skeeter turned hard to the right, toward La Madre Springs and Lost Creek. They rounded another curve, and the burros returned into view.

"Maybe it's feeding time at the visitor center," Juan said. "Looks like me when my girlfriend cooks dinner."

"Always a casanova," Lee said.

"Does BLM know about them?" Nate said.

"Pretty sure."

"We're here, Cap'n" Juan said.

Lee slowed the truck. The sign for Ice Box Canyon appeared, and Lee steered into the parking lot. Two other cars were in the lot: an empty dark-blue Subaru Outback and a gray Saturn.

"We're here," Lee said.

A dark-haired woman in a puffy coat was in the Saturn. When the Skeeter pulled up, she opened her car door, climbed out, and walked to the truck. The wind blew her hair. She kept her hands in her coat pockets. Her tennis shoes and jeans were too urban to be hiking on a day like this.

Juan said, "Pretty girl."

"Remember you have a girlfriend," Lee said. He stopped the engine and opened his door, reaching up to make sure his lucky pen was still there. Before he could say anything the woman started speaking.

"I'm so glad you came," she said.

The wind blew colder, chilling Lee. "You're the one who called in the missing person?"

"I am. My name's Susan. Susan Mercer."

"I'm Fire and Rescue Captain Lee Tommen. This is Juan Carasco, and this is Nate O'Reilly."

The woman kept her left hand in her coat pocket while she shook the hands of the firemen.

"So, who's missing?" Lee asked.

# REVELATION

"Here's the car," Susan said. "I'm worried about whoever is driving this car."

Lee stood, quiet. Already, he doubted this woman. The word 'whoever' told him Susan did not know the person or people in the other car. *Was this a false complaint?*

"Ma'am," Juan said. "Do you know who owns this car?"

Susan paused. She fumbled with whatever was in her coat pocket. "Um, no."

Figured, Lee thought. "How long has he been gone?"

"I don't know," Susan said.

"Well then, why'd you call 911?"

Lee, Juan, and Nate waited.

She struggled to get the words out. "I…I just have a feeling."

"Oh, brother," Juan said.

Lee studied the mountains across the valley.

"Please, you'll have to trust me," Susan said.

"Ma'am. We're still waiting for a reason to." The storm blew harder.

Juan stepped aside to Nate, made a "she's insane" gesture with his finger, and walked toward the truck.

"I'm not crazy," Susan said.

Lee stepped forward. "Ma'am, you called 911 to report a missing person. Exactly who is missing?"

Susan's face flushed as she rubbed the back of her neck, still fumbling with her coat pocket with the other hand. "I told you. It's the people in this car."

"Are you sure there's more than one person?" He remembered his pocket. His lucky pen was still there, though it wasn't helping today.

Susan studied the trail that led into Ice Box Canyon. "There's something wrong. I'm worried about whoever went in there."

Juan stepped toward Lee. "Captain, if you want to report it as a false alarm…"

"Just a minute." Something *was* wrong. Lee didn't want to ask Susan about it in front of his men, but he had trouble disagreeing with her.

Juan said, "Should we let Red Rock Search and Rescue handle this? They've got people ready to help. All we need to do is call."

"Nate, call Dispatch. Do a search on the license plate. Tell me if anybody has reported it missing."

"I'm on it, sir." Nate climbed in the truck to avoid the wind so he could make a clear call to Dispatch.

Susan said, "I'm sorry I can't be more clear about this. But there's more going on."

Lee took a deep breath. He needed to be thorough. Show compassion. Get enough information to write up a good report for Sawvel. Then head back to town. "Ma'am, I know you feel that way. In fact, since the earthquake this morning, lots of people are on edge."

Juan raised his eyebrow. Lee winked at Juan, hinting to go along.

"It's not the earthquake," Susan said.

"What do you mean?"

Susan fumbled with her coat again. "I…I've had dreams."

Juan put his hands on his hip and looked away.

Lee motioned to Juan to settle down.

# REVELATION

"Ma'am, what's in your coat pocket? You keep fumbling with it." Lee expected her to hide whatever she was fumbling, but she pulled her hand out with the item.

"It's my Rosaries," she said. "I bring them wherever I go."

Juan rolled his eyes.

"Tell me," Lee said. "What's back there?"

"I don't know."

Nate shouted from the truck. "Captain, I have some info."

Lee said to Susan, "Excuse us a second, ma'am." He motioned for Juan to come.

Juan gave his Bradley Cooper look at Susan, who raised her eyes. Juan went back to Lee and met Nate at the truck. "Cap'n, she's crazy," Juan said.

"This whole day is crazy," Lee said. "But we have to play the cards we're dealt."

Nate said, "Are you ready for this?"

"What's the story?" Lee asked.

"That Outback is stolen."

"Since when?"

"About two weeks ago. It was reported in San Diego. Detectives thought it made it across the border and was torn apart and sold as spare parts. They seemed surprised to hear it wound up here."

"Who reported it?"

"Some guy named Crochet. He's 58 years old. I guess he teaches at a college in San Diego."

"So we don't know who is in that canyon."

"I couldn't say," Nate said.

"Stolen vehicles aren't our jurisdiction," Juan said. "That's PD."

"I agree. Let's go back and let the lady know."

The dark clouds spread across the sky, blocking out the morning sun. The wind whipped through their legs. Rain droplets fell. Susan's black hair blew across her concerned face as she held her Rosary. She appeared to be mumbling something as they approached her.

"Ma'am, I'm afraid we can't help you."

Susan didn't react to his statement.

He said, "It turns out this Subaru was reported stolen in California. We're not detectives, but we'll get some on the way. They'll handle the situation."

"I'm afraid it will be too late then."

"Why do you say that?"

"It just will."

Lee was pretty sure he and Juan had the same thoughts of leaving to get back to the station. The wind blew colder.

A rumble came from over the mountains, hinting at lightning.

"Ma'am. It's best if you go home."

"I can't. My car won't start. Plus, I have to go in there. If you won't help me, I'm going in there to investigate myself."

Her clothes were more fit for an outdoor mall experience, not a hike up the canyon.

Juan was right. Though she had an athletic build, her clothes told Lee she had no clue about hiking in Ice Box Canyon. Her coat was for urban shopping. Her tennis shoes were for sidewalks, not climbing up boulders. It's a public park. Sometimes people need to be accountable to themselves.

# REVELATION

Lee said, "Ma'am, you're not dressed to go up there."

"I know that."

"You'll be risking your life?"

"I have nothing left."

Juan mouthed, "Should we take her to a hospital?"

Lee shook his head.

The whole situation seemed strange. Something didn't sit right with him, and the woman, too.

As the dark clouds rolled over the mountain, casting a shadow on the desert floor, the dark green and brown sagebrush changed into hues of black and purple. Susan's hair whipped in the wind. Rain droplets wet his face. He didn't have an answer, and it bothered him.

"Captain, I have an idea," Nate said.

"You? What've you got?"

Nate went to the Skeeter truck. He opened a compartment and pulled out the drone. "We don't have much battery life, but this thing is designed to travel up to five miles."

Damned toys, Lee thought.

"Captain, can we fly this thing over the canyon?"

Lee doubted it would work, but he didn't know what else to do. "What about the wind?"

"It'll fly. I'll have to go high to keep the wind from blowing it into anything."

Susan was serious about going into the canyon. If she went, and he found out later something happened to her, he'd regret that he didn't keep her from it. He asked Susan, "Will you wait for us to at least try it."

Susan hesitated, giving Lee the impression that she was going to go up the canyon no matter what happened. Susan put her Rosary back in her coat pocket and fumbled with it before she said, "Okay. I'll wait." She went to her car, opened the passenger door, and grabbed her water bottle. She took a sip, then put it in her large coat pocket. "But I won't wait long."

Lee paused before he said, "Alright, kid. Let's see what you can do."

# CHAPTER 14

Nate opened the control box. The drone sat on the asphalt. The wind whistled through the drone's propellers though they remained motionless. Nate turned on the machine. "It should have enough battery life for one good trip."

"That thing has a camera on it?"

Nate showed Lee the control, and in the middle was a black screen.

"I'm not seeing anything," Lee said.

"That's the close-up of the pavement, Captain. We'll see more when it takes off."

Nate touched a few more buttons on the control. He went to the drone and inspected its parts. He said, "Everybody back up."

Lee and Juan stepped back, but Susan ignored the drone and looked to the west at Ice Box Canyon.

The wind whipped through them, and Lee shivered. His coat wasn't going to help if he didn't generate some body heat, and soon. Susan and Juan shivered also.

Nate touched another button, and the drone's propellers whirred, making a loud noise.

Nobody else was around, which was good. The last thing he needed was for some curious tourist to get in the way.

The drone shot straight up into the sky, the wind pushing it northward. Nate said, "I'll have to fight the wind, but I can handle it." He turned the control, and the drone zipped upward and westward toward the cloud-covered peaks of Ice Box Canyon.

"Here's the screen," Nate said. Juan leaned forward. Lee studied the screen in Nate's hand.

The screen's view showed the shadow-covered desert floor, moving top to bottom as the drone flew past. He didn't see anything but the trail, trees, rocks, and water. Little white specs streaked past the landscape.

"What is that?" Juan asked.

"Looks like snow," Lee said. He took his eyes off the screen. He heard the drone, but it was hard to find it in his view against the gray and red canyon walls. He spotted movement, a small black dot in the middle of the canyon. "There it is. Don't hit those walls."

"We're good so far. I'll slow it down just in case." Nate moved his eyes to the screen. He worked the camera angle to raise it forty-five degrees. They watched the trail and any oncoming cliff walls.

The wind in Lee's ears drowned out the buzz from the drone, now too far away to be heard.

As Lee watched the screen, he was amazed at the clarity of the picture. Technology had come so far, he thought. Would the future of firefighting and rescuing be done by machine?

"Captain, I'm not seeing anybody. We're more than halfway through."

# REVELATION

"Keep going," Lee said.

The screen went fuzzy, then came back. "Woa! What happened?"

"Could be the canyon walls. It might be making the radio signal a little erratic."

Juan studied the screen over Nate's shoulder. "Nothing so far, Cap'n. And the picture's getting fuzzy. Someone could be under those trees and we'd never know."

"If someone is in there, they'll hear the drone," Nate said. "I imagine the noise is louder in there, too. You know - echos."

Juan nodded.

Lee watched the screen. If someone was back there, where was he? The owner of the car reported it stolen. Was the thief in the canyon?

Hiding.

If hiding was the game, then a flyover won't reveal much.

"We're almost near the end," Nate said. The screen kept fluttering and coming back. "And that's a good thing as I don't know if we have all that much battery life left."

"Wait," Juan said. "I see something."

It was a small colored item on a flat rock. "See that thing there, Nate? Fly down there and get a closer look."

"Yes sir."

The screen drew closer as Nate lowered the drone. He angled the camera downward. The drone hovered a few feet above the colored item.

"What is that?"

"It looks like a coat, or a piece of cloth."

"No," Lee said. "It's a pack. See the straps?"

"Who wears a pack with that kind of color?"

Susan said, "It's a woman."

The three men raised their eyes. "Huh?".

She said, "It has to be a woman. And she's not prepared to be up there." She continued to fumble with her Rosary.

Lee said, "Nate, raise the drone, see if you can't get a wider angle of everything back there."

Nate nodded. The screen showed the canyon floor as the item appeared smaller in the distance. They saw the rocky trail, bushes, the stream, there was a tree-

The screen flashed bright yellow and went black.

"Where'd it go?"

"What happened?" Juan said.

"Nate?"

"I…I don't know, sir."

"Look!" Susan said.

A bright orange light lit up the black clouds above the canyon, and an odd silhouette moved within them. Lee caught it for a split second. Then it was gone.

"What the hell!" Juan said.

"Lightning?" asked Nate.

"Captain, the canyon is on fire!"

Lee's heart thumped in his chest. And then a voice came from the canyon. He could not make out the words, but it was deep and dark. Lee did not know the language. It spoke for a moment. Then the voice ended.

Lee froze. His feet stood firm on the asphalt.

"Captain," Juan said. "Did you hear that?"

# REVELATION

Lee couldn't move, like a rabbit frozen when a coyote passed it in the desert.

Juan's eyes were big, and his face turned white.

Nate stuttered, "Sir, have you heard anything like that?"

"Just the storm," Lee said, but he worried it wasn't. Something else was at play here, but he didn't want to scare them. He was already scared enough. They wanted answers though. He should tell them the truth - that he didn't know.

But control mattered more. He decided to lie. He heard tremors in his voice as he said, "Lightning causes forest fires. My guess is lightning hit our drone. That explains the flash. What we heard? Just thunder."

Juan and Nate stood still.

Susan huffed and stepped away from them. Did she know he lied? Was she one of those sixth-sense religious nuts?

The dark clouds moved above them, pressed by the winter wind. Small pieces of ice fell upon them, resting on their hair and shoulders. The falling sleet turned the desert shades of white.

The cold wind stung Lee's cheeks.

Susan waited, but she was getting impatient. She stood firm except for the occasional shiver. Her face seemed more determined like she knew something he didn't. What did she know? Why was she here? "I don't believe you," she said.

"Captain, what's the plan?" Juan said. His arms folded around his chest as he tried to keep warm.

Lee wanted some help. "Nate, find out when the police are coming."

Nate said, "Yes sir," and he returned to the Skeeter to get on the radio. The sleet fell upon them while they waited.

"I am going up there," Susan said.

"Ma'am, you'll freeze to death," Lee said.

"I'll wait in the car until the storm passes."

"You'll be waiting a long time. Why don't you go home and come back with better shoes, and during better weather?"

"I told you, my car won't start. There's no time, anyway."

"Time for what?"

"Captain," Nate said.

"What'd you find out?"

"No one can come. They said that all units are unavailable."

"What's going on in the valley?" Juan asked.

"They didn't tell me."

"Everyone's nuts over the earthquake."

Nate said, "Captain, while we're here, should we go up to investigate? At least we'll have responded, found out what's in that pack, and retrieved our drone."

Nate was by the book, and Lee had to admit that one quick trip in and out would check off the missing person call box. "What kind of hike is it to get back there?"

"I looked it up while you were talking. It's a moderate hike for some. Others say it's easy, but that's in good weather."

"At least we'll be moving," Juan said. "My legs are getting stiff."

Lee shook his head. "Nate, you sure Dispatch said no PD?"

"Yes sir."

Lee scratched his head. What was going on in the city? Regardless, they were on their own. He said to Juan, "You up for this?"

Juan smiled. "That's why they pay me the big bucks."

"I'm going, too," Susan said.

Lee cursed under his breath. "Ma'am, it's not a good idea. We train for situations like this every day. We'll be in and out in no time. If you come, it'll slow us down."

"There's more going on. I need to look for something else back there."

New info, Lee thought. "Okay. What, exactly?"

Susan fumbled with her pocket again. She shuffled her feet, showing signs of restlessness.

I'm done with her, Lee thought. "We have a job to do. Nate, how long is it to the rear of Ice Box Canyon and back?"

"An hour in, and an hour out."

"Okay. Notify Dispatch we have to investigate the canyon for what looks like a rescue. Don't tell them about the drone. If we find somebody, great. If not, when we get back we'll notify Red Rock Search and Rescue and they can explore this canyon when the weather's better."

"Yes sir."

"Oh, and Nate."

"Yeah?"

"Go in the Skeeter and find a blanket for Susan. She needs to get warm."

"On it."

"Juan, what if you and I go? Nate can stay here with the lady?"

"I'm not staying," she said.

Nate returned with a blanket. "Here you go, ma'am."

"I'm not staying," she said again

Lee said, "Ma'am, you need to stay. I'm going to have my man, Nate, stay here with you. We'll get back and let you know what we find."

Susan said, "Thanks for the blanket." She wrapped herself in it. As the wind blew, she turned into it and walked toward the trail. Her water bottle sloshed inside her coat pocket as she walked. After her feet left the pavement, her footsteps crunched the small rocks on the trail toward Ice Box Canyon.

Lee swore.

"She doesn't know how to take orders, Cap'n," Juan said.

"Alright. You men going to be warm enough?"

"We have our gloves and coats."

"Do we have any other warm clothes in the truck?"

Nate said, "When I heard the weather report, I packed some extra clothes and water just in case."

Nate's recent training kept him focused on the checklists, and right now Lee was glad he was.

"Good thinking. Do me a favor. Grab the smallest coat you have. We'll let the lady have it. Let's also grab our rescue packs. No telling what we'll find. Dress in layers. We're going to need all of them."

They went to the Skeeter, grabbed all the warm weather clothes they could find, including gloves and caps. They strapped on their red rescue packs, harnessed over their shoulders and around their waist.

They checked their radio belts strapped across their shoulders. Bottles of water jutted out of the pack's rear side pockets. Nate grabbed his spare coat. He held it under his arm.

# REVELATION

Everything felt bulky. Lee's lucky pen was pressed against his chest. Lee said, "Alright, men. Let's make this quick. Three in, three out."

"Captain?" Nate said.

"Yeah?"

"Don't you mean four?" Nate nodded toward the trail entrance.

Down the hill, Susan was fifty yards ahead of them. White sleet stuck to the blanket wrapped around her shoulders.

Lee adjusted his shoulder harness. He checked his water bottles. One, two, three, four. Juan and Nate had the same, making twelve between the three of them.

"Cap'n," Juan said. "You sure that was lightning we heard?"

"No."

"What else could it be?" Nate said, strapping his rescue pack around his waist.

"Come on," Lee said. "Let's get going." He stepped on the trail, toward the threatening cliffs covered by the dark, moving clouds, with the wind blowing in his face.

# CHAPTER 15

Lee, Juan, and Nate hurried down the trail. The wind chapped Lee's lips, but he was glad to get moving again. Standing in the parking lot only made him colder.

A rumble came over the mountains. "Captain, my guess is the drone hit the cliff," Juan said. "The wind pushed into it."

"Hell if I know," Lee said. "Nate, do drones make explosions like that when they crash into rocks?"

"I don't remember that in training," Nate said.

Lee's crunched rocks under his boots. He liked this part of the job, being outdoors. It helped him forget his problems.

Lee's cell phone rang, and it brought him back. It was Chief Sawvel.

"Hold up, guys." Lee held the phone to his ear. "Yes sir."

"Where are you?" Sawvel asked.

"We responded to a missing person call on the loop," Lee said. "We asked Dispatch if someone else could take it, but they said everybody is covered up."

"What've you found out so far?"

"We met the woman who called it in. She's determined to check it out. We saw some unusual activity up here. As cold as the wind is, we don't want to be up here long. We need to investigate one thing, and then we're coming back."

Sawvel didn't seem concerned, at least not about him. "Hurry it up. The whole city seems to be at each other's throats."

"Do you need us to abandon the call?"

"How long will you be?"

"Shouldn't be more than two hours," Lee said. "What's happening down there?"

"Call after call. We're convinced the earthquake got everyone's blood pressure up."

Lee nodded. "Same up here."

"Don't take long. We'll need you before the afternoon, I'm afraid."

Juan and Nate leaned in, hoping to hear. Lee put his finger up, motioning for them to hold on.

"It sounds like it's bad."

"Just unusual. I've never seen people treat each other this way," Sawvel said. "It's like decorum went out the window."

"We'll confirm when we've accomplished our mission," Lee said. "Then we'll head back right away."

"Don't dilly dally. If today keeps going like it is, we're going to need you."

"Roger that," Lee said. He ended the call. Juan and Nate stood on the trail, the wind kept blowing. "He says things are blowing up in town. Seems they're getting drowned by all the calls from Dispatch."

"What's going on?" Nate asked.

"He didn't say. Just said people aren't treating each other very well."

Juan pointed ahead. Susan had covered a good distance and she was close to the canyon walls. The blanket wrapped around her urban coat whipped in the wind. "We've got to get going."

Lee said, "The sooner we end this call, the better."

The three men marched westward to Ice Box Canyon. As they approached, Lee thought how he had never been to Ice Box Canyon. He had once taken Joan and Jenn hiking near Calico Hill One, right by the Visitor Center. But most of his time was in town, working on his new career.

Susan put some distance between her and the firemen. Once she made it inside the Ice Box Canyon walls, she slowed down. She appeared to be waiting for them as if she was afraid to continue.

"What's she waiting on?" Nate asked.

"Us," Juan said.

Lee and his men came to the base of the canyon walls. The wind died down, blocked by the cliffs. Susan sat on a rock, her blanket still wrapped around her. She took a sip from her water bottle. Nate approached with the spare coat and offered it to her. She dropped the blanket and put on the warm coat over her own. Then she picked up the blanket and wrapped it over her shoulders, then she sat on a small boulder.

"Don't get used to that," Lee said.

"Maybe I will," Susan said. "I never thought about working for the fire department."

"Best job in the world," Juan said.

"How're your feet holding up?" Lee said. He had hot spots where his boots were rubbing.

"I'm alright," Susan said. "I'll be glad to get this over with."

# REVELATION

"Okay, ma'am. Get what over with, exactly?"

Susan sat still, unflinching. She held her breath.

"Well?"

"I told you. I'm worried about those people up there."

"You said you don't know who owns the car. You don't even know if there's more than one person. How do you know something's wrong?"

"You lost your drone. Didn't you see the fire?"

"Yes. But what drove you to call before all that?"

Susan tightened the blanket over her coat. "Call it a feeling."

Lee walked up to the rock she sat on. He put his hands on his waist and leaned forward. "Ma'am. If you're coming along with us on a rescue mission, I have to make one thing clear."

"What's that?"

"I'm in charge. My men and I have been trained for just this situation. When we issue a command, it's not a suggestion. Got it?"

"Captain, do you go to church?"

Lee stood still. "What's that got to do with anything?"

"Do you?"

"No. Don't need it."

"Then you're not trained. At least not for this." She stood on her feet and walked along the trail. A cool creek ran out of the canyon. She walked alongside it, around a boulder.

"What the hell's that supposed to mean?"

Juan shrugged.

"Strange," Nate said.

"Come on," Lee said, and the men followed Susan into the canyon.

# CHAPTER 16

Lee followed close behind Susan, where he caught up with her. The large canyon walls loomed overhead, to their right and their left. The clouds above rolled past the heights of the canyon walls. Small bits of sleet fell upon his head. Susan walked wrapped in the blanket. Juan, physically fit, kept pace. Nate stayed behind a few paces. Lee figured he did so as a matter of seniority. He was a smart kid for not wanting to disobey his command.

As they caught up with Susan, Lee said, "Ma'am…"

"My name's Susan," she said.

"Alright. Susan. What did you mean back there?"

Susan said, "This isn't going to be a normal call."

"So far you're right," Lee said.

Susan nodded. She kept walking.

Lee's phone buzzed again. It was Sawvel. "Hang on, guys. It's the Chief.

He answered the phone. "Yes, sir."

"Bad news....You've got to come back." His voice cut in and out.

"Everything alright?"

REVELATION

"Unfort … no. As nuts as … have gotten down here in the valley, the County Mana… has given specific … for all emergency … to return to the city."

"You're cutting out, sir."

Juan and Nate waited with Lee as he spoke. Susan had walked a few steps but stopped.

Lee's tone changed. "It's not far back to the truck," Lee said. "Probably twenty, twenty-five minutes."

"Good," Sawvel said.

Lee turned off his phone. "Men, we have to go back."

Susan sprinted to Lee. "No. No you can't!"

"Ma'am, I was just given orders."

She grabbed his arm. Lee pulled his arm back, surprised at her touching him.

"I'm sorry."

Susan stood. She stared into his eyes. The light reflected from her dark pupils.

"Come on, guys," he said. He took several steps to get back to the truck.

"You *know*," she said.

Lee stopped. *Why does she keep saying weird things like that?*

Susan stepped forward. "You feel it, don't you. Something is wrong back there, and you know it."

Juan and Nate motioned like they were heading back, but Lee remained standing where he was.

"You know, don't you."

Lee didn't answer. The wind and the rain were up ahead, with the truck and the uncertain future of whatever chaos awaited them in the city.

"Captain?" Juan and Nate waited.

The canyon walls closed in behind Susan. Something was back there. He didn't know what, but his intuition said danger, and it was big.

"If you go, you'll know you left," Susan said.

"Of course I'll know I left. I want to leave. I don't want to find whatever's back there."

Susan's eyes lit up, and she raised her eyebrows. "You do know."

"Tell me what it is you're talking about." He shuffled his feet. He was ready to keep going if she didn't explain herself.

"I don't know exactly, except that something is back there."

"What is back there!"

"I said I don't know."

Lee stepped away and said to Juan, "You're right. She's crazy." He took three steps toward the Skeeter.

"If you go, your family will be in danger!" Susan raised her voice.

Lee, Juan, and Nate stopped. "Danger from what?"

"Fire," she said. "Something back there has to do with fire."

"How do you know?"

"I just know!"

Juan reached out and touched Lee on the arm. "Captain, we have orders."

Lee knew what Juan was saying. Sawvel gave him a command. But his gut told him something else was happening, something he couldn't explain. Susan was right. He did feel something. But how could he disobey an order based on 'something'?

"Susan, I have an order from my superior. You give me no rational justification for my disobeying his order, except for a hunch. If I disobey without facts, I'm disciplined at best, which I'm already going to get. At worst I'm terminated from a job I love."

"I know how you feel."

"Oh, how would you know?"

"Because I lost my job to come here today," she said. She stood firm, wrapped in the blanket that covered her urban coat.

"Why? How can I justify going up there? Sending my men up there?"

A tear formed in Susan's eye. She said, "You can't, except that feeling you have inside. I know you have it because I have it, too."

"That's not enough to go on," Lee said.

Juan leaned toward Lee. "Captain, why are you arguing with her?"

"Because she's right," Lee said. "There is something up there."

"Trust me," Susan said. "I don't want to do this either. I'd rather be in the valley, at work today, trying to build a future. But I had to come."

Juan let out a sigh. "Captain, what do you want us to do?"

Lee put his hands in his pocket. The ground was wet as sleet fell upon them, but they were shielded from the high winds by the red and brown cliffs. "How far are we to the back of the canyon?"

Nate said, "Not far. Maybe thirty, forty minutes."

"I'm sorry to do this, guys. But we need to take our chance. We need to recover that drone. We need to see if anybody has claimed that brightly colored pack we saw. And then when we don't find anybody, we need to come back right away, bring this lady out of the canyon, and report this missing person search and rescue as complete."

Juan said, "You know this will mean disciplinary measures. The Chief won't like it."

"I know," Lee said. "I'll deal with Sawvel."

"He'll deal with you," Juan said.

"Captain?" Nate said. "What will that mean for us? If we go with you, what happens to us?"

Lee said, "I don't know. You were following my command."

"Captain?" Nate had his hands in his pockets, working to keep warm.

"Yes?"

"You're doing the right thing."

"I don't understand it," Juan said. "But I agree."

"I thought you were trying to get me to follow orders?"

"I was," Juan said, "but I follow you, first."

Lee sucked in a deep breath of the cold air. He knew this would not go over well. Behind him, Susan stood still, wrapped in the blanket. "Okay, guys. We're all in on this."

"Yes, sir." Juan stuck his hand out.

Nate put his hand on top of Juan's. "I'm in."

"Alright," Lee said. He put his hand on top of Juan's and Nate's. "Ma'am, you might as well come join us."

# REVELATION

Susan walked toward the men. Then she pulled her hand out of her pocket under the blanket and put it on top of Lee's.

"Four in, four out," Lee said.

"Amen," Susan said.

Lee remembered his lucky pen and felt embarrassed.

After a moment of hesitation, the men nodded. Then the four of them hiked the trail together.

# CHAPTER 17

Ten minutes had passed, and they came to a large boulder. Sleet covered the rocks, and a cold stream passed by them on the right. They had passed puddles of water, and they had stepped over mud, under barren tree branches, and through gaps in the rocks as they continued on the trail.

They stayed silent as they went, except for a grunt or a helpful word of caution. Lee thought of the trouble he would get into if he was not back when expected. He checked his cell phone, but there was no answer or communication. He said, "You guys getting any communication from the valley?"

Juan and Nate both answered, "No sir."

"Will we be able to communicate when we get in there?"

Juan said as he moved around a boulder, "We should get some coverage. It may be delayed, though. Text would be best."

"We'll need to test it," Lee said.

"I just sent you a text," said Nate.

Lee laughed how when it came to technology Nate was always first. He expected his phone to buzz, but nothing came through.

"I'm not getting anything," Lee said.

"It must be relaying through the airwaves."

Lee kept walking. Susan was behind them now. They were making good time, and he was glad she kept up.

"Susan," Lee said. "So what exactly are you seeking up here?"

Susan did not answer. She walked over a branch. Though she was out of her element, she didn't complain.

"Are we going to find people up here?"

"I don't know."

"You're not looking for people, are you?"

Susan stepped around a boulder, and she leaned against it. "No, I'm not."

The men stopped and turned around. Susan remained where she was.

"What then?"

"A fountain."

"A what?"

"A fountain," she said again. "A hidden fountain."

Juan swore. He shook his head.

"Take that back," said Susan. "You don't know what you're saying."

Lee moved down the trail, past Juan and Nate. "Okay, Susan. What is this hidden fountain?"

"I don't know." Her face grimaced, and a rumble of thunder rolled overhead as the dark clouds blew above them by the wind. Sleet stuck to her blanket and hair.

"You don't know a lot," Lee said. "Nate, how far to the top?"

"About twenty minutes, I'd imagine."

"We don't have time to wait," Lee said. He motioned back to the lead, ready to get this mission over. With any luck, they'd be done and back and, though late, perhaps able to avoid any serious disciplinary action.

"I heard a woman's voice."

The three men stopped.

Susan leaned on the rock.

"I heard a woman's voice. Several times. I've had dreams, dreams that seemed more real than we are standing here today. Every time, I see a vision of these canyons in the mountains, and the woman's voice tells me to seek the fountain. I see a fountain, and usually that's all I see. Then I wake up."

Juan whispered, "We may need to check her into a mental hospital when we get back."

Lee offered a weak smile. Susan needed help. She carried Rosaries as her crutch because she was confused and scared. He whispered back to Juan, "Just go with it."

Juan nodded. In their firefighting and rescue calls, they had seen normal people act strange. These people were often wrong, but they believed what they believed, and during the crisis they refused to listen to reason.

"Susan, what do you mean when you say 'usually'?"

She hesitated. Then she said, "Last night, there was more. After I saw the fountain, I saw a fire. A hot fire, so hot it would melt the strongest steel. I don't know where it came from, only that it was there."

"Is that why you called the fire department?"

"It had crossed my mind, yes."

"Captain, we don't use a water truck," Nate said.

## REVELATION

Lee chuckled. There was Nate's lack of experience, stating the obvious. Would the kid adapt to an untrained situation?

"Susan, is there anything else?"

"Yes, there is."

"I'm not surprised," Juan said.

"Go on," Lee said.

Susan wrapped her blanket closer around her. "Every time I've had a dream, I've come up here to look for the fountain."

"In this canyon?" Juan asked.

"No. I've gone to all the others, though. I obeyed, and I went the day after each dream. They were so real, I had to go. Anyway, this is the last one. I don't know if the fountain is here, but I have to try to find it. I've lost so many jobs because of this."

Juan and Nate stayed quiet, not sure what to say.

Lee said, "You know, my uncle used to say when you're up the creek, make sure you still have your paddle. I never knew what he meant by that, but that didn't make him a bad guy."

Susan hinted at a smile.

Nate said, "So, are you a prophet or something?"

"I hope not," Susan said.

Juan said, "I don't believe in God."

Susan frowned. She didn't like hearing that. She said, "I didn't ask for this."

"No one does," Lee said.

"How about you, Captain. Do you believe in God?"

Lee fumbled for words. Now he wished he didn't have a lucky pen at all. He had been trained to avoid religious and political topics while he was on the job. "Maybe," Lee said. "If he's up there, it doesn't mean he's down here."

Susan asked, "What do you mean by that, Captain?"

"I'm just saying that I have to make my own choices, and I own them. What happens to me is because I decide."

Susan let out a small laugh. "That hasn't been my experience."

"I want to believe in God," Nate said. "I don't know much about him, but I like the idea."

"Rely on your training, kid, or your life's at risk," Lee said.

"Yes sir."

"Now wait," Susan said. "No one said prayer was a substitute for action."

"No offense, ma'am. But you're the one who keeps losing jobs."

"Only because I'm willing."

"Well, I'm not," Lee said.

Susan rubbed her neck, then said, "Captain, I don't like these dreams, but I choose to listen to them because I believe there's a purpose in them."

"A purpose? Lady, you said over and over again that you don't have any idea what we'll find up there."

"I know that," she said. "But I trust. Just because I don't understand doesn't mean I'm not receiving instructions."

Juan leaned against a rock. "All this is making my head hurt."

"But what if there is a God?" Susan said. "You rush into fires not wondering if you'll come out alive?"

"That's right. I rush into situations relying on my training."

"Captain?" Nate said.

"What is it?"

"I hear something."

REVELATION

Everyone stood still. A crack of thunder echoed through the canyon. Lee flinched on instinct as the rumble vibrated between the cliff walls.

# CHAPTER 18

The echo bounced between the canyon walls, and then it was gone. The clouds rolled past the cliffs, hiding the rims of Ice Box Canyon. They moved like a silent magician ready to uncover what was behind his cape. When an opening appeared in the clouds, they revealed rock. The canyon cliffs rose to magnificent heights up steep colorful walls.

Lee's team had a hundred yards to traverse to reach the end of the canyon. He studied the cliffs. Did a boulder fall and hit the drone? The odds of that were low.

It could explain the voice, though, what he heard. A rolling boulder could have made the sound.

Lee hated not knowing. It meant he was vulnerable, and he hated feeling vulnerable.

Whatever Nate thought he heard, it was probably a loose rock. "You just heard the thunder," Lee said.

"No. That wasn't it," Nate said. He remained still, his ears and eyes pointed up.

"I'm not seeing anything,"

"Wait.".

# REVELATION

"We need to get going." Lee stood tall and stepped on the sleet-covered trail. His boot slipped a little. The last part of this trip was going to be slow.

Juan followed. But Nate stood still, his eyes watching through the clouds. Susan stood next to him, also watching.

"Nate, you coming?" Juan asked.

"Yeah. Something moved up there, though."

"We heard it," Lee said. "Just thunder. Shook a rock loose."

"No. I thought I saw something."

Susan said, "I thought I did, too."

Juan caught up with Lee. "She's infecting Nate with whatever she's got."

Lee's mouth held back a smirk. "Why not try your famous grin? Could calm her down."

"I don't think it will work on her."

Lee shouted, "Nate. Come on!"

Nate pointed at the high cliffs. "There. I see it!"

Lee and Juan didn't see anything. Just the clouds rolled past the cliffs, nothing more.

Lee said, "Okay-"

"Look at that. The kid's right!" Juan said.

"What do you see?" Had Lee's eyes aged?

"Bighorn sheep. There's one moving along the cliffs."

Susan smiled. "I see it."

Lee asked, "Where?"

Juan pointed. Under the rolling clouds, a desert bighorn sheep clung to the side of the cliffs. It had a muscular body. Its coat blended in with the rocks to make it appear invisible. Its light-colored coat on its hindquarters was shaped like a crescent moon.

Its legs were bent, placing its hooves on a rock that could slip away with any step. If the creature fell, its body would smash onto the solid rocks at the base of Ice Box Canyon.

The Bighorn sheep would not fall, though. It was as agile as an ant climbing up a wall.

"Amazing," Lee said. The creature's head was crowned with beautiful circular horns. Lee thought of the Los Angeles Rams, how they donned that shape on the player helmets, but the horns on this animal were majestic. No need for imitations. This creature had power in its neck, shoulder, and legs that were unmistakable, and real.

"How does that thing not fall?" Juan said.

"He has a gift from God," Susan said. "It's how he made him."

"There's more than one." Nate hadn't moved from his standing position. The grin on his face reminded Lee of Nate's youth like a young boy excited to see the wax animal exhibits when he went to the museum. "There's a bunch of them".

"Sure are." Juan covered his brow with his hand, blocking out the sleet.

"How many do you see?" Lee squinted. The creatures blended in with the rocks.

He searched for their movement.

One of them moved. It came into focus. Once he found the shape, several more appeared.

It was a herd.

They moved along the cliff face in the direction of the canyon's entrance.

"Is that their normal behavior?" Juan adjusted his rescue back harness over his shoulders. "It looks like they're wearing anti-gravity boots. Either that or they're sticking to the cliffs?"

Lee admired the herd's movement, their ability to walk the cliff face like it was a stroll through a neighborhood.

"Okay. Enough nature watching. Let's get this job over with."

"Captain, remember the burros?" Nate said.

"What about them?"

"These Bighorn are moving in the same direction."

Lee lifted his eyes. The sheep moved away from the back of the canyon, towards the entrance. They wasted no time.

"What burros?" Susan asked.

"We saw some burros running across the desert while we were on our way here," Lee said.

"They left a trail of dust behind them," Nate added. "Never seen anything like that before."

"A trail of dust?" Susan said. She put her hand up to her chin. "My grandfather was Native American. He used to tell me stories about wild desert animals. Not once did he say he saw a burro run."

Nate said, "Cap'n, where are they going? Are they scared of us?"

The animals seemed intent on heading east, out of Ice Box Canyon. Lee didn't know if the thunder was driving them out, or the wind. Maybe they were migrating? "Maybe the weather has them spooked," he said. Another rumble of thunder echoed between the canyon walls as he said it, justifying his statement.

"Cap'n," Juan said. "Do the animals know something we don't?"

Lee glanced at Juan, then he turned to Susan again. She was quiet, her brow bent with worry. What did she know?

"Let's go," Lee said. "Not too far now. Let's get what we came for, and let's get the hell out of here."

The four of them stepped back onto the path. The sleet fell on Lee's face as he marched across the makeshift trail, traversing wet, loose, and slippery rocks. Up ahead, the canyon walls closed in. Several trees and waterfalls were between them and the end of Ice Box Canyon.

# CHAPTER 19

The cold penetrated Lee's coat as they trod through the sleet. Moving helped him stay warm, but the damp clothes were having their effect. He knew it wouldn't be long before the cold overtook them.

"Captain," Juan said. "Can you feel your toes?"

"Can you?"

"Barely."

Susan pulled out one of her Rosary beads and held them with her hand under her blanket. She moved around a boulder, but slipped and fell to her knees. She let out a small scream, and she swore, but she held firm to her beads.

"Ma'am," Lee said. Susan was still on her elbow and knees, the blanket muddy on its edges from falling into the sleet-covered dirt. "You may need both hands from here on. Why don't you put those beads back in your pocket?"

"That's not a good idea," she said.

Lee put his hands on his hips. "Ma'am,"

"It's Susan."

"Whatever. Look, we're trying to get you in and out of here alive. Don't make it any more dangerous than it needs to. I don't want to have to carry you out of here."

"I'm holding the beads," she said.

"Susan," Lee said. "There's not much time,"

"No, there isn't."

"You can say your prayers when we get out of here," he said.

"No. I need to pray."

Nate asked, "What are those beads for, anyway?"

"It's a Rosary," she said.

Nate said, "What's a Rosary?"

Susan said, "It's a form of prayer. It reflects on the life of Jesus, and it asks for his mother Mary to intercede for us."

"Does it work?"

"Sometimes."

Juan laughed.

"What's so funny," Susan said.

"Sometimes doesn't work in our business."

Lee said, "Nate, let's go. If she stumbles, we'll get her on the way back."

"I'll be fine," Susan said.

"Then don't slow us down," Lee said. He imagined Sawvel sending up a police squad to bring him in. He didn't like that idea. He shifted his boots and stepped over the creek that ran alongside the trail. "Rocks are slippery. Be careful." He splashed water as his boots shifted on some wet rock. His pants got wet.

Juan followed close behind. "Captain," he said. "We need to move faster. I'm sensing something."

## REVELATION

"What do you mean?" Lee said. Things were strange since they entered the Canyon, and Susan was right when she called him out on what he was sensing. Call it intuition. He didn't believe in prayer. Action carried weight. But all he had with him was his lucky pen, which he now regretted bringing. He didn't mind that she was trying to pray.

So long as she didn't slow them down.

He went under drooping tree branches. The sleet was now covering everything. The wind had died down inside the canyon, but a cold chill hung in the still air in between snow-covered cliffs.

A strange smell hit his nostrils.

"Is that sulfur?" Juan said.

"Sure smells like it."

"Is there a natural gas leak up here?"

It had the strong odor of rotten eggs. "Can't be sewer," Lee said. "Gotta be natural gas." Lee touched his nose until he was used to the odor.

Lee imagined the drone and the pack were close by. "Keep going. We're almost there."

He stepped under and through more drooping tree branches. The creek ran from melting sleet and rain, making a pleasant sound. With cliffs shielding the wind, he thought this was a pleasant setting. Silent.

Then a chill ran through him. The chill was much colder than the wind. He shuddered as it ran through his torso and hips. A cold like that had never touched him before..

Susan brought her Rosary up to her lips and kissed it. She said the prayers louder. "Hail Mary, full of grace…"

"Shhhh," Lee said. They were being watched. This time, Susan obeyed. She scanned the area, searching. The cliffs didn't move. The clouds rolled as they had since they entered the canyon. Thunder rumbled in the distance. But something was different.

"We're not alone here," Juan said. His brow was sweating. It wasn't because of the hike.

"Did you feel that chill?"

"Yes sir," Juan said. He took a few soft steps forward, passing Lee. He worked to get a better view of what lay ahead.

The four remained quiet. The creek was the only noise, except for the falling sleet that hit their clothing. The area was turning white. Lee worried that the drone and the pack wouldn't be so easy to find if they had been buried in ice.

Then Juan's face went white. His eyes widened, and he let out a yell. He ran into Nate, knocking him over and into a rock.

"Get him!" Lee shouted.

Juan leaped over Nate's falling body. Nate grunted as his torso fell into the cold creek water.

Lee pumped his arms, his rescue gear clanging as he chased his man down the trail.

# CHAPTER 20

Nate hurried to his feet, his boots splashing water. Susan ducked out of the way. Juan ran into a drooping tree branch and hit his head. He fell. Nate dove on top of Juan. Juan tried to throw Nate off, but Lee jumped on the two men. They wrestled in the sleet.

"Get out of here!" Juan said. "We have to get out of here!"

"Hold him down!" Lee grabbed Juan, who tussled with the two. Juan flailed like a bird in a net, tearing his coat sleeve on a stone.

"What's gotten into him!" Nate said.

"Hold him!" Lee wrapped his arms around Juan. Juan struggled, punching Lee in the rescue pack and ribs. "Juan. Juan! Calm down!"

"We have to get out of here, Captain. We're in trouble!" Juan's teeth clenched. His eyes were wide, and his neck muscles strained through his shirt.

Blood seeped through his coat, but Juan paid no attention.

"Juan, relax," Nate said. He grabbed Juan's legs. The three wrestled under the drooping branches. One of Juan's water bottles fell from his emergency pack. Its cap fell off, spilling the contents.

"Juan, we're here. We're here together."

"It's not good. It's not good," Juan said. "We're in trouble here." Juan's effort lessened.

"Juan," Lee said. "We're firemen. We're always in trouble."

Juan's dark pupils showed fear, but his senses reappeared. "I'm sorry, Captain."

Lee held him still, uncertain if Juan was serious or trying to get Lee to release his grip so he could escape and run. "What's going on, Juan?"

"I saw something," he said. "Something horrible. Something I never want to see again."

"What did you see?"

Juan held his breath. "I don't want to say," he said.

"Okay," Lee said. He knew he couldn't force it. Juan would get excited about things, and often overdo them, but this was the first time Juan turned tail and ran.

Nate released his grip and knelt beside the two men. "Captain, what should we do?"

"I'm okay," Juan said. "I'm sorry."

Lee wasn't sure he should let go. "Can I trust you?"

"Yeah," Juan answered.

Juan's muscles relaxed. Lee allowed himself to loosen his grip. Eventually, he let go and rolled over.

Juan said, "We need to hide."

"Where?" Nate said.

Lee furrowed his eyebrows at the young man.

Nate shut his mouth.

Juan rolled over on his side. He put his arms over his midsection.

REVELATION

"Where did you have in mind, Juan?"

"Somewhere. Behind a boulder. In a cave. I don't know."

Susan walked over to the men. She held her beads. "Is he alright?"

Lee held up his finger, not saying one way or the other. "Can you get up?"

"I'm not feeling all that good, Cap'n. Like I want to throw up."

"You just sit for a moment."

Nate got up and sat on a nearby rock. His clothes were wet and muddy. Susan stood next to him, mouthing the words to her prayers. Nate studied her, curious.

Lee knelt beside Juan. He didn't want to get out of arm's reach in case he sprinted away again.

Juan said, "I don't know what it was I saw. But it was evil. Pure evil."

Lee didn't know what to say. He had been in homes ablaze with fire, and those flames had the look of a living evil creature.

"Captain. Is it hypothermia?" Nate said.

"It's not that," Juan said.

"You wouldn't know it if it was."

"It's not that."

Lee put his hand on Juan's shoulder. "You've had a pretty rough day," Lee said.

"Yes sir."

"Can you go on?"

Juan nodded. "I'm sorry captain. I know I saw something. It scared me to death."

"What will you do if you see it again?"

Nate said, "Captain, There's something-"

Lee shushed him. "Juan, what will you do?"

Juan calmed himself. He put his hand on Lee's shoulder. "Kick its ass," he said.

"That's more like it." Lee stood up and helped Juan to his feet. Juan was shaky, bent over with his hands on his knees. Lee offered some water, and Juan took a sip, spit it out, and swallowed some more. Then he hunched over again and spat.

Susan said, "I'm praying for you."

Juan put his hand out and touched Susan on the shoulder. "Ma'am. Just in case. Did you bring along any extra beads?"

Lee shook his head. Well, that was a reversal, he thought.

"I do carry a spare," she said. She put her right hand into her coat pocket and pulled out a Rosary, with a small wooden cross and light blue beads. Juan held out his hand and accepted them. She placed them in his palm.

"I thought you weren't religious," Lee said.

"Not until two minutes ago."

A clap of thunder cracked and echoed between the canyon walls. Lee flinched, threatened by the storm. He studied Juan, Nate, and Susan. "Can we finish this?"

"Four in, four out," Juan said. "We need to find that pack, though. I'm worried about whoever came in that Subaru."

Lee gathered himself. His clothes had mud on them, and they were wet. Hypothermia could have affected Juan. It could overcome any of them at any moment.

"Are you cold, Juan?"

"Not so bad, Captain."

"Can you tell us what you saw?"

# REVELATION

Juan leaned against the rock next to the trail. He stood up, his face tense.

"I saw a dragon," he said.

Lee raised his eyebrows. Nate and Susan had their mouths open, with surprise on their faces.

"That's what I saw, Captain. A red, fire-breathing dragon!

# CHAPTER 21

Fury made himself invisible. The human saw him, and that was enough for now.

The dark clouds moved through him as though he was not there. But he was there. His spirit eyes, filled with hatred, glared at the four humans in the canyon.

The morning's events came quickly. The first two humans he had devoured. He had made himself physical and chomped down on the man before he knew what had happened. He relished the taste of the man's blood. The man's soul, dark and red from a life of selfishness, cowered once it left his body. The soul screamed at Fury. Then the shadows moved, and other demons, minor ones but part of the Rebellion, exited the cracks in the rocks. They grabbed the man. The man resisted, but he was no match. Soon, he was pulled into a crack within the rocks, his pleading disappearing as the shadows dragged him into the abyss.

Fury next went after the woman. She was different. Her soul was also red and black, but it was shifting. There was some regret inside her, a recognition for repentance, for needing forgiveness, for realizing she had made mistakes and she needed to make better choices.

# REVELATION

Fury could not have that. She would make the Count. He had to act right away.

Then the dog saw him. Animals, being a part of Creation, but not tainted with sin, saw spirits.

The dog tried to warn the woman, but she was too confused and angry. Her sin would not let her open her heart to what the dog was trying to say.

Fury materialized and hovered above her, blocking out the sun. The woman screamed at the top of her lungs.

Fury had clamped down upon her flesh, devouring her instantly. Her soul remained, standing atop the rocks.

The shadows moved, and the minor demons slithered from the cracks. To Fury's disappointment, she begged for forgiveness from on High.

A light flashed through the black clouds like a meteor coming through the atmosphere. It was an angel of the heavenly hosts. The angel was bright.

The woman cried.

Fury glared at the angel.

The angel glared back.

Fury reared his head back, ready to send the angel and the woman into Oblivion. Fury lunged with his dragon jaws, but they clamped down on nothing.

The angel had grabbed the woman's soul by the hand, and flew her like a rocket through the dark clouds, leaving a bright blue streak through a brief opening that exposed the sky. Then the opening closed again, and the clouds were dark.

The woman had escaped. Though Fury had consumed her flesh within his fiery torso, Fury had missed a chance to send another soul to judgment, to add one more to the Count. He clenched his claws to the rocks, which crumbled under the strength of his grip.

He spread his wings and flew up above the clouds. As the clouds spread before his power, he went through them and hovered below the blue sky. The morning sun was bright, but Fury focused his vision high into the next realm.

Somewhere up there was Michael, the General of God's angelic army. Michael had pierced Fury during the Rebellion, sending him to his cell and trapping him for centuries. Fury would have his revenge.

But also up there was the woman. Fury feared the woman. It was the woman who caused the Rebellion. When the Prince of Light refused to acknowledge God's plan to be born of a woman, a creature, and that she would be esteemed above the angels, The Prince and one-third of the angels rebelled. War had broken out. The woman, not yet created, would defeat the Prince.

Fury had not yet seen her. He was in his cell when she was born. He was in his cell when the Son was born from the woman's womb. Though she was a creature, the angelic hosts revealed themselves to simple shepherds and sang glorious songs about the Most High.

Fury snapped his jaws. If not for Michael, the Rebellion would have succeeded. Since he was in his cell, he could not become a god and corrupt man into violence.

Instead, her Son was born and had lived. He died as the Lamb of God, sacrificing himself for sins and opening the Gates of Heaven.

# REVELATION

The woman was assumed into Heaven. She was with him now.

She could crush the serpent's head with her prayers to her Son.

Yet, Fury had been released. That meant that man was rejecting God. If there was one weakness of the Most High, it was that He loved his creatures enough to respect their free will, even if they sinned against him.

"Free Will. Ha!" Fury said. "What kind of God takes his power and grants a portion of it to the minds of creatures? A powerful god would keep all his power, and lord it over his subjects. A God that respects free will is no God. He is weak. He must be replaced."

Fury thought of Adam in the Garden. How easily, how quickly Adam sinned against God. The Prince had exposed God's weakness through the free will of man.

And yet God wanted angels to honor a woman? Creatures were weak.

The Most High's weakness was his love for his creatures. Death now entered the world because of sin. So did judgment.

Fury joined the Prince and rebelled. The Rebellion would have won. If only Micheal hadn't pierced him.

There was a glint to the east. Above the city, the sun's reflection bounced off a moving object in the air. Inside the object sat hundreds of humans, their souls consisting of varying colors. Most of them were gray. Some were black. Some were red.

Others had bluish hues, representing their connection with God.

Fury laughed at man flying. As the metal carriage moved, Fury focused his eyes. He could knock down that object in an instant, and each soul he'd send to judgment.

Below the flying carriage, the city awakened. Metal carriages drove on wheels, their engines run by heat and motion. They moved on paved roads that navigated between large buildings.

Fury was not interested in the buildings, or how they were constructed. He was more interested in what was inside them. People were in them, and each one reflected the state of a soul.

Most of the souls in the city were gray, or turning black. They were indifferent to God.

Some were varying degrees of red, signifying their anger against their fellow man. Fury grinned. A large portion of the city was indifferent. But these red ones, they would be his first followers. One of these he'd possess, making the man a priest and king. He would gain control. Then he would proclaim Fury as their god.

Mixed within the black and red, however, were the bright ones. They had their shades of blue. The brighter they were, the closer they were to the Almighty. These confused him. They were a threat to him. Fury wanted to ruin them, but he knew not the ways of deception. Adam and Eve had the brightest souls in the Garden, but the Prince knew how to deceive them into sinning against God. It worked, and Adam's soul turned black upon the sin.

How would Fury handle these bright ones? The sight of him might be all he needed to turn their souls black.

He lowered himself below the clouds and perched on the canyon cliffs. A tree moved, its branches jerking.

REVELATION

The dog was entangled in the tree. When Fury lowered himself, the dog panicked and tried to run, but was caught. Fury would destroy the dog soon. Anything connected to man had to be destroyed.

The clouds swirled around him. The shadows blocked out the sun, and the wind blew with the coldness of his spirit.

To the east, a small blue vehicle sat in a parking lot. It had to be the carriage that brought Fury his first two victims.

But then he saw headlights. Another carriage pulled up. Inside the carriage was a bright soul. A woman. There was something with her, though. It was far brighter than anything he had seen since the Rebellion. It was brighter than Michael's sword. Not as bright as the Almighty, but enough to cause Fury confusion.

Fury squinted. The light inside the carriage warned him of danger. He could not tell what it was. He knew only that it endangered him.

The woman remained inside the carriage. She did not get out. After several moments, he noticed headlights.

A second carriage appeared. This one was red.

Three souls were inside it. All three were gray, like most of those in the city.

These were men.

When they arrived, they got out of their carriage.

The woman approached them. The bright object inside her pocket went with her.

The three men showed no indication that they knew the power in her pocket.

They spoke with her, and soon they launched a device. It flew through the wind toward Fury. As it neared him, it lowered.

He spread his leathery wings, stretching them from north to south inside the clouds.

The device flew, bouncing with the wind.

It looked for something. A small lens moved, and it reminded him of the pupil of an eye. The device gathered intelligence. It showed the people what was in the canyon.

The device lowered.

The lens focused on the spot where Fury had devoured the man and the woman, the spot where their souls had met their end.

Fury materialized into his dragon form, his wings still spread. The dark clouds swirled around his leathery membranes and his impenetrable scales. He reared his head back and launched a stream of eternal fire at the device.

The device exploded and fell into a heap of ashes. The wind scattered the ashes across the canyon.

The humans would never find the device. Perhaps its destruction would prevent the woman, and the bright thing in her pocket, from coming near him.

He gathered his wings and watched. What was in the woman's pocket? Why did it glow? Why did it hurt his eyes?

He would breathe fire upon the mortals. But the light the woman carried made him cautious. He had not seen this light before. It was from the Almighty, but different.

Would it be a call, a device that alerted Michael and his army to come to their defense? If he incinerated them, would the Heavenly army swoop down, attack, and imprison him again?

## REVELATION

He spread his wings, and he lifted his head. Thunder rumbled across the distant valley. He gathered flames inside his torso, but he did not release them. The flames sputtered between his teeth.

He had to be cautious. His aggression had cost him during the Rebellion. He would not let that happen again.

Not until he knew what that item was.

The bright object carried a divine grace, something from the Almighty. The object in the woman's pocket was there to protect them.

Yet he doubted the men, mere mortals with their gray souls, understood it.

The clouds swirled around him.

As he considered his next move, the bright light caught his attention. He watched in horror as the woman left the men and carried the bright object in his direction.

She was coming into the canyon!

Fury roared and flew to the top of the mountain. He did not expect to confront a member of the faithful so soon.

Was that the Creator's plan, to challenge him with a woman immediately upon his freedom? He did not know, but he knew the scriptures. He knew about the enmity God had put between the serpent and the woman.

He perched above the canyon.

He would not let a creature defeat him.

He had to decide his plan.

The three men followed the woman. As she walked the trail leading into the canyon, Fury thought of the events. She had arrived first, but she had stayed with her carriage. She left the carriage when the three men arrived. Had she called them somehow?

And now, she was walking first into the canyon. And the men followed her.

Fury suspected that the woman needed the men. The men were her strength, her help. Did she not know the power that was in her pocket?

Very well. Fury knew that he had to attack weakness. The woman's strength was with her.

The party's weakness was the gray souls, the souls indifferent to God. The men.

He would test their strength. He would test their courage. He would test their faith.

As they approached, he waited. He lifted his wings, and he roared. A bright flash of thunder struck the canyon, and the boom echoed between the rock walls.

Bighorn sheep flinched from their positions on the cliff and scattered eastward and away from Fury.

The humans paused from the weather, the lightning, and the thunder, but they pressed forward.

He returned to his spirit form. The bright light in the woman's pocket hurt his eyes, burning them.

He scanned the valley. Was this whole thing a trap? None of Michael's soldiers were in view. A few guardian angels were in the city to the east, but none that matched his strength and quickness. Many demons roamed the city as well, but they did not come to him. Perhaps they did not know of his release.

He paced above the canyon, growing frustrated. The Bighorn sheep hugged the canyon walls. He grew impatient, turned into his physical form for a second, and destroyed one of them, biting it in half. Its remains fell to the bottom of the canyon.

The bite did not satisfy him. Only the taste of human flesh excited his senses.

He turned invisible again. The cold wind whistled through him.

He listened to the men and the woman conversing. They spoke in a foreign language, a language that did not exist in the Beginning.

He squinted past the bright light coming from the woman's pocket and studied the men.

One had an aura of leadership. He walked with authority. But he carried something in his chest pocket, something that contained an unholy meaning.

The other man was cocky and self-assured. He behaved that way to hide his fears.

The youngest of the men was calm and had a slight bluish tint to his spirit. He had not the years to be disillusioned with life.

The cocky one would be his target. Fury did not want to get close and attack, as he was unsure of the bright light with the woman.

He decided to play a trick. He glowed his eyes red, burned the flames within his gut, and revealed himself to the cocky one.

The man's fear overtook him.

He ran like a frightened rabbit.

The other men chased him down and tackled him.

For a brief moment, they separated themselves from the woman by a short distance.

Fury saw a quick opening. He moved toward the men and opened his jaws.

But then the woman went to the men, and the bright object in her pocket burned Fury's scales. They sizzled, and he flew to the top of the canyon. He tried to glare at the woman, but she held the bright object in her hand and said a prayer.

The bright object grew brighter. He put his large forearm over his eyes, his large claws covered his reptilian face. Invisible fire spewed from his mouth. His giant wings folded behind his spiny torso, while his elongated tail swished the air hidden by the dark clouds. Rocks fell from their positions on the cliff and bounced into the canyon.

The woman glowed a bright blue by the power of her prayer and the object in her hand.

Fury clenched his teeth. The woman was dangerous. She could defeat him.

He would have none of it.

Fury knew he had to defeat this woman and these men first. If it came to light that Fury could not defeat four humans alone in the desert, the Prince would destroy Fury himself.

Fury would find their weakness. He would learn about the object.

He would separate the men from the woman.

And he would devour them all!

Men are mortal. He would exhaust them and then ruin them. They have no bearing on the power of the angels. Fury imagined the taste of their blood upon his tongue.

# REVELATION

The new Rebellion would begin.

It would begin with the four in the canyon. It would begin once he sent their souls to immortal judgment!

## CHAPTER 22

"I'm ready, Captain." Juan put the Rosary into his pocket. He brushed himself. He swiped off the mud and inspected his torn coat. He noticed blood where he had ripped it. The sleet fell harder upon them.

Lee looked up at the clouds. They were darker and threatened thunder. He heard the wind above as it whistled through the rocks. "We need to get going. The sooner we finish this mission, the better."

"I'm with that," Juan said.

Lee stepped forward. The sound of the sleet echoed through the canyon. He hoped they would find the pack and the drone under the fallen ice.

Susan held her Rosary. She said her prayers louder this time. Lee had imagined it would be a distraction, but he found it soothing.

Juan said, "Can you teach me to say that with you?"

"Sure," Susan said. "Do you know the Our Father and the Hail Mary?"

"I should," Juan said. "My grandmother was Catholic. She used to say Rosaries all the time."

# REVELATION

"Didn't she teach you?"

Juan limped over a fallen branch. "No. My mother had joined a gang. It didn't go well for her. She had me out of wedlock. My father was nowhere around. I remember that we were homeless often. That's why my grandmother prayed so much."

"Didn't you stay with her instead of being homeless?" Susan asked.

"Sometimes. But then my mother and grandfather would fight. He never forgave her for having me before she was married. So we left, and came back, and left, and came back."

"I'm sorry to hear that," Susan said. "What happened to her?"

"She fell ill while we were on the streets. I was a teenager, going to school. But she got sick and died. Someone told me it was pneumonia, but I think it was drugs. Anyway, I vowed right then I was not going to let that happen to me. I couldn't save her, but I'd save others. That's why I became a fireman."

Susan massaged the beads in her hands. "I'll teach you."

Ahead, near a tree, the sound of a log cracked. Lee put his hand up behind him. He motioned for everyone to stop. He listened. He heard the sleet and the wind. *Did the wind move the branch?*

Then a soft whine came from the direction of the tree.

Nate whispered, "Cap'n?"

"Shhh."

Lee waited, watching in the direction of the sound.

Another crack, and branches moved. Heavy sleet fell from the branches.

"Come on!" Lee said, his voice raised. Lee took long strides to get to the tree.

The branches jerked as they approached. He heard a bark. Then a growl.

He came to the tree.

A gray, black, and brown dog bared its teeth. It growled, its ears pinned back.

Juan, Nate, and Susan came up behind Lee. "What is it?"

"It's a dog," Lee said.

"What's he doing here?"

"Hell if I know."

Susan put her Rosary back in her pocket. She walked around Lee, gently crouching.

"Careful, Susan. He looks angry,"

She made herself less threatening. Her voice pitched higher as she said, "It's okay, boy. We're not going to hurt you."

"How does she know it's a boy," Nate said.

"Shhh," Lee commanded.

Susan came closer.

The dog leaned forward. It raised its ears and stopped showing its teeth.

Susan put her limp hand close, a few feet from the dog.

The dog stretched its head, sniffing Susan's hand.

"He's stuck. Looks like his leash is caught."

"Nate, go around and untie its leash."

Nate walked around. The dog sniffed at them.

Nate unhooked the leash. "The handle was stuck in the tree."

"Hold onto him," Lee said.

"He's got a collar," Susan said. She stroked the dog gently. "There, there," she said.

# REVELATION

The dog panted. It got up and attempted to walk past Susan and Lee down the trail. The leash went taut, and Nate slipped and fell on the sleet.

Juan tried to grab the dog, but Susan had reached for its collar. The dog stopped, and she soothed it again, getting it to stay.

"What's the tag say?" Lee said.

Susan leaned close. "It says 'TAHOE'. And there's a phone number on the tag."

Lee bent down. The dog's tongue dripped with saliva.

"He's nervous," Susan said.

"Of us?" Lee said.

"He was nervous before we got here."

The dog's collar was a shiny blue tag, shaped like a bone. Lee noted the phone number. "That's not a Nevada area code," Lee said.

Juan came in closer. "It's California."

"San Diego?" Lee asked. He remembered the report that the blue Subaru had been reported stolen. "California car. California dog."

Juan said, "I have an idea, Cap'n."

"What's that?"

"Call the number on the tag. Maybe you'll get the owner."

Lee nodded. He pulled out his phone. Sleet fell on the screen, and he brushed it away. He called the number.

There was no connection.

"Let me try that again." He tried the number again.

"I've got no bars, Cap'n," Juan said..

Lee swore. "Me either." He put down his phone.

"The canyon walls must be blocking the frequency," Nate said.

"That means we have no real-time communication with the outside," Juan said.

"All the better to get the hell out of here," Lee said.

"Captain, what will we do with him?" Nate held the leash, brushing himself off after his fall.

"Leave him here for now while we search. Let's tie him up. Find the owners. We'll tell them where he is once we find them."

"What if there are no owners?" Susan held onto Tahoe's collar. She rubbed her palm over the dog's gray, black, and brown coat. Tahoe licked his lips.

"Well, somebody brought him in here," Lee said.

"Maybe we should let him loose?" Juan said.

"Not while we're investigating the area. I don't want anything to get in our way."

"He could help," Susan said.

"Look at him. He's ready to run."

"I'll hold him," she said.

"You'll slow us down,"

"I'm not under your command."

Lee put his hands on his hips. "Okay," he said. "Nate, give her the leash." Lee surveyed the area. They were near the rear of the canyon, and the investigation for the drone and the pack shouldn't take much longer. He said to Susan, "Stay here with him. Don't let him loose. He may be microchipped. We'll want to check him when we get back to Vegas."

"I'll hold him, but I'm not staying."

REVELATION

Nate bent under the low tree branches and handed Susan the leash. Lee expected the dog to run, but he stood next to Susan, panting.

Susan stood up. "We'll be alright," she said. She rubbed Tahoe with long smooth strokes. She pulled out her Rosary. The cross swung under her grip.

Lee shook his head. Then he took a big step over a sleet-covered rock, and found his way back on the trail, followed by Juan, Nate, Susan, and the dog.

# CHAPTER 23

The trail came to a rocky ledge, one they would have to climb. Lee grabbed a slippery root and pulled himself over. Cold sleet fell on his pants and coat.

"It's tricky," he said. He gave Juan his hand and pulled him up and over.

Susan came to the ledge. Tahoe panted next to her. His eyes darted from place to place. "What do I do with him?"

"You wanted him," Lee said.

"He may help me find what I'm looking for."

"The fountain?"

"Yes."

Nate bent down. "Let me try something."

Tahoe growled.

"Okay. Maybe not."

Lee said to Susan, "You can stay here with him."

"No, I have to get up there."

"Bringing him was your idea," Lee said.

"Give me the leash," Juan said.

Susan handed him Tahoe's leash.

"Captain, we'll pull him up by the harness."

# REVELATION

"You're crazy," Lee said.

"Be glad I'm on your side."

The two men pulled Tahoe's leash. Tahoe didn't fight when they lifted him. When they had pulled him to the top, Juan held the leash and walked Tahoe a few steps away. Lee reached down and helped Susan climb the slippery rock, while Nate waited below her to make sure she didn't fall. When Susan made it up, Lee and Susan helped Nate over the ledge.

"We're there." Juan walked Tahoe on a flat rock area.

The canyon walls surrounded them. Lee surveyed the area. To the west, the walls curve to the left. The dark clouds rolled past them, closer now with the increase of their elevation. The sleet fell. The wind whistled above them.

Large stone cliffs surrounded them on three sides. The only way out was the way they had come.

Nate pointed. "Captain. There's the pack."

A hint of yellow stuck above the white ice that had fallen to the ground. Lee moved to the pack. His feet slipped, but he kept his balance. When he got there, it was soaking in an overflowing puddle. Lee picked it up. It was a colored rainbow fanny pack. He held it at arm's length. "Do you guys see anybody?"

"Negative, Captain," Nate said.

"Me either," said Juan.

Susan walked in Lee's direction. She shook her head, then she scanned canyon walls, studying them.

"Here goes." He opened the pack. He reached in. He pulled out an uneaten sandwich. It looked to have been made within the last day, perhaps this morning. He pulled out a granola bar. Also uneaten. Then he saw a pink plastic cover. He pulled it out. "It's an iPhone."

"Really?" Juan asked. Tahoe pulled on the leash, but Juan held firm.

Lee held it up. "Who leaves their phone behind?"

"Nobody I know."

Lee examined the pack. Inside, there was a half-empty water bottle. The cap had been opened.

"Somebody had used it this morning," Lee said. *Where was she?*

The sleet fell upon them. He was getting cold.

Water ran through the crevices all around them. Every step Lee took splashed in a puddle or slipped on a wet rock. "Nate, where's the drone?"

Nate clamored over some boulders near the northern canyon wall. "Should be around here, Captain."

"Where is it?"

"I don't see any sign of it, sir."

"Someone's not going to be happy if we don't bring back their toy."

Tahoe barked. He jerked the leash, but Juan held him tight.

"Any sign of people?" Lee shouted. Though his voice echoed between the walls, the falling sleet drowned it out.

"No. It's like they vanished."

"Nate, any sign?"

"No sir!"

"Susan, you see anything?"

Susan faced the rock walls to the south. Her hands touched their cold surfaces.

# REVELATION

"Susan?"

Susan whipped around. "No. But I need to keep looking."

"That's a negative. The weather is getting bad. We've got to go."

Tahoe barked again. Juan tugged on the dog's leash. "He's ready!"

"Me, too." Nate said.

Susan moved laterally with the wall, feeling the individual cracks before moving to the next one.

"Ma'am?"

She didn't answer.

Tahoe barked again.

"We're never getting out of here," Lee said.

# CHAPTER 24

Susan wasn't listening. Lee raised his arms, frustrated. "Susan. No missing persons under my watch. Let's go!". He marched across the sleet-covered rocks toward Susan. He grumbled, "She's going to have to come back, and that's going to be that."

He walked beside her. He'd try the respectful tactic. If that didn't work, he'd get more forceful. He didn't want to have to do that. "Susan," he said. "Susan, we need to go."

"It's here," she said. "I can feel it."

"What's here?"

"The fountain."

Lee scratched his forehead. She probably was crazy. Force was out of the question. He hoped he'd convince her instead.

"Ma'am, the weather is bad. We're not dressed for this. Aren't you cold?"

"Very," she said. "But I found it!"

Lee watched the wet sleet and water trickle off the canyon walls. "Great. Let's leave. You can come back when the weather's better and drink all you want."

"I need to be sure."

"Susan, be reasonable."

# REVELATION

"No," she said. "The woman told me to come look for it this morning. I have to find it."

"The woman?"

Susan didn't answer.

"Susan. I am responsible for my men. And because you're here with us, that also makes me responsible for you. Now, it'd be a good idea if all of us got out of here alive."

Susan's fingers slid over the rocks. "I would hope so. Of course, there's never any guarantees."

"Well, that doesn't make me feel any better."

"Me either," she said. "But I have to find this. I've been looking for the fountain for months. I've lost so many jobs. If I find it, perhaps my life will return to normal."

"See if you can find it later."

"Help me find it now," she said. "Please."

Lee rubbed the back of his head. *This woman is driving me crazy.*

Nate climbed up a ledge near the northern cliff. He surveyed the canyon both south and east. His head was down. His feet kicked a small rock that rolled and splashed into a puddle. He raised his head toward Lee and shrugged. Nate had not found the drone.

Juan scanned the area where they found the pack. Tahoe pulled on the leash toward the canyon exit. Juan held the pack to Tahoe's nose so he could sniff it as if Tahoe was a hound dog on the hunt.

Tahoe paid the pack no interest. He pulled on the leash again, trying to leave the canyon, and Juan pulled back.

Susan pressed her fingers into a crack in the stone wall.

"Ma'am," Lee said, "We're leaving. That's my order. You need to come with us."

"I can't."

"You'll die if you stay."

Susan didn't answer. She felt the cold rock walls with her fingers, inch by inch.

"That's it," Lee said. "Men, we're leaving. The lady has decided to stay."

"Yes sir," Juan said.

Tahoe barked.

Nate saluted Lee from the ledge. He crouched to find his way to climb down it.

A rumble echoed above them.

Nate looked up.

The dark clouds swirled.

Lee said, "Nate, get down off that ledge before that lightning gets you."

There was a second rumble, but it was not like thunder. It sounded like crunching rock, rolling.

The clouds opened above Nate, and a large boulder the size of a truck fell through them. It rolled down the cliff, spinning sleet and snow and fog.

Nate froze.

"Nate! Look out!" Lee sprinted two steps but he was too late.

The boulder crashed on the ledge where Nate was. The boulder crushed the ledge, then tumbled end over end towards Juan and Tahoe. Juan jerked Tahoe's leash, pulling the dog from danger as it rolled past and settled on the trail.

REVELATION

Lee's heart skipped inside his chest. He scanned the ledge area where Nate had been.

"Nate!"

He leaped away from Susan. He stepped into a puddle and slipped, his rear and rescue pack breaking his fall. He got up and ran to the ledge.

Nate wasn't there.

He climbed up it. Nate's body lay motionless on the ground. "Nate!" He crawled to him.

Nate's leg had been smashed in several places. Blood covered the ground.

Two of Nate's water bottles were smashed, and water spread upon the rock and soaked into Nate's clothes.

Nate's eyes were open, but he was quiet.

"Oh, don't be dead!" Lee knelt next to Nate and put his ear down, hoping Nate's chest would rise or that he'd hear the sound of a heartbeat.

Neither happened.

Lee did CPR. He pressed hard, pumping Nate's chest several times before blowing air into his lungs.

Nate's eyes widened as his lungs expanded. He let out several yells. Lee bent down and held him. "Nate!"

"Momma! Momma!"

"It's alright."

"Momma!"

"It's alright, kid. It's alright."

Juan had arrived next to Lee. Tahoe barked.

Lee said, "He's alive. He's in shock. His leg's smashed. He's going to lose a lot of blood. I just gave him CPR to come back. Quick, try to call for help."

"There's no cell reception, Captain. I'll try texting."

"Do what you have to do. Just get him help!"

Juan handed Tahoe's leash to Susan and he ran down the trail to call for help.

"It hurts!" Nate screamed.

The young man's femur stuck out of his skin as red blood flowed onto the white sleet. Lee took off his belt and tied it around Nate's thigh.

Tahoe barked below the ledge. Susan lifted her head. "What can I do?".

"Lady, get your beads out and start praying. We're going to need all the help we can get."

Susan nodded, and her head ducked below the ledge.

The dog kept barking.

"Sending a text message now, Captain!" Juan held his phone high, hoping something would pick up the reception.

"Get a helicopter here, asap!"

"Can they do it in this weather?"

"Tell them to!"

"Captain?" Nate's eyes opened. "Everything hurts so bad. How is it?"

"Not good, kid. We're going to have to carry you out of here."

Juan crawled up the ledge to Lee and Nate. "Sir, no response yet."

"They'd better get here soon. Or else we'll make a board to carry him out of here."

"Oh geez. He's bleeding bad."

"He is." Nate's skin was discolored. "His leg, we can stop. I'm worried about internal bleeding more, though."

"I can't move my arm," Nate said. "My shoulder hurts."

"Could be dislocated."

"How much time do we have?"

"Won't be much. Two hours, more or less."

Juan paused. "Captain, that's not much time. It'll take at least one hour to get him out of here."

Lee swore. "I know that. Just get a chopper here as soon as you can!"

"Yes sir!"

Juan climbed off the ledge. He hurried down the trail, pressing buttons on his cell phone and holding it high to get a signal. He slipped, but kept his balance, as he held his phone pointed at the canyon entrance.

"Captain," Nate said. "I'm afraid."

"I know you are, kid." Lee was afraid, too. He didn't have any idea this would happen today. He worked to get the tourniquet out of his rescue pack. Supplies fell on the blood and sleet-covered rock.

"Cap'n, where'd that rock come from?"

"I don't know, kid."

"Captain?" Susan had edged near the ledge. "Can I do anything?"

Lee worked his first aid, everything he could think of, on Nate. His leg bled, and he splinted it the best he could. The sight of bone sticking out of the leg made him nauseous, but he held everything in. His adrenaline pumped through his body. Nate didn't deserve this. He may never walk again if he lives through this. He noticed bruising on the exposed skin on his neck. He hoped it wasn't internal bleeding.

"Captain?"

Susan was still there. "Just keep praying," he said. "Tell whoever you talk to upstairs that Juan needs to get a helicopter here pronto!"

# CHAPTER 25

After splinting Nate's leg, he discovered his arm was also broken, and Lee splinted that, too. Lee had done his best. They didn't bring the EMS board into Ice Box Canyon, but it wouldn't matter.

There was no time.

A bad bruise was on Nate's neck, confirming Lee's concern about internal bleedin.

They needed a helicopter.

The rumble of thunder overhead echoed within the canyon walls. And the falling sleet made him cold.

"Captain," Nate said. "I'm going to die."

Lee got close to Nate. "Don't think like that, kid. You're going to make it. Four in, four out. Remember that?"

"Cap'n?" Nate was turning color.

"Susan." Lee said.

She lifted her head.

"Give me your blanket."

She nodded, and unwrapped the blanket around her. She handed it to Lee who covered Nate with it, trying to keep him warm.

Tahoe barked below the ledge. She held his leash with her right hand and said her Rosary with the other. The repetitive prayer was calming, Lee had to admit. He remembered his lucky pen in his pocket.

He reached into his coat collar and pulled his lucky pen from his shirt pocket. It was silver. He flung it, and it flew thirty yards down the canyon, where it hit a wet rock and fell into a hole.

If there was a God, he needed to save Nate. And Juan needed to get that cell reception.

Lee opened his phone. There were no messages, not even from Sawvel. The cliffs blocked any cell reception. "Where the hell is Juan?"

"Cap'n?" Nate said again. His voice was getting weaker. "What's it like in Heaven?"

Lee clenched his jaw. "Don't know, kid."

"I'm afraid."

"We're getting you help. Hang in there."

"It hurts. Everything hurts."

A tear formed in Lee's eye. I'm not going to cry, he thought. He wiped his cheek with his wet coat sleeve, making his face wetter. If Juan's not successful, we're going to lose him.

Tahoe barked again.

"Can you shut that dog up?"

Susan pulled Tahoe close to her. "He feels the energy here. It's not good."

"That doesn't help us," Lee said.

"You need to pray," Susan said.

"Praying isn't going to heal this boy."

"You don't know that," she said. "I'll pray for both of us."

# REVELATION

Lee decided not to answer. All his focus was on Nate. He said, "Do you want some water?"

Nate closed his eyes but made a slight nodding gesture.

Lee pulled out his water bottle, leaving the two left in Nate's rescue pack untouched. He didn't want to move him as he couldn't know the extent of his injuries. He brought the bottle to Nate's lip and gave him a few drops. The boy swallowed, his throat gulping with each drop.

"Captain," Nate said. "I didn't mean for this to happen."

"I know."

Susan said her Rosary. She prayed, and Lee listened to the rhythmic cadence of the Hail Mary's, interspersed with the Our Fathers.

"Cap'n" Nate said. "Does she have any extra beads?"

"I don't know." Lee leaned over the ledge. "Do you have any extra beads?"

"I gave my spare to Juan," she said. "How about I give him mine?"

"That would be good."

She reached up and handed the beads to Lee. Before he put them in Nate's hand, he studied them.

There were over fifty beads, held together by tiny metal connectors. They formed a circle except for four beads and a cross that extended from the rest.

He liked holding the beads, but Nate had asked for them. He raised the blanket. Sleet and rain rolled off it as he lifted it.

The cold surrounded them.

He found Nate's hand and, without moving it, rested the Rosary beads in his palm. He closed his fingers over Nate's hand.

"Thanks," Nate whispered.

Lee swore. "Where's Juan?"

Tahoe barked again. The trail wound through the canyon before them. The sleet-covered the rocks. Dark clouds swirled in the sky, and five hundred-foot cliffs rose to the north and the south, but Juan was not able to be seen. He had to be halfway down the trail by now. That is if he hadn't slipped and fallen.

To his right lay the giant boulder. It rested in the middle of the canyon, near where they found the rainbow pack. Where was the rainbow pack, anyway? What about the boulder? It had come through the clouds without warning.

He remembered the slight rumble, which he had thought was thunder.

Then it came down without any warning. And right on top of Nate. How did that happen? Was it bad luck?

Something bothered him about the boulder. It was like the rock aimed for Nate. Of all the times to be in all the wrong places, large boulders don't come flying out of the sky and come landing on people. He had never heard of anything like this.

Susan continued her prayers, even without her beads. He peered over the ledge and saw her sitting next to the cliff wall, holding Tahoe with her arm over his fur. The dog looked up at him, still panting, still afraid.

Lee raised his eyes to the swirling clouds. Was God up there, above the storm?

Lee didn't believe in God. But even if there was a God up in the sky, he wouldn't be able to see him through the dark cover of the clouds.

REVELATION

A wave of emotion went through his torso as he knelt on the rock. He clenched his fists and shut his eyes. He bent down and put his face near the sleet-covered rock, near Nate who lay with his eyes shut. He fought back the tears for two seconds. Then he raised himself, wiped his eyes, and controlled his emotions.

"Four in. Four out," he said.

Nate gave a weak nod, his eyes still shut. His face grew pale. "Four...in...four...out."

# CHAPTER 26

Fury's claws grasped the rocks at the top of the cliff, and his tail swung like a cat on the prowl. The dark storm swirled around his neck and wings.

How was the young man still alive?

When the young man separated himself from the protection of the two bright objects and stood on the ledge, Fury knew he had his chance. He lifted a large boulder in his hands and rolled it at the young man. Blinded by the two bright, strange items, his aim was off. An edge of the boulder chipped the cliff wall on its way down, knocking it off course.

Now the boy lay dying, and the woman, holding the bright object in her hand, sat next to him. Fury could not approach and finish the job.

Worse, the woman prayed. Her soul glowed blue. Her prayers were like hammers hitting his head.

He swung his head trying to avoid the pain.

*What was that object?*

The dog by her side watched him, panting.

He flew higher and rested farther up the mountain. The hammering lessened as he distanced himself from the woman.

# REVELATION

He did not know their language. There was one language at the time of the Rebellion. Now there were others. He would listen and learn their language.

Fury spread his wings and raised his head. Purple lightning bolts shot from the black storm clouds and struck the mountain peaks.

He planned to destroy the ones below, especially the woman. The power with her was great. He glared at the storm. Michael was up there, above the storm, preparing the Almighty's army to defend his people. The woman's light was so strong that it might aid her prayer and call upon Michael and his angels to ambush him when he least expected it.

The membrane on Fury's back glowed orange where the scale on his shoulder was missing. It was where Michael had pierced him during the Rebellion. Fury refused to return to his prison.

There had to be a weakness among these four. There had to be a way to get the woman.

Down the canyon, near the entrance, the second bright light glowed. The cocky one carried it, separated from the group, no doubt to find help. Fury licked his lips. He launched into the air and with two mighty flaps of his wings landed atop the cliff wall near the cocky man. He stretched his neck lower to observe him.

The object in the man's pocket glowed.

The woman had given him the second object. No doubt he had asked for it after seeing Fury in all his form. She must have brought two with her into the canyon. If there were two, there could be more.

Fury squinted his dragon eyes, ascertaining the man's condition. The man's soul had shifted. It was no longer gray but contained hints of soft blue around the edges. Fury smashed his tail to the earth behind him. He could not lose another to Heaven.

The earth shook under Juan's feet. He balanced himself, hanging onto his phone. He spun around, expecting to see the dragon again, but he did not see it. All that was there was the sleet-covered rocks and cliff walls and sagebrush. "Another earthquake? I hope that's all it was."

He took a sip of water from one of his bottles, finishing it. It was empty, but he stuffed it back inside his pack. He lifted his cell phone. There was a signal. He had sent a text, but there was no response. He called the direct line to Dispatch.

Someone was watching him, like eyes bored into him, and saw his soul. "There's no dragon. Get it out of your head. You're imagining things," he said. He felt vulnerable down here.

The sleet fell sideways as the wind blew into the canyon. The desert before him was covered with shadow and white sleet.

"Come on. Pick up. Pick up!"

He remembered the Rosary Susan gave him. He reached into his pocket. The beads slipped between his cold fingers. Somehow, it made his fingers warm. He hoped they'd work. Nate needed a helicopter.

A voice answered. "Dispatch. How can I help?"

"Yes. This is Juan Carasco CCFD from Station 53. I'm calling from Red Rock's Ice Box Canyon. We have a man down in the canyon. Multiple injuries. Life critical. We need a helicopter evac, pronto!"

"All units are occupied," said the voice.

# REVELATION

"Listen to me," Juan yelled. "Our man was crushed by a boulder. He's going into shock. We need life support now!"

"Just a second."

Juan wanted to swear, but he remembered the beads in his pocket. The wind hit his face. The temperature dropped near the canyon entrance.

The voice on the device said, "Ok. We were able to reroute. We have a life flight helicopter on its way."

Juan clenched his hand and fist-pumped. "Thank you!"

He hung up the phone. He had to run back and let the Captain know. But he froze.

Something watched him. Whatever it was, its eyes were full of hate. His legs froze. There was a predator in the area, and he was the prey. He couldn't rationalize it. He just knew.

The Skeeter was there in the parking lot. He could run there and wait. Maybe launch a flare when the chopper arrives? Show the pilot where to go?

No. His team needed him. "Four in, four out."

He sprinted west into Ice Box Canyon.

Fury crushed a stone with his claw. One precise throw and Fury would crush the man's head like a melon. But would Michael swoop down to protect him, and the woman?

The light in the man's pocket grew brighter. Now the man ran back into the canyon. His call must have been successful.

Help would come.

More souls.

More flesh.

Fury's lips curled. Before he would attack the city, he would begin his destruction here. He would study these modern people. He would learn their language, their advances, their weaknesses.

And he would watch the skies, ever on guard for an ambush from above.

He formed a plan. Once he learned, he would attack.

And then he would slay them all!

# CHAPTER 27

"Hang in there, Nate," Lee said. Nate didn't respond. His breathing shallowed while his eyes remained closed.

"Come on. Stay with me!"

Nate groaned.

He's still a kid, Lee thought. Heck, I was his age when I met Joan. He had been an accountant, working with numbers, bringing home the bacon every few weeks. He and Joan had lived comfortably.

But he hated it. He was destined for more.

Then Jenn was born. She gave him a new motivation, a desire to earn. At first, it seemed to work. But the calling, as he named it, returned. Even though he earned money and was climbing up the corporate ladder, he was climbing up the wrong ladder.

One day, he got up the nerve to tell Mary his thoughts. "I think I need to become a fireman." He expected her to come back with all the reasons why it was a bad idea, why it would be bad for Jenn, why it would put the house at risk.

"You should," she had said.

He was floored. "Really?"

"You've changed," she said. "You used to take chances and be adventurous. I miss that. You're almost forty. Why not?"

He had looked away and rubbed his eyes with his forearm, hoping she wouldn't see what he was doing. He could do anything in the world, so long as he had her support.

"Captain?" Lee blinked. Nate's eyes were still closed.

"What is it?"

"Everything's spinning."

"He's going into shock." Lee leaned down and spoke into his ear. "Stay with me, Nate. Stay with me!"

Nate's face drooped.

Lee raised his hands, not sure what to do.

Susan sat below the ledge, her arm around Tahoe.

The cold sleet covered the canyon.

"Where the hell is Juan?"

Susan stood up. "I need to search the canyon."

"Find Juan. We need that chopper asap!"

Susan stepped backward and slipped on the cold sleeted rock. Tahoe jumped back to avoid her falling on him.

"I'm sorry," she said. "Something tells me I need to find that fountain."

"Forget your fountain. He's failing!"

Susan stepped away, pulling the dog's leash.

Lee paid her no more mind. All he wanted to do was take care of his man. "Four in. Four out. Four in. Four out!"

Nate didn't respond.

Lee reached under the blanket and found Nate's closed hand.

Nate still held the Rosary.

# REVELATION

Lee put his hand over Nate's and squeezed. If those prayer beads did anything, now was the time to do it.

Nate's breathing was shallow. The bruise on his neck got worse. Definitely internal bleeding. "No way," he said. "No one's dying on my watch!"

Maintain control, he told himself.

He'd find a way.

He knew he would.

There would be an answer.

There was always an answer.

Susan Mercer inspected the canyon walls. She felt bad for leaving the Captain and Nate on the ledge, but while she prayed, she thought something was sending her to the other side of the walls.

She pulled on Tahoe's leash. The dog was distracting her. He was very nervous, but she held the leash firm with one arm while feeling the soaked rock wall with her fingers on the other.

Before the boulder fell, she had noticed something on the cliff wall. There was a formation that seemed familiar, like deja vu. She had to check it out.

The sleet fell. Her body shivered from the cold. She no longer had her blanket. Sleet and rain that fell from the sky soaked her dark hair.

Tahoe shook his fur, and water flew through the air. The poor dog needed a blanket, too.

She returned her attention to the stone wall. The rocks in the back seemed familiar. Why?

She slipped and her shoe skidded on the slick rock surface. Tahoe had better balance being on all fours.

The cliff walls were not unusual, except for a piece of stone that jutted out. The stone was three feet long. It stuck out like a slash against the walls. As she came closer, the slashing rock was red. That's funny, she thought. The rock was a different color, darker than the surrounding rocks on the cliff.

She put her hand on the red rock. She was able to grip it. She pulled, but her hand slipped off. Her fingers stung from the cold wet sleet and the hard rock surface. She tried again. Was this it? She tried pulling, but the rock didn't budge.

If she pulled down on the upper end of the slash, would it move? Holding Tahoe with the leash in her left hand, she reached up and grabbed the red slash with her right. Managing to hang on this time, she relaxed her legs and let gravity pull her down while she hung on.

The rock didn't move. Her fingers slipped and she fell on her backside, splashing sleet and water. Tahoe flinched, but he didn't run. He stood near her, observing. She squeezed her fingers around the leash handle in case he tried to run.

Susan climbed back to her feet. The red slash, the jagged rock jutting out of the canyon. It seemed familiar. How come? Did she dream it? She didn't remember it in last night's dream. Was there another dream she had?

Several large rocks rested near her toes. She bent down and picked up a rock that seemed sturdy, but one she gripped with her hand. She raised her arm over her head. While still holding the leash, she brought the rock down on the jagged red slash.

## REVELATION

The impact caused her to lose her grip on the rock in her hand, and it fell. The rock bounced off the cliff rock wall and hit her shoulder. She let out a small yell, closing her eyes and ducking her head. Tahoe pulled away, twisting her arm, but she held on. She brought the other hand up to hold her shoulder as the throbbing pain set in. The sleet made everything too wet, too slippery.

Lee wouldn't leave Nate, but she needed help. "I found something!"

Lee didn't respond. He focused on the young man.

Susan believed she could help Nate. If only she found what she was looking for.

A man's voice came from down in the canyon. Juan scrambled up over the ledge, first on his belly, and then up and half limping, half jogging over the rocks. "They're coming. I got through!"

Lee, still on his knees next to Nate, lifted his body. "How long?"

"Not long. Maybe five minutes. Rescue chopper is on its way."

"Thank God," Susan said. Now that Juan was back, maybe he could help. "Juan, can you help me?"

Juan said, "Let me see Nate first." He was thirty yards away from Lee and Nate. He moved over the cold wet rock in their direction.

Lee, still kneeling, spoke to Nate.

She was on her own. The red slash was something important. Perhaps she was mistaken. She stepped back again. What was it about the rock? She studied it. If it was on a clock, it would point to about three-thirty on the hour hand. Was it pointing to something? She moved her eyes, imagining a line extending beyond the slash.

A terrible roar came from above. She cowered, falling to a crouched position, her hand resting on the cliff wall for balance.

Tahoe jerked the leash. He tried running away, and it pulled Susan over onto her belly, scratching her elbow and her knee. Her chin scraped on the rock floor. "Hang on, boy," she said, but the dog kept pulling her over the sleet-covered rock. "Tahoe. Tahoe!" The dog wouldn't listen. She jerked the leash back, pulling on Tahoe's harness.

The roar came again from somewhere in the clouds above. It sounded so loud, like the Tyrannosaurus Rex in Jurassic Park when she went to see it in the Imax theater in Dolby.

Except this was twenty times worse.

Tahoe pulled. She gripped the leash with both hands. The dog tried to scramble up the cliff wall to escape. She held tight on the leash as she crawled against the wet rock wall.

Rocks fell from high up in the cliffs. Not boulders as what had hit Nate, but large enough that Susan covered her head, praying that nothing would hit her or the other men. Some rocks smashed into pieces upon the hard rock floor, others bounced, threatening to hit her and the others on the rebound.

Her hand was shaking. Lee fell to his belly, covering Nate.

Juan stopped running and crouched. The rain and the sleet fell on Juan's uncovered head, and water dripped down his coat.

"What the hell was that!" Lee shouted.

Juan pointed to the clouds. "It's the dragon!"

REVELATION

The dark clouds had lowered, covering the tops of the canyon. The clouds sifted like a fog around the upper rock formations.

Lightning streaked across the sky like purple veins.

Susan reached for her Rosary. Her pockets were empty.

She had given her Rosaries to Nate and Juan.

Exposed and unprotected, she wished she had her hands on one of them now.

# CHAPTER 28

Fury perched on the canyon rim. The dark clouds flowed around his spines and his wings.

The man who carried the bright item and had called for help had run back to the others. Fury was listening to them, learning their language. His eternal spirit managed to pick up on what they said. He gathered their names.

The leader was Lee.

The injured one was Nate.

The man who made the call was Juan.

And the woman, they called her Susan.

They even gave a name to the dog - Tahoe.

Fury pieced together their language structure. There were verbs and tenses and nouns. The more he listened, the more he'd understand.

While Juan was separated from the others, he was in the open, vulnerable. He carried one of the objects. Oh how Fury wanted to chomp on Juan, tasting his blood. But the fact that he carried the bright holy item, he stayed away.

# REVELATION

Should he tempt fate? Should he rush Juan while he was separated, end the man's life, and see how the holy item affected him?

Patience, he thought.

Juan had called for others to come. He would wait.

He watched Lee, Nate, and the woman they called Susan below. Nate still lived, but the glow of his spirit dimmed. It would not be long now. The holy item in his hand had prevented his demise so far. Would it last?

Fury noticed a change in Lee. His spirit was not as dark as it had been. The dark item that had been in his pocket was gone. Fury searched the canyon. The black item, with its unholy meaning, lay in a crack thirty yards from Lee. Lee must have thrown it, and doing so changed the color of his soul. It wasn't much, but enough to rumble the fire within Fury's belly.

The woman was different. Susan's spirit was bright, illuminating. She was a believer in the Most High. She was a believer in the Son.

And she believed in something else. Was it the woman, the one that caused the Rebellion, the creature that bore the Son?

Fury hated believers. Weak as Susan was, she could bring others to the faith. It was happening to Lee, Juan, and Nate, as the colors of their souls shifted from gray to a hazy blue.

He had to reverse that. Remove the woman, and the men would be lost for eternity. Remove the woman, and he would increase the Count.

Fury studied Susan. She fingered the walls while holding the panting dog. She seemed intent on searching for something in the rocks. *Why? What was she trying to find?*

While the glow of her hazel spirit hurt his eyes, he observed the cliff walls. Water trickled through the rocky cracks, and ice had formed from the weather. There were shadows everywhere as the sun's rays did not penetrate the clouds.

A pebble fell from the cliff wall, revealing a light. It was a very small light, less than that of a candle. It seeped out of a pinpoint crack in the cliff.

The light, small as it was, was hard to look at.

Holy light!

That was it.

The Almighty wanted the woman to find the light.

That was his plan.

Susan fingered underneath the small light. Her mortal eyes could not see it, and yet her praying had led her to a spot underneath it.

He must stop her.

Susan had picked up a rock and hit the rock wall. She fell, but she stood up. Her head was a few feet from the small light. Did she see it?

No. She was human.

He couldn't let her find it. Should he attack? Should he launch eternal fire and burn her to a crisp?

Would Michael's legion swoop down on him if he did that? He would be distracted, vulnerable to their swords showing images of Heaven piercing his hide and sending him back to his cell.

Her eyes and fingers were getting close.

He had to do something.

# REVELATION

He materialized. The weight of gravity pressed him down, pushing his mighty claws into the hard rock below his feet. His tail whipped in the clouds. They could not see him through the dark clouds and the falling sleet.

Fury spread his wings. Lightning flashed, and the wind picked up.

He extended his large, reptilian head. He bellowed a monstrous roar. It echoed terror along the mountain peaks and bounced between the canyon walls of Ice Box Canyon.

Rocks rumbled and vibrated. Several cracked from the force. They fell from their locations, bouncing off the rock walls, and crashing onto the canyon floor.

His roar traveled across the valley, covering the east and west. Those in the eastern city had to have heard it.

He waited. The people below stayed in their places. They were frozen, unmoving. They lifted their arms to shield themselves from falling rocks.

Yet each of them was protected by light.

No matter. He had to stop the woman, the one they called Susan. She could not find the light.

He gripped the side of the canyon wall. His large claws dug into the rock.

Gravity forced his massive weight into the mountains.

He dropped his head.

Susan was underneath him.

He flicked his tongue.

Her bright soul made him squint, but he moved closer. Flames oozed between his teeth. If the clouds raised a few feet, she would see his head. She would panic at the horrible sight of him, like the one they called Juan had done a short while ago. Fury opened his mouth.

A sound came from the east.

Fury lifted his head.

The sound thumped, growing louder and louder.

He focused his vision through the clouds. A machine flew toward him. Two men, each with graying spirits, sat in the machine.

"It's here!" Juan shouted.

"Thank God!" Lee said.

Fury licked his tongue, and he imagined the taste of blood.

# CHAPTER 29

Lee scanned the clouds as they rolled above the canyon walls. Rocks fell close to him and Nate as they crashed into the wet rock surface floor, breaking into multiple pieces. Others bounced with loud thuds and rolled with the force of gravity until they found their new resting place. The falling sleet lessened, but the air chilled to dangerous levels.

The sound of helicopter rotors filled Lee with hope. "That chopper can't get us out of here fast enough," Lee said.

Juan pulled a flare gun from his pack. He shot it straight up. The bright light rocketed into the clouds, brightening the mist in the sky for several moments.

Lee admitted to himself he was glad Juan brought the flare guns.

The sound of the helicopter blades drew closer.

Nate moved his mouth. "Water."

"He didn't hear the roar," Lee said. He brought his water bottle to Nate's lips while keeping an eye out for anything above.

Juan hurried to him, ducking. A couple of rocks fell to the floor, crashing to the ground. "Captain, let's get out of here."

"Will they be able to fly in here?" Lee said.

"Don't know. It's a tight fit. I'd bet they'll drop a ladder and pull us up one by one."

"Good." The clouds continued to roll, though the sleet had slowed. Icicles had formed on some of the rocks. With the temperature dropping, they could suffer from hypothermia. "If they can take all of us, great. Worst case scenario, they take Nate and the lady, and leave you and me to hike back to the Skeeter."

Susan focused on the rock in front of her, feeling it with her fingers. "Woman's crazy," Lee said. He shouted in her direction. "I want the helicopter to take you back, too." Lee said.

"Not yet!" she shouted back.

"It's cold. Best you have the doctors take a look at you once Nate gets to the hospital."

"What about him?" She motioned to Tahoe.

"We'll figure it out. I'll get him out of here, then take the truck back to the Station."

Lee's breath was showing in the chilled air. He lifted his head, unsure of the powerful sound they had just heard, but welcoming the sound of the helicopter. The clouds above remained dark. A rumble of thunder echoed between the walls.

"I'm not liking this weather," Juan said.

"Instrument training," Lee said.

"Let's hope."

The helicopter drew closer, the sound of its rotors coming down at them from above the canyon rim. The wind swirled around it, whipping the misty dark clouds and exposing the helicopter's underside. Bright lights flashed from the outside, helping the pilot see. A man in a jumpsuit and a helmet stood and

# REVELATION

waved from an open door. He held onto a cable that ended in a crane. He was attaching an EMS board, readying it for lowering.

"Best sight for sore eyes I've ever seen," Lee said.

"Me too," Juan said. He reached down and pulled out one of his bottles of water to take a celebratory swig.

A lightning bolt flashed, and a dark shadow flew above the helicopter.

The shadow was the size of a house. Its neck was like that of a serpent. Two giant bat-like wings extended from its center. Its tail ended with a spear and whipped in the air. The shadow whizzed past the canyon walls. Then it disappeared.

Lee fell onto his back next to Nate. "What in the world?"

Juan didn't see it. "What?"

Was Juan right? Lee didn't want to say. The weather, the cold, and the lightning were too much. His eyes must be playing tricks on him. "Nothing," Lee said.

"Captain. You saw something?"

"Go get Susan."

Juan nodded. He ran up the wet rocks, bottle still in hand, to where Susan stood.

Lee leaned down to Nate. The boy groaned. "Hang in there," Lee said. "We're going to get you out of here."

Tahoe barked, loud and with urgency. Susan kept her fingers on the rocks as trickling water flowed past them, but turned her head to see why he was barking.

Juan was running in her direction. "Tahoe, it's just him," Susan said. Then she noticed Tahoe wasn't barking at Juan, but at the helicopter in the sky.

Juan rushed up to her. "The helicopter can take Nate back. Maybe it can take all of us. If not, you need to go with them."

"I'm close," she said. Her fingers caressed the red jagged slash that jutted out of the rock. "Here, hold him." She thrust Tahoe's leash into Juan's hand. He grabbed it and was jerked by the dog's pull. Juan dropped his bottle of water, which rolled against the cliff wall.

"We're responsible for you. It's not safe!"

"I have to be sure," Susan said.

The helicopter grew louder. The man with the cable was lowering himself down.

Juan said, "What about that noise?"

"I don't know," Susan said.

"I know what I saw," Juan said. "I may be crazy, but something got those hikers."

Susan removed her fingers from the wet wall. She didn't say anything.

The helicopter noise grew louder. Juan had to shout. "Think about it. Who leaves a pack, and a cell phone, and a dog?"

Susan nodded. "Did you feel the earthquake this morning?" she shouted.

Juan nodded. "I did."

"So did I. That's why we're here."

Juan paused. He pulled out the Rosary beads in his pocket. "Here," he said. "These are yours."

Susan reached down and put her hand on Juan's, covering his cold hand and the beads with her own. "You keep them."

Juan said, "You shouldn't stay. There's something in here."

## REVELATION

"I won't be long. I just need to find what I'm looking for. It's here. I feel it."

"The Captain saw something. He saw the dragon. He won't admit it, but he did."

Susan put her fingers back on the wall.

"Come with us. It's now or never," Juan said. The helicopter sound echoed loudly in the canyon. The rotors forced a wind that blew their clothes and faces.

Susan nodded, then returned to the wall, her wet hair blowing with the wind.

"You've got two minutes. You won't make it if you stay." Juan pulled Tahoe toward Lee and Nate.

Susan peered over her shoulder. The metallic glint of the red and white rescue helicopter hung in the clouds, and a man with a helmet dangled on a swinging cable between the canyon walls.

Fury flew high above the storm clouds in the bright sun. Below him, the dark clouds covered the earth like a hurricane. He let the wind move under his wings. In the clouds, purple lightning flashed, streaking across the horizon.

The men in the machine hovered between the cliff walls, while clouds swirled around the blades. The machine, stationary in the air, was an easy target.

Fury hung in the air, observing. The woman's light glowed brighter, She remained by the holy light in the canyon wall. The other men were apart from her, yet they each were near holy items that glowed with radiance. Their souls were changing color. More blue entered into their aura.

Despite Fury's threats, there had been no indication of defense from Michael's army. Though the woman prayed, and there was light from the items she brought into the canyon, Fury had not seen a member of Michael's guard. The only angel he had seen thus far was the one who rescued the female hiker.

He scanned the sky.

The storm raged below him.

Human flesh was down there.

They issued him a challenge, a challenge to his god-status.

There was no threat from the Heavenly Hosts. There was no sign of a trap.

He would wait no longer. His turn has come. His brows furled, and his tongue flicked as the wind whipped past his house-sized body. He lifted his bat-like wings. From high above, he lowered his head and dove like a missile into the storm clouds toward the rotors.

The helicopter hung in the air. The man on the cable swung, working his way down.

Lee kept Nate covered with the blanket. He checked both his splints, but the bruise on Nate's neck had spread into his shoulder and chest. Nate's face was pale. His breathing was shallow. "They're almost here. Hang on for me."

Nate remained motionless. His eyes closed.

The wind blew the helicopter, and the pilot adjusted its flight. The hanging man swung on the cable. The sleet slowed, but the clouds rolled over the canyon walls. The helicopter windshield was weathered. The pilot brought the helicopter low while the man on the cable swung underneath it.

Lee felt hope. They were going to make it.

Juan pulled Tahoe next to the ledge Lee and Nate were on and he tied Tahoe's leash to a large stone. The helicopter wind was blowing his hair.

Lee shouted, "What did she say?"

"'No.' She said 'No'. I told her two minutes!"

Lee nodded. "Help me."

They surrounded Nate, preparing him for when the EMS board came. Lee would keep Nate's head still, while Juan would lift his side, as they had done with the lady who had broken her ankle that morning.

Juan shouted, "Ready."

Lee gave the thumbs up. "Let's get the hell out of here!"

Above the sound of the helicopter rotors, louder than the constant thumping, a roar echoed from the clouds. It shook the rocks in the canyon, and a sound vibration hit Lee's head.

"What the-?"

There was bright orange and red light in the clouds. The moisture spread the light in a circle, but the center was all heat and energy. Then it hit; a stream of fire struck the helicopter from above, piercing its carriage and exploding the blades. The fire bore through the carriage, hitting the dangling man. His body was incinerated except for a leg, which fell lifeless onto the ground.

The helicopter exploded into a fireball. The pilot burned as flames erupted through the windshield glass. The helicopter and the cable dropped, slowly at first but faster with the acceleration of gravity.

"Look out!" Lee shouted, but it was too late. As the helicopter crashed onto the canyon stone trail, shrapnel exploded in all directions. Pieces of the helicopter flew everywhere.

Before Lee could move, a piece of shrapnel flew through the air, spinning. It stuck into his quadriceps and went through the other side. He screamed as pain and heat pierced his leg, while his pants soaked up red.

Then the clouds opened and a creature fell onto the flames, crushing the machine. It had a long neck, four legs, and large bat-like wings.

The creature was the size of a house.

Flames spewed out of the creature's scales.

An intense heat warmed the canyon. The sleet and the ice around Lee and Nate melted, and water rained down upon them. Lee's skin and shirt burned with the presence of the monster.

It was the most hideous beast he had ever imagined. It was evil. Pure evil. It was the dragon, the one Juan had seen. Its eyes bored into him, but it squinted like its eyes were in pain. Lee tried to move, but his leg was stuck. The muscles wouldn't move.

The dragon roared. It fought the pain and bored its yellow eyes into Lee like it saw inside his soul.

Lee shivered.

He smelled soot and sulfur.

It was difficult to breathe.

The thought came to him: He would die. They all would die.

The creature's massive head pointed at Susan and then Juan. Tahoe pulled on the leash, stuck to the rock next to the ledge, barking, and yelping.

# REVELATION

Juan fell from the ledge and cowered into a corner, frightened and unable to move.

Tahoe pulled his leash loose from the rock, ran up the hill at the back of the canyon, and disappeared behind a boulder.

Susan stood, her back to the wall, her palms pressed against the rock. The creature lumbered toward Susan like a giant anaconda but with legs that crushed stone. It appeared unable to look at her, as its eyes squinted like it was facing a bright light. But it stepped in two massive movements in her direction.

Juan lay on the ground, frozen.

Susan stood still.

The creature opened its mouth. A deep voice came from its throat. Its lips moved as it spoke.

"I know your plan!"

The creature pointed its head to Lee. Fire burst from between its teeth.

Its wings spread. The creature flapped its wings with a giant stroke. Rocks and boulders fell as the wind from its wings blasted Lee, forcing him onto Nate's immobile body. The fire from the torched helicopter blew against the far canyon wall. Nate groaned. Lee shouted as the pain in his leg twisted his torn muscles. One of Lee's water bottles slid from his emergency pack and rolled off the ledge and behind a rock.

The creature launched itself into the clouds, where it disappeared.

# CHAPTER 30

The heat from the helicopter and the melted rock singed Lee's exposed skin, overcoming the dampness and the cold.

He tried not to think of the dead pilot and crew. His leg throbbed.

He put his hand down. He touched the hot metal sticking out of his leg and burned his hand. Pulling it back, pain shot up his leg and into his hip. He hurt everywhere.

He had to move slowly. He pushed himself up.

Nate was quiet. He breathed, but barely.

A bolt of lightning flashed across the dark clouds. Lee shuddered. The thunder echoed in the canyon. Lee cowered next to Nate, ducking his head until the rumble subsided.

When it was over, he lifted his head. He had to take stock. What did he have?

He was still alive.

He didn't know if he could move. One leg worked. If he stood on his good leg, maybe he could.

Nate was still alive but needed immediate help. That wasn't coming from outside. Right now, Nate needed shelter.

So did he.

# REVELATION

Where was Juan? Juan, who was right after all. He did see a dragon. As Lee thought of the dragon, the creature's characteristics haunted his memory. It was so horrible, he tried to block it out of his mind. "Don't think about it," he said. But it was hard. He had never seen a being so filled with hate and malice and destruction and ruinous fire. If he closed his eyes, he'd see the dragon; the scales, the wings, and those eyes, those haunting, piercing, hate-filled eyes. They had bored into his soul like a brain surgeon's drill penetrating a skull.

And that voice. The thing actually spoke. What did it say?

*I know your plan.* What the hell did that mean?

And he spoke in English. Each syllable pounded through Lee's ears and into his mind like amplified telepathy. The creature was filled with power, a power determined to destroy, and to rule.

Of that Lee had no doubt.

Nate needed help. His breathing was getting worse.

Lee had to find shelter.

He also needed to warn the city.

Hell, maybe the world. With a creature like that on the loose, mankind was in serious trouble.

He thought of Joan and Jenn. Joan would be at home, taking care of her chores. Perhaps she was in the grocery store, walking down the aisles and picking up dinner for her and Jenn. He wouldn't have been home tonight anyway as he had begun his forty-eight-hour shift. Joan and Jenn would sit down to dinner. Joan would discuss Jenn's day, and perhaps after Jenn did her homework they would watch a movie before bed.

Right now Jenn would still be in class. What class did she take this time of day? He didn't know. As much as he wanted to control things, he hadn't asked her what her order of classes was. He tried to dictate her future, making sure she made good grades and chose a future that would keep her safe.

Why would he do that? He had left a cushy corporate career to become a fireman. He loved the thrill of the adventure, of being a hero. He took enough risks for everyone, or so he thought. He worried about Jenn's choices, that her risks could harm her.

He was one to talk. Look where I am now, he thought. *Look where we all are.*

This monster from the sky, it'll destroy all of us. All mankind.

Somehow he knew trying to kill the monster was folly. He didn't know how he knew. He just did.

"Captain." Juan was climbing up the ledge. "Captain, you ok?"

"Am I glad to see you!" Juan appeared in one piece except for his torn coat and a cut on his forehead. "I'm alive, I think."

"Cap'n. Your leg!"

"Yeah," Lee groaned. "It's quite a sight."

The piece of metal in his leg stuck out on two sides. His pants were soaking in red. Out the back of his leg, the shrapnel rested on the ground.

He twisted his body to look at the exit wound, but the pain prevented him. "Focus on what we have," Lee said. "We've got to get Nate help. He's fading."

Juan examined the piece of the helicopter sticking out of Lee's leg. Juan bent back down and heaved.

"I need you to be strong," Lee said. "Fix me up so I can tend to Nate. Then you are going to have to call for more help."

Juan lifted his head. He wiped the drool from his lips. "Sorry, Captain. I couldn't help myself."

"Listen. No matter what, we stay in control. We're not in this business because we'll always win. We're in this business because we always fight."

Juan's eyes brightened. He nodded, like a football player who just heard his coach's pep talk. "Yes sir."

"Tell Susan to find a place to hide. Then you have to get more help since our communication lines don't work here."

Juan licked his lips. "But, Captain. You saw it. What is that thing?"

Lee didn't know, except that it was the most horrible creature he had ever imagined. A dragon? Probably. It had the head, the wings, the legs, the tail, and all that fire that exhumed its body. But there was more. It was not of this earth. Was it from outer space? Under the earth? No telling. "Evil incarnate," Lee said.

"It looked at us," Juan said, "Susan, too. But for some reason it seemed...blinded."

"I noticed that."

"If it's alright with you, I'm going to pray with her."

Lee remembered the Rosary in Nate's hand. He didn't know what a Rosary was, or how to say one, or how they worked. "Tell her to find a hiding place, and you make your call to get help. Then tell her to pray until we're out of this hellhole."

Juan took a deep breath. "Captain, what do you want me to tell Dispatch?"

Lee shifted his weight, and pain shot up his side. He braced until the pain went away. "Tell them the truth," he said. "Tell them the truth."

Susan pressed her body against the wall like a cornered rabbit. The creature had taken several steps in her direction, each one telling her he would devour her. But the creature had to shut its eyes as it approached her. It moved its head like it was in pain, but it fought the pain and moved closer.

When it spoke, its voice was powerful. Evil power bent on ruin.

What did it mean? *I know your plan?*

Hate seethed from the creature's every move. Every syllable it spoke was death.

She sat alone, her back against the wet rock walls. Thunder rumbled overhead. Water trickled off the stone, into her dark hair, down her back, and onto her shoulder.

She was warm. Though the helicopter burned, the dragon left heat in the canyon that melted the sleet and the ice. She breathed in soot and sulfur. Ice Box Canyon carried the heated moisture like a sauna. Her face was warm like she suffered a sunburn.

The sound of trickling and dripping water filled her ears. The water puddled and meandered through the rock floor of Ice Box Canyon, leading down to the trail that went into the valley.

Juan limped in her direction, splashing the water as he neared. "We need your help," he said.

She remained seated but lifted her eyes. "We're in trouble."

"Yes we are. We all are. But we need you."

"That creature is evil."

Juan stopped. He bent down, his brown eyes pleading with her. "Yes. But we're still alive."

# REVELATION

She looked behind Juan at the smoldering wreckage. Flames and smoke rose to the rolling clouds. "What about them?"

"Both dead," he said.

"How's the Captain?"

"Not good. Shrapnel got him in his leg, bad."

"We need to pray."

Juan pulled his Rosary bead from his pocket. "I don't know how this works, but it's better in your hands than mine."

"It's yours."

"Tools should be in the hands that know how to use them," Juan said.

She hesitated.

"Look, when we get out of here, you can give it back to me."

She reached with her hand.

Juan lifted her from her seat and gave her the Rosary. The beads in her palm were a warm comfort for her. She pressed the Rosary back into his palm. "It's yours. Let it help you pray."

"I don't know how."

"Trust it."

"But you know how-"

"You're right. I do know how. Take it with you while you go down the canyon."

Juan leaned in close. "We're going to need you. You need to find a hiding place, somewhere for all of us."

"I have to find the fountain."

"Would you forget the fountain for a moment!"

Susan leaned back.

"The Captain is trying to keep a man alive, but his leg is immoble. We need shelter. I have to call for more help. You have to find a place to hide until help comes."

Susan closed her eyes. The trickling water rolled down her back as she leaned against the rocks. "Okay," she said. "But promise me you'll be careful."

"I'm a fireman," Juan said. "Danger is part of the job."

"Why do you say things like that?" she said.

He shut his eyes tight, then opened them again. "Find the hiding place. Then we'll worry about the fountain?"

Susan glanced back to the wall above her, where the sash pointed.

"Look, when I get back, I'll help you find it myself," Juan said.

Susan nodded. She knew he was right. The fountain had brought her here, but now that they had seen the dragon, her dreams had been correct. She'd find the fountain with God's help. But also in His timing. "Okay. Where's Tahoe?"

"I don't know," Juan said.

"He ran past me, up here somewhere."

"Find a hiding place. I have to run for help."

"I'll do it."

Juan put his hand on her shoulder. "Thanks," he said. For good measure, he held up his Rosary, and he grinned his Bradley Cooper smile at her.

She smiled back.

"Hey, it *does* work." Juan said. "I'll be back." He turned and ran into the smoke, past the smoldering helicopter and the large

REVELATION

boulder that had hit Nate, and he disappeared from view down Ice Box Canyon.

Would she see him again? She hoped so.

# CHAPTER 31

Nate's breathing slowed. The young man had gone into shock. Lee spoke in Nate's ear, "Wake up," but he didn't answer. Nate needed that helicopter. A quiver of fear shot through Lee's chest. What control did he have? Who would have thought his day, his life, would come to this?

Lee wanted to shake Nate to wake him up, but his training warned him of a possible spinal injury. What did that matter if Nate died from shock? He wrestled whether or not to try to wake him.

At least the cold had left. Whatever that thing was, and as bad as it smelled, it had heated the canyon.

Melted water fell on him like it was raining, trickling through the rocks and crevasses. The sound of the water echoed in the canyon.

The dark clouds rolled above them like smoke under a ceiling. But the sleet had stopped.

He sat up and examined his leg. He swore.

It hurt. The shrapnel stuck out of his thigh at both ends. Red had soaked into his pants, and pooled upon the ledge where he lay. He was losing a lot of blood.

He unhooked his emergency pack from his waist. Opening his first aid kit, he found a tourniquet and tied it around his upper thigh. He worked to patch his wound, but the patch did nothing. He hoped the blood would coagulate and slow the bleeding.

"I'm not dying without a fight," Lee said.

Nate groaned. His breathing went into short spurts.

"Hang in there," Lee said. "I'm here with you." The boy's coloring was changing. How much longer did he have? Lee had no idea. He raised his eyes to the clouds. "God, people say you're there. But it's hard to believe that right now."

He moved his leg, and pain hit him, causing him to yell. He laid back down. His abdomen moved up and down as he breathed in the smoke-filled air. The smoke and the clouds misted the cliffs above him. He watched the clouds that hid the creature that attacked them from above.

Susan leaned against the rock wall, underneath the red slash. She wanted to find the fountain and get on with everything.

But she had given her word.

Juan was right. Men were dead and dying because she had called for help.

She wished she had her Rosaries. She tried to pray. "Hail Mary," she said. But that was all she mustered.

She pushed herself away from the rock wall. She watched the clouds, expecting the dragon to swoop down, devour her with one giant chomp from its massive jaws, and that would end everything.

Was it her time to die? She couldn't say. The dragon terrified her. But what of it? An accident could kill her on the freeway. So long as she believed and hoped in God, what did it matter? The worst that could happen was she'd die and go to Heaven.

In the meantime, she had a mission. Find the fountain. She was close.

But the men needed a shelter, a hiding place.

There'd have to be a detour.

God expected her to help others. Jesus commanded us to love one another.

She would help the men first. Be obedient to that. Then return to find the fountain.

"Where is Tahoe?" she said out loud. She lifted her hands to direct her voice. "Tahoe! Tahoe!"

She waited. The trickling water echoed in the canyon. There was a large stone boulder that jutted out of the left side of the back of the canyon. Tahoe did not appear.

She stepped away from the wall and toward the top of the canyon. A sloping rock went up to a higher ledge near the rear of the canyon. She stepped upon the sloping rock, her foot getting covered with water, soaking her shoes and socks.

Everything she wore was wet. Her hair dripped water and slung like whips across her face with every motion.

Her shoe lost its footing, and she fell onto her hands and knees. The water ran through her fingers, and the hard rock scraped her knees. Her skin stung from the impact. She crawled on all fours to the top of the slope.

When she reached the top, the boulder was larger than it first appeared. She still couldn't see around it. "Tahoe?" she said. "You there?"

# REVELATION

There was no reply. She stood up. Ice Box Canyon, from this angle, was like the bottom of a bowl. Water had carved out this area, headed north, then flowed east toward the valley and away from the mountains. Smoke and haze filled her view. Within it, Lee laid on the ledge next to Nate. It looked like he was doing something with his emergency pack, patching himself.

And somewhere in the canyon, Juan was trying to get help. She liked Juan. Would they get to know each other more one day?

The Captain tied a tourniquet around his leg.

That's when Susan noticed all the red on his pants and on the ledge. A chill ran through her, the kind that happens when you're not prepared to see a bad injury. She had to help him. He didn't deserve this.

She turned around and faced the rear of the canyon. "Tahoe?"

She took a sip of water from her bottle. The water went down the wrong pipe, and she coughed. The smell of the beast hung in the air. Even up here, the dragon stench lingered. She remembered her dream from last night. She remembered the fire, and the urgency to find the fountain.

Was the dream only last night? So much has happened since this morning. The fire in her dream had been so hot, the air so putrid.

And it all just happened. Fire and odor. The odor was awful like it would rot her lungs.

She stepped further up the rock and found herself on a higher ledge. A pool had formed in the rock where a bowl-like formation had formed. It was smooth, and she saw her reflection in the water. Her hair drenched, her clothes soaked. She frowned. The heat had left the canyon and the cold was coming back. The air chilled her.

Then she heard a noise. It came from her left. She stepped over a rock, and there was Tahoe's leash. It was sticking out of a crack in the rock. She went to the leash. Tahoe was inside a small cave. It wasn't much, but it was hard to get in, and it might hold the team until help arrived. "Good boy!" she said.

Tahoe panted. She leaned in. The dog licked her face, then he licked his lips and panted some more. She brushed her hands over his wet fur. "You found a place. Good dog. You wait here. I'll be right back."

She crawled out of the entrance of the cave. Lee and Nate lay down on the ledge. Neither man moved, and she worried that they were dead.

She had to get to them.

She found a hiding place. She had to let them know.

# CHAPTER 32

Fury's claws dug into the canyon cliff walls high up in the clouds. He spread his giant bat-like wings, proud of his destruction of human life. The two souls in the flying machine were gray and darkening. Fury's flames came at them. Their souls left their bodies and stood amid the helicopter's burning ashes.

Their souls stood, bewildered. The helicopter wreckage burned all around them. They said nothing as the chaos surrounded them.

Neither quite knew that Fury had incinerated their mortal bodies.

The shadows moved inside the cracks amongst the boulders. While fire danced around the souls, the shadows also danced, moving with the flames in an arrhythmic cadence. The shadows approached the two men, and at once pounced upon them.

The men fought and screamed, trying to escape. Neither succeeded. First, one was pulled into a crack, and then the other. Their screams echoed and then vanished.

Fury loved the screams. The living humans did not react to the screams. The living could not hear them, but he could. Each time a soul rejected the Almighty, the soul fell into recognition of eternal despair and hatred. The screams became both. Fury knew their pain. He longed for the screams but knew they would never fulfill him. He needed and hated them all the more for it.

His fire consumed the flying machine. He laughed that mortals thought they flew like spirits. How could the Almighty honor these creatures so much? They had no power, no wisdom, no immortality. They were worms compared to him and the angels.

Fury watched the mortals from above. Nate's life was fading. Lee suffered a serious wound in his leg from the explosion that had rendered him immobile. The light from the object glowed around them, though. Fury still could not look at them.

Juan carried his light object to the woman. They conversed next to the light from the rock. Susan glanced at it a time or two, but her face still doubted what her heart was telling her. Her spirit glowed bright, fueled with the power of prayer.

Juan tried to give her the holy item. It radiated between them. She refused it, though, and he kept it in his hand.

Juan ran past the smoldering machine, rounded the corner, and hurried down the trail. The radiant glow of the holy item in his pocket went with him.

Fury scanned the skies.

He had expected Michael's attack, yet none came.

No swords coming at him glinting scenes of Heaven. No shields showing scenes of Calvary. If they would come, they would have come by now.

Or, were they limited by the prayers of men? Fury grinned. He flew high into the sky and watched the souls in the city.

Some souls glowed brightly. They prayed.

Most did not. They were indifferent, wrapped up in their entertainment or their desires.

Perhaps that was it. Fury doubted Michael's angels would aid an unpraying man, regardless of the token in his pocket.

His eyes turned to Juan, running alone in the canyon. The glowing light surrounded him. His soul had hazel blue edges, but for the most part, remained gray.

Juan did not pray.

Fury opened his mouth, and flames exited between his teeth. He flapped his mighty wings and flew in the air toward Juan.

He arrived in the air high above Juan, then he stopped and hovered.

He squinted at the bright glow of the object in his pocket. He now doubted it would protect the man if he did not pray.

He lowered himself within the clouds and lighted upon the northern cliff wall. The dark clouds surrounded him. He spread his wings, and a lightning bolt flashed across the sky. Thunder echoed across the valley.

Juan hurried, now holding the phone. He pressed buttons and held the phone in the air, then pressed more buttons and held it again, all while he ran. At one point, Juan tripped and fell, dropping the phone. He got back on his feet, picked up the phone, and ran again.

Fury nodded, as the item in Juan's pocket did not prevent his fall. Launching fire at Juan would give Fury a minor satisfaction. Fury wanted more; he wanted to taste blood. It had been too many hours since he had tasted blood, and he wanted Juan's.

Before, Fury had been prevented from breathing fire upon the four of them, but that was when Susan was with them, holding the item, and praying.

Now, Susan was nowhere in sight.

Perhaps the item was destructible. Perhaps it glowed but had no power without prayer.

It was worth the risk. Fury had to know what this weapon was that glowed and blinded him.

Juan reached the place where he made his call earlier, and again, he pressed his fingers on the phone. He put the device to his ear.

"Yes. This is Juan Carasco, CCFD. The EMS chopper you sent blew up. I repeat, it blew up!"

Fury lowered his head and tucked his wings. He reached his claws into the cliff rocks like a squirrel climbing down a tree. Quietly, slowly, he descended.

"No, don't send another one. We have a monster out here...Yes, a monster. A fire-breathing dragon!" Juan's voice grew louder.

Fury closed the gap. His eyes burned, and he focused them on the canyon walls rather than the glow coming from Juan's pocket.

"I know you lost contact with them. That's why I'm calling. Don't send another one yet. First, there's a threat to the city up here. Send someone from Nellis. Send some F-16s! We need firepower. No. I'm not crazy!"

The rocks gave to Fury's powerful muscles. His head and back were now visible below the storm clouds. Fire escaped through his scales, but he didn't make a sound.

# REVELATION

Thunder rolled across the valley. The storm clouds swirled like a hurricane. Bighorn sheep scrambled from their positions on the cliffs to get away from the dragon, but Fury paid them no mind. His intent was Juan.

"Look, get someone. Yes, we need EMS. But there's no evac unless we neutralize the danger. Trust me, we have a dragon up here. No, I'm not making this up! Just send help from Nellis."

Fury climbed down behind Juan. Juan still had the device to his ear.

"Okay, you know what, blame me. Yes, I shot them down. I have a tank up here. Send some fighter jets, I'll get them, too!" Juan hung up the phone. "Of course they don't believe me. Who would!" he said, frustrated. The eastern sky was covered with dark swirling clouds.

Fury closed behind him. His large muscular body was silent like a predator ready to pounce.

His flaming scales moved through the storm air with ease. His snake-like tail raised in anticipation. His leathery burning wings spread with excitement.

Juan sniffed the air. He lifted his eyes and searched the sky.

Fury put his large right claw on the ground. His rear feet dug into the rock.

He spread his wings. He imagined tasting Juan's blood on the tips of his forked tongue. He moved slowly, getting ready to strike. Juan stood within striking distance of his gaping jaws.

Juan bowed his head and lowered himself, pulling out the glowing holy item. He went to one knee. "Lord God, have mercy on me, a sinner."

The holy item that Juan held shot a streak of blue power at Fury's chest, burning his scales.

Fury moved with the speed of light. He lunged at Juan, roaring as he extended his massive head and flaming jaws.

A bright blue light surrounded the kneeling Juan, shielding him.

Fury's teeth slid off the shield. Before he had closed his mouth, he knew to retreat.

Juan lifted his head, interrupting his prayer. His head went from side to side, sensing something happened behind him.

Fury flew into the sky, his tail whisking a tree. He was in the clouds before Juan saw him. He perched on the canyon rim, hidden in the clouds. He glared with hatred at Juan, whose soul now glowed blue. He was now like Susan, and his light hurt Fury's eyes. He dug his claws into the southern cliff walls, crushing rock. Juan had prayed, and Fury's eyes retreated from the blue light that enveloped his soul. Fury scanned the heavens. None of Michael's angels rushed to attack him, to defend Juan.

Yet Juan now had protection from that item in his pocket. An item Fury did not understand.

Juan turned and retreated into Ice Box Canyon. His blue light surrounded him.

As Fury watched, he crushed the rock under his claws. Before the day was over, he would devour the woman of light.

## CHAPTER 33

Lee waited. That was all he could do.

He lifted his cell phone. There had been no messages. He guessed someone had tried to reach them, but the canyon blocked all cell phone reception. If he made it out alive, and if he survived this ordeal, he figured he'd be fired.

"Captain!" It was Susan.

He lifted his head and winced at the pain in his bandaged leg.

"Oh my God. Is that from the helicopter?" she asked.

"Yeah. Just another part of the job."

Her face turned white. "Should we take it out?"

"I'd like that, but don't want to make it worse. I'd rather a surgeon do it."

She dropped her head below the ledge. He heard her make a sound like she was heaving. He studied his wound. For some reason, he was able to stomach it.

When her head reappeared, she said, "I'm sorry. I'm not made for this."

"Neither am I."

"How's Nate?"

"Still breathing, but shallow. We need to get him out of this weather."

"I found a place."

"Where?"

"Up the rock. There's a flat surface up there, and to the left Tahoe found a cave."

"Tahoe did?"

"He's in there now."

"Smart dog."

She motioned toward Nate. While his body was under the emergency reflective blanket, she saw his face. His coloring was pale. "How do we get him to the cave?"

Lee rolled, keeping his injured leg straight. The metal shard dragged on the ledge floor, and the pain welled inside his thigh. He let out a deep shout. He gathered his balance and sat up, his legs straight ahead. "We'll have to drag him."

"What do you mean, 'we'?"

Lee scooted toward the edge of the ledge. "We're going to have to roll him onto that blanket, and drag him up there."

Lee rolled over onto his one good knee, moving while trying to keep his injured leg still. His leg was throbbing. Swelling formed in his thigh and quad. He tried not to use his bad leg, but the slightest twitch shot pain through him. He put his emergency pack back on, being careful with each move not to cause more pain.

He slid around to Nate's head. The young man was close to death. Still, he had to try. He grabbed the blanket and pulled it off. Nate's leg was crushed, and bandaged, and disfigured. Gangrene wasn't far behind. Susan put her hands to her mouth as she gasped.

Lee decided to leave Nate's rescue pack on him, not sure about the extent of his spinal damage. Best to drag him to safety as is, he thought. "I need you to help me slide him onto this blanket," Lee said.

Susan didn't answer. Her eyes were wide.

"Get it together. He needs you now." Lee spread the blanket open. "Get him on this thing and let's drag him up there."

"He's holding the Rosary," Susan said.

Lee nodded.

He reached down and opened Nate's hand. He grabbed the Rosary and handed it to Susan. "Here."

"What do you want me to do?"

"Hold it for him."

Susan nodded. She put it in her pocket.

Lee said, "I'm going to handle his head and neck. Together, we're going to slide him onto the blanket. I'd roll him, but there's not enough room."

Susan crawled up on the ledge. It was tight.

Nate's body rested against the cliff walls. Had he not been so close to the cliff, the boulder would have crushed him in a direct hit. "What now?"

"Get on the blanket. Try to pull his belt so that his midsection gets on the blanket."

She moved around him.

Pools of red covered the ledge and got on her jeans.

"Go slow. And don't freak out on me." Lee put both his hands around Nate's head and lifted. The boy didn't make a sound. But he still breathed in and out. The bruise on his neck had spread to his ear.

Susan pulled, at first, but increased her tension. "Will we hurt him?"

"Probably," Lee said. "But until help does come, he needs to be out of the elements."

"Shouldn't we help you, first?"

"Later. Get him on the blanket." He noticed his voice elevate as he fought back the pain.

The two edged Nate onto the blanket. Lee instructed Susan to climb off the ledge. They had to drag Nate off the ledge and keep him from falling.

Lee went to the edge of the ledge. Keeping his leg straight, he sat down, leaning to one side to keep the shrapnel from catching the rocky floor. His bottles of water sloshed in his emergency pack. He slid off the ledge. Pain shot up as he twitched his wounded leg when his foot hit the ground. He swore as he moved and the pain went through his body.

"Be careful," Susan said.

"I'm trying."

"I mean watch your words. If you mean to talk to Jesus, you'd better be specific."

"I'm in no mood to worry about that right now." He grabbed the blanket and pulled. Nate's immobile body slid toward him. "I'm going to get under him and try to control his torso and his head. I need you to hold his legs." As Nate slid, Lee wrapped the blanket around his legs. Doing his best to keep the young man stable, he pulled while shifting underneath him.

Susan did as she was told, holding the bloodied blanket but keeping the legs elevated.

Lee balanced on his one good leg, keeping his back against the ledge wall for support. As Nate slid off, Lee said, "Hold him up, I've got his back." He lowered Nate to the ground. As he did, he watched Nate's bruise. The internal bleeding was taking its toll. Even if they got Nate to the cave, he would not live to see the sun go down. Lee was surprised he wasn't gone already.

The thunder rumbled overhead. Lee hopped to the blanket where Nate's legs were. "Good job," Lee said.

Susan dusted her wet hands. "What now?"

"Grab the blanket, and let's pull. Be sure to watch as we go so he doesn't slide off."

Susan grabbed and tugged.

Lee did as well. He tried hopping on one foot and ignoring the wound in his leg, but that didn't work. Getting on all fours, they both pulled and tugged and maneuvered up the wet rock slope.

Nate's body moved upon the blanket over the rocks. One of Nate's two remaining water bottles became free, and it rolled down the slope and floated on the water until it stopped by a rock.

Water flowed underneath them, covering their hands and shins and soaking Nate's clothes.

Lee said, "Where's the cave?"

She pointed left. "There."

Lee got to his knees and pulled the rest of the way.

His wound was getting to him.

He was losing energy.

When they came around the bend, the cave was there. Tahoe stood in the darkness, his tongue and eyes reflecting the outside light. "Hey, boy," Lee said, trying to lighten the mood. Susan was right. The cave was just about big enough to fit all of them. He went inside. He noticed streaks of red mixing with the trickling water where he was. He was losing blood and getting weak. From inside the cave, with Tahoe behind him, he pulled. Nate's body slid inside. Susan supported Nate from the outside, then climbed into the cave with them.

Once they were in, Lee examined the wound on his leg. The blood had soaked his pants. He had no idea what to do.

"Will you lose your leg?" Susan said.

"If that's all I lose, it'll be a good day."

Shadows darkened Ice Box Canyon. The clouds were sleeting again.

He closed his eyes.

The image of the dragon had filled his head. He tried to remind himself: Four in, four out. But another question penetrated his thoughts.

How will any of us make it out alive?

# CHAPTER 34

In the dampness of the cave, Susan knelt next to Nate. Lee rested on his side, trying not to move his punctured leg. It throbbed with pain each time he breathed. The cold damp cave let very little light in. Tahoe stood next to Susan. The dog had slowed his panting, but his eyes and ears were alert. Lee's rescue pack pinched his skin. He unclamped it, and the pinch went away.

"Will he make it back?" Susan said.

Lee didn't like the alternative. If Juan did, they'd have a shot. Or would they?

The dragon reeked of power and evil. As a fireman, he had seen flames tear up rooftops as he rescued screaming women and children. He saw smoke and fire devour entire structures. Fire like that cared not about its victims. When flames reached high into the rooftops, when they latched onto burning victims and would not yield, he learned that fire acted as a living thing. When it was loose, it was evil and needed to be destroyed.

But the dragon was a thousand times worse than anything he had ever witnessed. Its whole purpose was to destroy every bit of humanity on the earth. He wasn't sure how he knew that, but he couldn't get the idea out of his head.

When it spoke, chills ran all through Lee's body. As the dragon spoke, he forgot about the shrapnel in his leg, and the pain, for a moment.

But what about Juan? He was out there.

Alone.

"Juan is a good man, and a good firefighter," Lee said.

"That's not what I asked," Susan said.

"Let's not think about that."

Susan put her open hand on Tahoe and smoothed his fur. "Is he Christian?"

"I don't know."

Susan sat back, brought her knees to her chest, and wrapped her arms around her legs. "Getting cold again."

"Yeah."

"Why hasn't that thing killed us?"

It had made such short work of the helicopter pilots, yet it hesitated to attack them. "I don't know."

"Did it kill the people with the Subaru?"

Tahoe stood next to Susan, his leash still tied to his collar. He came into this canyon with somebody, and they hadn't found that somebody yet. "That's my guess, but who knows."

"What happened to the pack we found?"

Lee remembered that he had left it where he found it after examining its contents. Then, Nate got injured, and all hell broke loose. "It's under the helicopter."

Nate's breathing grew more shallow. Lee laid next to him, one arm resting on his elbow.

"I'm a Christian." Susan watched Lee for his reaction.

"So."

"So, that's why we're not dead yet."

"Christians get killed all the time," Lee said. "Haven't you ever heard of martyrs?"

"Yes, I know that. But this is different."

"What makes you say that?"

"Because that thing's not real."

Lee held back a snort because he knew his pain would hurt like hell if he did. "No offense, but what did we just see? It looked pretty real to me."

"I know that. It's just, it's not a real creature."

"Are you going to start telling me to believe in unicorns and magic fairy dust now?"

"Or dragons?"

Lee kept his mouth shut. The sleet fell outside among the shadows.

Susan shook her head and rocked back and forth. "No, I'm not asking you to believe anything."

Lee grew impatient. "What is it, then?"

"It's a demon."

Lee studied the woman. He had believed she was crazy. She had called them on a missing person case. He didn't believe her at first, but she was right. She had told them about prayer. She had mentioned a fountain, and a woman, but neither of those had come true. Now she's mentioning the dragon is a demon? "Why not?" Lee said.

"I'm serious."

"I'm not saying you're not. Hell, until an hour ago I never believed in dragons, either."

"My dream last night showed me fire. That's what we just saw."

"Did it show you how to defeat it?"

"Only the woman's voice, which told me to look for the fountain."

Lee shook his head and bit his lip. "Well, when we first met I thought you were insane. Right now, if you tell me there's a fountain somewhere, maybe there is."

"We're close," Susan said. She shifted her weight. "It's important, too. Like it will help us."

Lee tried to imagine how a fountain would help, but nothing came to mind. Would the water put out the dragon's fire? Maybe. It wouldn't matter. He knew he'd fight, but the odds of winning this one were nil.

Susan pointed at Nate. "It will help him, too."

Nate's complexion worsened in the dark of the damp cave. They had put the blanket over him. Lee wished the boy would say something, anything. The kid was a good kid. He was so inexperienced, but he worked hard and did what he was told. Lee pained over Nate. What would Lee tell his family? He had never lost a man. This man was under his charge.

It was his fault. He studied the metal sticking out of his leg. The pain was awful, but the aching in his heart was growing worse. He deserved the shrapnel. He deserved to lose his leg.

Susan pulled her Rosary beads out of her coat pocket. They clicked together as she held one end but let the others fall. "Will you pray with me?"

"No."

"Do you mind if I do?"

REVELATION

He didn't understand this. He had to get a plan together. Where was Juan? Was he dead? He'd never know hiding in this rock. "No. I don't mind. Go ahead."

Susan closed her eyes and she said her prayers, beginning with the statements of belief. As she went, Lee asked, "Is that Catholic?"

Susan opened her eyes. "Yes."

"You look Native American. How'd you become Catholic?"

"I wasn't always."

"No?"

"No. You could say I was spiritual. Many of my people are." Susan leaned forward, holding her legs tight. "I guess it was my father. He became an alcoholic, and my family suffered a lot because of it. He believed in spirits. Why did he suffer? Why did the spirits let him suffer?"

"I'm sorry to hear that," Lee said.

"No. Don't be. He made his choices."

"But how did you become Catholic?"

"One day, when things were bad at home, I was driving to get away. And I had that question in my mind. Well, I made a turn, and I saw a Catholic Church. I don't know why, but something told me to go inside. So I did. And when I did, the first thing I saw was this man hanging on a cross. And I understood why suffering was a part of life, and why it has meaning."

"So you walked in and never left?"

"It wasn't like that. I decided to learn more, open some books, and ask some questions. I went through the classes, and became Catholic about a year later."

"When did you start having dreams?"

Susan shivered. "About six months ago."

Lee watched her. She was still attractive, despite the weather and the cold. Her hair was stringy as it fell on her shoulders. She had to be in danger of losing her body heat. "I know you want to find that fountain, but we've got to get you somewhere warm."

"I'll be okay," she said.

Lee didn't believe her. He didn't believe any of them would be okay when all this ended. "So, who is this woman that keeps speaking to you?"

Susan raised a slight smile. "It's Mary. Her voice is so beautiful, and I get such a warm feeling every time I remember hearing it."

"Who's Mary?"

"The mother of Jesus."

Lee didn't understand. Why would the Jesus's mother come to this strange woman in a dream? He doubted that it happened. He did believe that Susan believed it, but was it as she had said? Maybe, he thought. After what he had witnessed, he wasn't sure about much of anything anymore. Lee winced at the shrapnel sticking from his leg. "What's this fountain look like?"

"It's strange, but a formation in the rocks, like a lowercase 't', but without the small point sticking out."

The cave was elevated, so they could see the lower levels of the far wall, opposite the wet slope. The dark clouds cast shadows on every crack and crevice, though, and it made it hard to distinguish anything. "Do you want to go out there and look, knowing that thing's out there?"

"I have to. But I don't want to."

"Why'd you say you were close?"

# REVELATION

"A slash in the rock. A piece that jutted out, and went like this." Susan moved with her hand indicating the direction of the slash.

There was a red piece of rock on the opposite cliff wall. It was a strange color compared to the rest, though the poor lighting made it blend in. "I see your slash," Lee said.

"But that's not it. I tried hitting it with a stone, but it didn't break."

"Maybe it's not supposed to." Lee said.

"Why do you say that?"

Above the slash, and to the right, there was a strange gap in the rocks. When Susan was standing below it, she wouldn't have noticed it because it was a gap that dug into the wall. From that vantage point, the gap would have blended in. But from where Lee was laying, through the cave entrance, the gap was clear. It was about two feet wide and two feet tall. Perhaps she was right. From where Susan sat next to Nate, she wouldn't be able to see it. But from where he lay he saw it.

"I see your fountain."

# CHAPTER 35

Susan shifted to the cave entrance. A crack of lightning lit up the canyon. Thunder echoed between the walls, causing Lee to jump.

He grabbed his leg in pain.

Tahoe ducked his head and crouched. Nate, still unconscious, didn't move.

"Where is it?" Susan said.

Lee pointed. "There's your slash, right?"

Susan nodded.

"Look above it, and to the right. See those cracks?"

Susan gasped, putting her hand to her mouth. Her voice squeaked. "It's there. It really exists!"

Lee twisted around. The pain from his wounded leg got worse. Infection was imminent. *No way Nate and I are getting out of here alive.*

He grunted but got to a point where he could move forward and out of the cave. Before Susan ran outside, Lee said, "Let me go out there. No telling if that monster is back. Best he gets me before you."

Susan waited.

Lee dragged his body toward the entrance so he'd see better. "I'll tell you one thing," he said. "Meeting you is making me question things."

Susan poised her legs to run. "What do you want to do?"

"I was going to ask you the same thing. When you get to it, what do you expect to find?"

"Water," she said.

"Well, the whole canyon's full of water."

"No. Water on the inside. That's what we're supposed to find."

"We're?"

She raised her eyebrows. "Well, we're a team, aren't we?"

"Yeah, but who's in charge?"

Tahoe pressed his fur against the rear wall next to Nate. He did not indicate that he would follow them. Should Lee leave Nate's side? What if he didn't make it? What if he didn't come back?

Susan leaned forward, the cave entrance seeming to pull her out.

Lee stretched his neck, peering out from under the cave. Was the dragon out there? Where was Juan? He thought in circles. The cold and the blood loss were getting to him. His mind turned foggy.

He shook his head. Someone had to make it out of this canyon alive, he thought. Nate is close to death. He's losing a lot of blood. And Juan? No telling where he is now. He never should have sent him to seek more help. He had seen the dragon first, and no one believed him.

But it was there. Lee saw it with his own eyes. The smoldering helicopter wreckage, the dead pilots, they were proof enough.

"Let me go first," he said. He limped forward. His pierced leg dragged behind him.

"You can't move," she said. "Let me go alone."

"No. You need someone to watch for cover." He made his way outside the cave entrance. It was a small cave, the entrance no more than four feet high. Nate was safe in there, as far as he knew.

The thunder rumbled. More sleet fell, chilling the air and re-icing the canyon. He took a step, and water splashed on his boots. He watched the skies. There was no sign of the dragon.

His rescue pack remained inside the cave. He had no weapons, nothing.

He saw a baseball-sized rock. He stiffened his injured leg as he bent down and picked it up. He knew it would be useless against the dragon, but he held on, feeling better having it in his hand.

Limping, he moved out in the open. The canyon walls seemed closer together as the danger closed in on them.

He paused, waiting. The sleet fell, and the water trickled. He heard the faint howl of wind blow inside the clouds. Far off thunder rumbled. He waited some more.

"See anything?" Susan whispered.

Lee raised his hand. "Wait."

He listened.

He heard no noise.

Then he motioned his hand indicating for Susan to come.

She hurried up to him.

"Go," he said. "I'll watch."

She ran and reached the slash. She inspected the walls and reached up with her hands, feeling for the cracks above her head. She was too short. The cracks were high. She found a large stone, braced it against the wall, and jiggled it. It was wet, but it might hold. She placed her foot on the stone and stretched her left hand against the wall for balance.

The stone wiggled but it didn't roll.

She put her right hand up and slid her fingers over the "t" formation.

She moved her hands over the cracks.

From the cave entrance, Tahoe barked.

The hairs on Lee's neck stiffened. "Any luck?" Lee said.

"Almost."

"Hurry."

Susan stopped.

A rock fell onto the trail. Lee waited. His muscles tensed. His heart pumped adrenaline through his body, lessening the pain. He watched.

Another noise.

Susan backed away from the wall toward Lee. He motioned for her to come.

There was movement. It was Juan.

"Thank God!" Lee said.

Juan rushed up to Lee and Susan. "I got through."

"Great," Lee said. "Did you see the monster?"

"Something strange happened while I was down the trail. I thought I heard him, but I only saw a tree move. Must have been some wind that made its way down the canyon."

"When does help come?"

"I don't know. I did what you told me to do. I told them to bring weapons, that there was a dragon."

"Did they believe you?"

"No. They knew about the downed chopper and confirmed no radio contact. But they didn't believe me when I said 'dragon'."

Lee's energy faded, and he put his hand on Juan's shoulder.

Juan pointed to the rock in Lee's hand. "What's that for?"

Lee dropped it. "Nothing," he said.

"You don't look good."

"I'm alive," Lee said.

"Where's Nate?"

"Come, let me show you." Lee took two steps toward the cave, but he felt weak.

Juan grabbed Lee, lifted Lee's arm, and put it over his shoulder.

"There," Lee said, lifting his arm toward the cave.

Juan aided Lee in that direction.

"Water!" Susan shouted. "I found water!"

Lee and Juan turned their heads. Susan pointed up the stone wall. A small trickle of water dripped from the center of the cross. "I removed a small rock and water came out!"

Lee had hoped for something more. The entire canyon was getting wet with sleet again, and Susan is excited about a trickle? "That's it?" Lee said.

"Cap'n," Juan said. "She found it. Should we try to get her out of here?"

"Yeah," Lee said. "But I can't do it. You take her. Leave me with Nate. Send help when you get back."

# REVELATION

Tahoe's bark echoed inside the cave. Lee, Juan, and Susan flinched.

Lee said, "Hurry!" and he limped toward the cave. Susan sprinted. Juan said, "Where?"

Lee pointed. "There!"

Susan took two steps, then stopped.

The smell of sulfur and soot hit Lee's nostrils like a tidal wave. The dragon!

Tahoe barked again.

Juan found the cave.

Susan sprinted her way up the slope, splashing water and slipping as she went.

Lee shouted, "Come on!"

Susan made it up the slope. She helped Juan carry Lee to the cave. Lee then told them to get inside. Lee put his hands on Susan's back.

Then a mighty roar echoed in the canyon. Lee put one hand on his ear. Susan stopped.

Heat and fire came from above. Another roar.

Susan screamed.

Lee shoved Susan into the small cave. He fell while yelling. Juan shouted something as he grabbed Lee's coat, but the roars were too loud, like a jackhammer going off inside his skull.

Juan pulled.

Susan screamed again.

Tahoe barked.

Nate lay silent.

Pain ran through Lee's leg. Juan jerked Lee's coat with a mighty tug.

An explosion erupted behind them. Heat hit Lee's foot on his bad leg. Then there was pain.

"Put it out!" Juan shouted.

Flames surrounded Lee's feet!

Juan jumped on it. He hit the metal stake piercing out of his bloodied leg. The pain of the impact on the shrapnel shot through Lee's leg.

Lee screamed.

Outside, the canyon stank with sulfur, soot, and fire.

# CHAPTER 36

Tahoe barked. Lee scooted his feet back as Juan put the fire out on his boot. Nate's blanket also caught fire though it was wet. The cave walls lit up in yellow and orange. Tahoe retreated, pressing his body against the moist wall and barking at the fire. Juan ripped off his coat and smothered the flames, bumping Nate who remained motionless. Juan's coat caught fire.

Lee's eyes widened as the fire burned the water-soaked cloth. *How in the world?*

Juan whipped his coat up and down and put out the fires. The cave went dark. The smell of smoke made Susan cough.

Then there was silence.

The three of them tried to remain quiet, holding their breath, but their adrenaline made it difficult. "That was too close," Juan said.

"Shhh," Lee said. He held up his hand. "Wait."

Tahoe whined. Susan put her hand over his muzzle so he wouldn't bark.

Moments passed. The sleet fell. A soft glow danced somewhere outside the cave, and there was the crackling sound of burning wood.

"Did anybody see it?" Lee said. "Any idea if it has a weakness?"

Juan sat back. He winced as he leaned his back against the stone-cold cave. "No."

Susan kept her mouth shut.

Lightning flashed outside, and a crack of thunder boomed from above.

Tahoe muffled a bark in Susan's grasp. She gripped tighter.

"Keep him quiet," Lee said.

"Cap'n" Juan said. "Nate doesn't look good."

Lee nodded. This cave may be his and Nate's burial place. But he needed Juan and Susan to get out to tell the story. Joan and Jenn would want to know.

"The water. That's what we need," Susan said.

Lee glared at Susan. "Did you see how the fire burned wet clothes? That monster's flames are too hot."

"It's not normal water."

Juan rubbed his shoulder. Lee figured he hurt it when they dived in the cave. "What do you mean?"

"It's just different."

Lee chuckled. "There she goes again."

"If you don't want to take me seriously…"

Lee paused. He leaned back, the pain and the weakness coming back. "We need to think. What are our options?"

Juan said, "Hide here?"

"We need that water," Susan said.

Lee slammed his palm on the ground. "I need something concrete!"

No one said anything.

# REVELATION

Lee lowered his voice. "Look. At least one of us has to get out of here. We need real ideas."

Juan shifted. "Wait and hope. That's all I got."

"Wait for what?" Susan said.

"I talked with Dispatch. They know about the helicopter. They didn't believe me when I told them why. But I told them Nellis needed to send some firepower."

"We wait here, and they may blow us all up," Lee said.

"Nellis Air Force Base?" Susan said.

"Yeah."

"Will they come?" Susan said.

"We have to hope."

Susan shook her head. "It won't work."

Juan said, "No living thing can withstand firepower from an F-16."

"I'm telling you it won't work."

"Why?".

"She thinks the monster is a demon," Lee said.

"It is a demon," Susan said. "I know it."

"Did you dream about this, too?" Juan said.

"I dreamed about fire," Susan said.

"One of us has to get out," Lee said.

"Let the F-16s come. They'll blow that thing out of the sky."

"Maybe," Lee said, though his doubts grew.

Susan pointed outside. "Look!"

The fountain's trickle of water opened up. The water gushed out of the center of the "t", splashing the rocks on the level below. "I have to get to it," Susan said. She moved to get past Juan.

"That dragon will eat you," Lee said.

Susan pulled up her Rosary, her small beads falling at the swing of her fist. "No he won't."

"You're crazy!" Juan said.

Lee said, "Wait." He shifted his position.

Juan grabbed Susan.

Susan pushed. "Let me go!"

"Think!"

Lee moved. The pain in his leg worsened. His vision went foggy. "Don't give us away!"

Juan and Susan tussled. Then Susan took her right hand and hit Juan on his shoulder.

Juan let go.

Susan rushed out of the cave and hurried over the sleet-covered rocks. She splashed in the pool as she went down the slope.

Lee, expecting fire, said, "Get back." He and Juan scooted to the rear of the cave. Tahoe barked.

There was no explosion, only the glowing orange, the sound of burning wood, and sleet and trickling water.

Lee had to admit that Susan was resourceful. She may have used all her cards, but she was playing with the few cards she had left. He moved past Juan and stuck his head out of the cave. He did not see the dragon.

"Wait here," Lee said.

"What are you doing?" Juan said.

"Just wait." Lee grabbed his emergency pack and clasped it around his waist. His three remaining water bottles sloshed in his emergency pack.

"That won't protect you."

## REVELATION

"Habit," Lee said.

While Susan ran to the fountain, he crawled out into the darkened canyon. Several trees burned against the cliff walls under the falling sleet, casting dancing shadows within an eerie orange glow.

Somewhere, a dragon lurked. And he knew the dragon wanted them dead."

# CHAPTER 37

Fury perched in his spirit form above the canyon like a gargoyle on the edge of a skyscraper. The clouds went through his spirit, though the soft orange glow of his outline sifted in their mist.

The mortals and the dog hid in the rock. They had found a cave.

The water, now pouring from the nearby cliff, made it hard for him to see. He wanted to swoop down and, with one swing of his claws, dig them out from the rock and send them to judgment. He imagined the holy items would shield Juan and Susan. But for Lee and Nate, they remained vulnerable.

The bright water poured from the stone wall, leaving a long trail of light as it mixed and trickled with the sleet down the canyon. The light grew, paining his eyes. He could not see as the light burned his pupils. He had tried to hit the mortals with the flames from his mouth, but he had to guess where to aim. He did not see their souls after he threw his fire. They lived, hidden.

The two holy items protected them. Juan carried one; Susan the other. The flames did not harm them. However, Lee carried neither, and if not for the cave, he would have been incinerated.

## REVELATION

He clenched his claws into the rock and straightened his batlike wings. Purple lightning flashed across the sky. He whipped his long tail, which snapped like thunder. The wind blew harder, and the sleet turned to snow. The dark clouds became black, and shadows covered the canyon.

Fury shouted at Heaven. "Your mortals cannot defeat me. You try to give them gifts, but they know not how to use them. They are helpless against me. The new Rebellion begins today. I will send them to judgment before the night is over!"

He waited. He expected the heavenly hosts to unite against him, to come and strike him. He prepared his claws. He stirred his fire. He lifted his tail, expecting an attack.

But none came.

"Have you grown weak? Have you grown frail? Has the power of the Prince surpassed you?" Fury's taunts went up. He waited, but God did not answer.

Fury laughed. Flames spurted from his mouth.

He knew not the power of this water. He shut his eyes and blinked.

God was doing something with these mortals. He was helping them.

They had to suffer for it.

Incinerating them would not be good enough. No, he wanted to taste their flesh upon his tongue, to feel them scorch inside his belly, to see their souls scream at the approaching shadows.

He materialized into his dragon form. The wind and the clouds whistled past his scales and his wings. He gripped the canyon rim, forcing his giant claws into the rock like a knife cutting through cheese. The stones crumbled within them.

He had to make a choice. Would he endure the pain from the light to devour the mortals? Should he risk the defense from the holy items that they carried? Michael had not yet come. God was absent. The mortals had three objects, the two holy items, and the water. The mortal fools knew not their power.

He had been too cautious. Years of capture had dulled his confidence. His caution had been ineffective.

He was an angel, a demon among the Rebellion, an archangel turned against the Almighty. Only one angel was greater than he, and that was the Prince of Light.

He had made an error in his caution. Force mattered most. Get to the mortals before they understood how to use their tools. No matter the burns. No matter the blindness.

Power would win. Aggression would conquer.

His move would be sudden. Their fear would render them helpless, hopeless.

So that was it. He would attack.

He stretched his elongated neck. He spread his wings.

Lightning flashed and streaked across the sky.

The canyon glowed in a holy light. The fountain water streamed down the trickling puddles.

The woman had left the confines of the rocks. Her spirit glowed. She ran toward the fountain like a mammal scurrying out of its burrow. The holy item glowed blue in her pocket.

Lee, with his injured leg, crawled from the cave. He got up, hopped, then stumbled and fell.

He did not carry anything holy. His spirit remained dull, gray.

Fury's eyes burned from the light, but no matter.

Lee was in the open.

# REVELATION

Now was his time. Fury stretched his wings. With a mighty push, he dived off the edge of the Ice Box Canyon rim. He imagined Lee's blood upon his tongue. The air rushed past him as he aimed at the painful light and the wounded mortal below.

# CHAPTER 38

"What am I doing out here?" Lee said. Snow fell all around him. He was barely mobile. At least Juan could move and run. But in his need to be in control, Lee felt responsible. He had to get Susan back to safety. He dragged his leg as he stepped on the slippery rock surface.

Susan hadn't been incinerated by the creature yet. She was now under the fountain, the water gushing from the crack shaped like a 't' formation above her head. "It's warm." she shouted, the snow falling on her face. "I'm not cold!" She rubbed her fingers through her hair. She smiled like a child who had learned the joy of swimming for the first time.

Lee's toe hit a dip in the rock, and he fell. The shrapnel caught the rock, and it twisted in his leg. He yelled and rolled down the slope. He put his hands on his leg as his momentum stopped on the lower level. He mustered the effort to sit up.

"Captain!" It was Juan.

"Don't come down!" Lee shouted back.

"Cap!" Juan's voice panicked. He pointed left.

The earth rumbled, and the rocks shook where he sat.

"Another earthquake?" Lee said.

# REVELATION

Sulfur and soot filled the air. The smell hit him hard.

"Lee?" It was Susan, her attention focused down the canyon corridor.

The heat burned the skin on his face and hands.

The falling snow melted into rain.

A flash of lightning raced across the sky, visible between the canyon walls. There was a low, deep, terrible growl. Lee's heart skipped a beat, and the hairs on his arms and neck stood up. He moved his eyes to where Susan was looking.

The dragon was the size of a house. It carried its weight on four powerful legs, its wings stretched high and scraped the canyon cliffs. The edges of its wings sliced through the rocks like spades through beach sand. The rocks crunched under its weight.

Flames sputtered between its solid red scales. An orange fire glowed through its belly. Its reptilian mouth grinned as the beast anticipated his meal.

But its eyes squinted. It had trouble opening the eye close to Susan. It turned away, like a man blind from the sun.

"Lee!" Susan said again.

Lee flinched, trying to get off the ground.

The wet stones made him slip. His emergency pack caught upon a rock.

He lifted his good leg and scooted backward, bearing the sharp pain in his leg and body. One of his water bottles fell from his pack and into a puddle.

The dragon opened its mouth. "Are you ready to meet your judgment?"

Lee didn't only hear the terrible words, they penetrated his heart. Fear spread through his chest and limbs.

Panic ensued.

He was losing control.

He fought to keep it, but it was escaping his thoughts. Those words - they were meant to be the last he heard.

Susan grabbed his coat above both shoulders and yanked. She pulled Lee under the water. It was warm, and he let it fall and wash his hair and head. The cold and ice didn't affect him. The panic and fear subsided.

The dragon roared. The sound waves knocked them both against the stone cliff. Susan screamed as both she and Lee put their hands over their ears. The putrid air of hell replaced the oxygen around them.

Then the dragon stopped. It squinted, hesitating. It roared at the sky like it expected a threat. What threat did it expect?

The moment lasted a second. It focused on Lee, though it struggled to see.

The dragon's eyes flashed. Its lips curled. Its throat gurgled with the anticipation of destruction.

It breathed in the air. It sucked in the atmosphere.

There was a brief pause.

Then, it closed its eyes and whipped its head at Lee and Susan. Flames of fire spewed from its mouth. The aim was haphazard, like a new fireman learning to handle a fire hose under heavy pressure.

The flames exploded at Lee. Everything seemed to slow. Devils with pitchforks and swords appeared within the flames. They had red eyes and sharp teeth that devoured everything in their path.

The fire was death.

# REVELATION

Susan screamed again, putting her hands to her face. Poor girl, Lee thought. She didn't deserve this. She was just doing what she was told. No one imagined a fate like this.

He thought of Joan, sitting at home, putting groceries away.

He thought of Jenn. He wished he had made more time for Jenn. Why had he been so hard on her?

The flames came at him, like the funnel of a tornado. Devils and fire and anger and shadows and hate and everything unholy came at him.

This is it, he thought.

He ducked his head, put his arms around Susan, and waited for the end.

.

# CHAPTER 39

The flaming devils, their eyes red and yellow, their mouths spewing sharp fangs and teeth, their hands wielding red pitchforks and swords, threatened an eternal pain. Lee yelled deep in from his chest, expecting death to wrap around him

Susan screamed, her voice loud and scared.

But the water fell upon them. The pain did not come. The fire did not eat his skin or roast his organs. Instead, his body tingled. He heard the flaming vortex, and he saw the hellish devils, and he reasoned each second would be his last.

Then it was over.

The putrid wind ended, and the flaming devils disappeared in smoke. A haze hung in the air.

Lee still held Susan. Her head was buried under her arms. He felt no pain. Lee expected he was dead. But the water splattered as it hit his hair. It trickled down his face and soaked into his clothes. He lifted his head.

The dragon stood in front of them. The creature's yellow eyes glowed with hate.

"Captain?" Susan had opened her eyes. "What happened?"

# REVELATION

The creature lifted his long neck and let out a roar, exposing its massive fangs. It launched fire into the storm clouds above. It spread its wings. Lightning flashed across the sky. It flapped its wings and lifted off into the swirling clouds. Its tail whipped as it disappeared into the storm.

Lee touched his arms. "I thought we were dead."

"But we're not." Susan stood up. The warm water poured down upon her.

Lee rose, keeping his back against the wall for support. His emergency pack scraped against the wall. He didn't feel pain as he leaned against the stone.

"Captain, your leg!" Susan said.

He looked down. His pants were still torn, and the red stains were still there, but the shrapnel that had been in his leg was not. Still red with blood, it laid on the ground on the wet rocks.

He put his hand on his thigh, expecting to touch a wound, but his skin was healed, as though he had never suffered an injury. "What the-?"

"You're healed."

"How did that happen?" Lee rubbed his leg. There was no pain, no bacteria, no sign of infection.

He rubbed the back of his leg where the shrapnel had exited. It, too, was completely healed. He moved his leg. Perfect. It felt strong.

"Now do you believe?"

Lee inspected his leg.

His muscles felt good. His strength was good. "This is amazing," he said.

Susan grinned. "This was why we had to find the fountain."

Lee laughed in a release of energy. A few moments ago he had thought he was dead. Now, he felt completely alive.

He let the fountain water pour on his face. It was warm and soothing. Safe. He pulled out a water bottle and emptied it. Then he filled it with the smooth clear water pouring from the fountain. The water was pure, with no minerals floating in the bottle. He drank it, and he laughed. "I love this fountain!"

"The lady from my dreams. It had to be Mary. She was right!"

Lee let more water fall on him, enjoying the splattering it made upon his forehead. He moved his leg. There was no pain, and he felt strong. He pictured Nate and Juan in the cave. "I have an idea." He filled his water bottle to the brim. "Come on!"

Lee ran to the cave, careful not to slip on the slick wet rock. His legs felt athletic like he could run a track meet. The sulfur and soot still hung in the air and entered his lungs, but he didn't care. He ran to the cave, and Susan followed close behind. When he arrived, Juan was sitting next to Nate and Tahoe. "You're alive?"

"Yeah."

"I thought you were toast!"

"Me too."

"You're moving!"

Lee grinned. "How is he?"

"He doesn't have long. He convulsed a few moments ago when the dragon showed up. I thought we lost him then, but we didn't."

Lee bent over Nate. The young man's breathing had slowed so much. He was dying. He pulled out his water bottle and poured it on Nate's chest, head, and leg. When he was done, the bottle was a quarter full.

"What are you doing?" Juan asked.

"Oh, hell," Lee said. "He emptied the rest of the water onto Nate's body, soaking his clothes."

"Your leg?" Juan said. "Where's the shrapnel?"

"That's it. The water healed my leg."

Tahoe wagged his tail. Susan entered the cave. "Did you give the water to him?"

"Just poured it all over Nate."

"Is it working?"

Nate's head lifted, his eyes opened wide, and his mouth gasped. His chest rose, breathing in air.

Juan, Lee, and Susan jumped. Tahoe barked, then wagged his tail.

Nate coughed, and then coughed some more.

He flipped over onto all fours and coughed, spitting blood.

Juan pressed himself against the wall, not sure what to do.

Lee put his hand on Nate's back, but he was too surprised to know what to say. Blood poured from Nate's lips, but his color had already returned. The bruise on Nate's neck faded away.

"My God," Juan said.

"Nate, you alright?" said Lee.

The boy had finished spitting, and he shook his head. "I missed the online training for this."

Lee laughed. "Best thing I've heard all day."

Tahoe licked Nate in the face.

"I told you," Susan said. "It's the water."

Lee rubbed his leg.

He felt no pain, like he was twenty years younger.

More importantly, his team was back. He turned to Susan and raised the empty water bottle. "I have to hand it to you, you knew something we didn't."

Susan smiled and pulled her Rosary from her pocket. "I just try to hang onto this. That's all I know."

Nate sat up and put his arms around Tahoe. Tahoe wagged his tail. "Where are we?"

"In a cave," Juan said.

Nate tried to get his bearings. "Man, I never want to go through that again. I just knew I was going to die."

"You were," Lee said, shaking his head. "I can't explain it."

"Faith," Susan said. "We need to have faith."

Juan and Nate looked at Lee.

Lee was amazed. His leg was healed.

Nate appeared fully healed.

Juan was alive.

Susan was right. His team had made it.

"What do we do about the dragon?" Juan said.

"So there is a dragon?" Nate asked.

That's right, Lee thought. The kid had been out ever since the boulder fell on him. "Yeah. Seems there is."

Nate's mouth dropped. "What's it look like?"

Juan said, "You don't want to see it."

"But, how will I recognize it?" Nate sat up and brought his legs under him. He crouched, ready for action. A tear came to Lee's eye. A moment ago the kid was bleeding internally, mangled, and on death's door. Now, the kid was going to be alright.

## REVELATION

"Trust us. You'll know," Lee said.

"Can we fight it with the water?" Juan asked.

"That's a good question." Lee said to Susan, "What do you think?"

"I don't know."

"Well, you're the only one who's been right so far."

"I don't know. All I know is I was supposed to find a fountain, and we did."

Juan shifted toward the cave entrance. "Let's find out."

"Whoa," Lee said, holding his hand up. "We don't know what we don't know. Let's plan a strategy."

Juan sat back down.

Nate had his arm around Tahoe. The dog had his tongue out, its eyes focused on what lay outside the cave.

Lee's mind was no longer foggy. He remembered his training. "What do we know?"

Juan and Nate didn't answer.

Susan said, "His fire he shot out at us, it didn't touch us."

"I saw that," Juan said. "I thought you were cooked."

Susan rubbed the Rosary beads in her hand. "Did you notice he couldn't look at us?"

"You're right," Lee said. "He seemed to have trouble focusing on us."

"Perhaps he's blinded by the water," Susan said.

"How does that happen," Juan asked. "We're not blind to it."

"Perhaps he sees things we can't. If he's a spirit, that would explain a lot," Susan said.

"But how can a spirit throw rocks and spew fire and take down helicopters?"

Lee said, "When I think of spirits, I think of ghosts. This monster out there, it seems pretty real to me."

Susan said, "Spirits were here before Creation. They are more powerful than anything on earth."

Lee held the water bottle in his hand. "Susan's right. If he's blinded to the water, maybe we can use it as a defense and get out of this canyon."

"Don't forget we have help coming." Juan shifted his weight. He appeared eager to get out of the canyon.

"Help?" Nate asked.

"I called for help. I think Nellis is sending some air support after the downed helicopter."

"You got through?"

"Yeah. Not here, though. Had to run down the canyon."

Lee stuck his head out the cave entrance. Water trickled down the cliff walls, and snow, heavier than before, fell onto the rocks inside Ice Box Canyon. "Look, I don't want to put us all at risk. I am going to go get more water, then I'll bring it back."

"Captain, we need to go together."

"No. We still don't know what we don't know. Susan and I may have gotten lucky. It's best that one of us take the chance in case he doesn't make it."

Susan said, "Let me go with you."

"No," Lee said. "Stay here. If something happens to me, they'll need your guidance."

"I don't like this," Juan said.

"Me either. But I'm doing it anyway."

"But your leg-"

"My leg is fine. Never better."

# REVELATION

Juan didn't move. Nate nodded. She held her Rosary beads and put her hand on Lee's shoulder. "Be safe."

The snow fell, collecting on the rocks, outlining the puddles and streams.

A flash of lightning lit up the snow, followed by a crack of thunder. Lee stuck his head out of the cave entrance and watched the rolling clouds. The wind above the canyon walls pushed the storm.

Was the creature up there, waiting for him?

He didn't know. But he felt like an athlete. Just two minutes ago he was close to death.

He held his breath. He checked his emergency pack to make sure it was still secure. He grasped the empty water bottle in his hand. He stepped out of the cave and ran like a deer.

# CHAPTER 40

Lee knew he was unprotected. If he only reached the fountain. He longed to be under it, to feel its warmth and security. Susan had been right this whole time. Why did he doubt?

At the top of the slope, he searched for any sign of the creature. He didn't want to see it. It was so evil, so hideous. Nothing he had ever seen in his life, not the burns of victims, not the pain of loss, nothing matched the evil in that beast. It oozed hatred. It intended the destruction of the earth.

Thunder rumbled above the canyon walls.

The dark clouds covered everything in their shadows. Snow dropped like a curtain. Except for the burning trees that cast their orange glow, the night would have covered the canyon.

Tahoe barked. It was loud, unsuspecting.

Lee stopped and shuddered. Was it a warning? Dogs had a keen sense of smell. There was already soot and sulfur in the air. How could the dog tell if the smell was from the dragon's last appearance, or if it warned of a new one? Did he know the difference?

Lee jumped down the slope, splashing through the running water.

# REVELATION

The air was cooling again. His wet clothes chafed his skin.

The snow fell thick upon the rocks and boulders.

He had to move. In a few steps, he was back to the fountain. The water warmed his arms. He welcomed it.

He heard a noise. Was that a breaking branch? He expected the dragon's attack.

But the dragon was not there.

Juan, Nate, Susan, and Tahoe remained quiet, hidden in the cave. All he heard was the trickling water and the burning wood and the soft landing snow.

"Okay," he said. The water poured from its 't' crack in the rock. He opened the cap from his water bottle and held it up to the fountain, filling his plastic container. The water was clear and pure. No minerals floated in it. After he filled the bottle, he put on its cap.

The earth shook, and Lee's feet slipped on the wet rock. A deep growl came from behind him. The sulfur smell hit his nostrils. Definitely new. His heart raced.

The dragon was on the slope, between him and his friends, staring at him. Though its yellow eyes squinted, they glowed with hatred. Its lips grinned, showing saber teeth. Then the dragon moved its head toward the cave.

Tahoe barked. Susan screamed. Nate said, "What do we do?"

"I don't know!" Juan said.

The dragon pointed its snout at the cave and squinted its eyes. Giant teeth showed underneath its scaly lips. Fire sputtered from its nostrils. It flexed its bat-like wings, and its snake-like tail whipped against the canyon walls behind it. Rocks fell at the impact of the tail, and the canyon shook.

The dragon laughed. By God the dragon laughed, Lee thought. It knew it had them trapped.

Susan screamed amid Tahoe's barking.

"Get the hell away from us," Juan shouted. The sound of a gunshot came from the cave. A flare shot out of the cave and hit the dragon between the eyes. Lee recognized it came from one of Juan's flare guns. It burned upon the dragon's snout. A red light hissed as red and orange smoke rose in the falling snow.

The dragon laughed again. It said to Lee, keeping its eyes from him like they stared into the sun, "You will watch your friends perish."

Lee didn't know what to do. His chest heaved as he leaned against the stone and held his hands pressed against the rock canyon walls. The warm water fell upon his head. He squeezed the water bottle in his hand.

The dragon pointed its snout. It squinted its eyes as they focused inside the cave.

Susan screamed.

Tahoe barked.

Juan and Nate yelled.

They're done for, Lee thought.

The dragon's tail whipped around and slashed the rock canyon wall like a knife cutting through clay. Rocks and boulders crashed to the canyon floor and rolled down the slope past Lee's feet, splashing through the water as they found their new resting place on the canyon floor.

The dragon lifted its head. Its neck curved upward like a cobra about to strike. It placed its front claws in an attacking stance.

## REVELATION

Lee knew he had to do something. But what? His heart raced as the panicked sounds from his friends echoed in the canyon.

The dragon sucked in the air. The orange fire in its belly glowed through its red scales.

His friends would be burned to a crisp without the protection of the water.

Lee squeezed the water bottle.

Water!

He stepped out from underneath the gushing fountain and he lifted his arm. He threw the bottle at the dragon. It spun through the air and flew toward the dragon's red scales.

The dragon filled its lungs. There was a moment of silence.

As it lowered its head, the water bottle exploded upon the dragon's side, on its shoulder above its left wing.

The dragon raised its head and let loose fire into the rocks. It screamed with pain as the water sizzled a hole in the creature's scaly armor. The dragon's fire turned the canyon wall into magma where it hit, and the magma fell to the canyon floor. The sound of the creature's roar vibrated between the walls. The soundwaves knocked Lee back into the rocks, where the fountain poured upon him.

The dragon's fire stopped.

The creature brought its head down and examined its new wound. Fire spewed from its injury. The scales had dissolved, showing a glowing muscular membrane that bled a bright yellow.

The dragon glared at Lee, this time not being bothered by the invisible light coming from the water. Its retinas sizzled, but its eyes had filled with hate, and the dragon ignored the pain.

As his friends cried in the cave, the dragon took two giant steps toward Lee.

It stepped on the slope and went close to the water, limping from its injury. Its tail crashed into the opposite canyon wall. Rocks fell and crunched on the canyon floor. Soot and sulfur filled the air.

"Now I know. The plan was you all along!" the creature said. Its tone was that of an enraged lunatic, hellbent on his destruction. Its breath hit Lee like rotting flesh.

Lee remained under the water. The dragon's eyes sizzled more as it glared at Lee.

Another sound entered the canyon. It was the sound of jets, followed by that of a helicopter. The sounds echoed through the canyon walls.

Nellis!

The dragon raised its long neck and head. Then it brought its head back down, its squinting eyes glowing hot white at Lee instead of yellow.

"More will die because of you," it said.

Lee knew he was right. How can I warn them, he thought.

Flames sputtered from between the creature's teeth as it spoke. Its breath stank like the inside of a sewer.

Lee covered his mouth.

The dragon lifted its head. Its leathery wings raised. Lightning streaked across the storm clouds. With a mighty flap, they thrust the creature into the clouds. Its tail whipped in the air. And it was gone.

# REVELATION

Lee sank under the fountain. The warm water splattered on his head.

*We've got to do something. But what?*

# CHAPTER 41

The fighter jets flew above Ice Box Canyon. The roar of their engines bounced between the cliff walls like the inside of a drum.

Lee stood up, soaking wet but warm under the running fountain.

Tahoe barked in the level above. Juan, Susan, and Nate argued about what they should do next.

Lee gathered himself and sprinted across the rocks, splashing water as he ran.

A rocket crashed somewhere in the dark clouds. Another jet flew past.

Lee ran up the slope. His feet slipped on the snow, but his legs felt strong.

There was a loud explosion. The creature screamed inside the storm.

Lee stepped along the slope and dove into the darkness of the cave.

Juan and Susan knelt, while Nate held his arm around Tahoe and gripped the dog's leash. Nate's blood-soaked blanket was shoved against the wall. Nate said, "We thought we were all dead. What happened?"

Lee said, "I thought so, too. He was going to breathe fire on you, but I filled a water bottle with the fountain, and I threw it at him."

Susan's eyes widened. "It hurt him?"

"Yeah. Got him on the shoulder. I saw it explode and dissolve some of his scales."

Juan leaned forward. "Does it bleed?"

Lee pressed his lips together.

"Does it?" Juan asked again.

"No," Lee said. "I didn't see blood. I saw…" he felt foolish for saying it, "I saw something else, like fire. His muscles glowed or something."

"He's a demon," She said. "That's got to be it."

Another jet flew past, and a missile exploded. All four of them flinched, ducking their heads.

"We've gotta get out of here," Juan said. "We're sitting ducks."

"No," Susan said. "We're safer by that water."

"You saw what just about happened to us," Juan said.

Nate kept silent, his eyes wide with his arm around Tahoe. Tahoe was nervous, his eyes watching the entrance to the cave.

"Juan could be right," Lee said. "With the creature distracted, we should make our escape."

"You can't outrun a demon," Susan said. The cross on her Rosary beads tapped her wrist as she moved her excited hands.

"That thing can get hurt," Juan said. "Nellis should come. I say we wait for the Air Force to shoot the dragon out of the sky and let's get the hell out of here."

"It won't work," Susan said.

"Cap'n, we don't have much time. And I know of no monster that'll defeat today's Air Force fighter jets."

"I agree."

Susan slammed her hand on the rocks. "You men don't get it, do you? This isn't flesh and blood we're dealing with."

Lee put his hand up. "Look, you've been right so far. But we do have to get out of here. We're trapped in here."

The creature roared, and three jets rocketed above them, drowning out Lee's voice. He shouted again. "We're trapped if we stay here. Let them do their job. Let's get out of here."

Nate nodded. He gripped Tahoe's leash and crouched, then crawled to the entrance.

"We need to stay," Susan said.

"Susan, if ever we had a chance, now is the time." Lee put his hand on the cave ceiling. He heard an explosion in the distance. "The fight is moving away from here. We have to go."

Juan crouched close to Lee. "I'm right behind you, Captain."

"Let's get to the fountain. Have your bottles ready." Lee stepped out into the canyon. A jet flew past, and he heard guns and flames. "Hurry!" His foot splashed in the pool, then he sprinted down the steps. He heard the footsteps of the others behind him. He got to the water. Juan had stuck his last water bottle under the fountain, and Nate did the same with his. Tahoe drank the water that spilled onto the rock. Susan stood behind Nate, holding her Rosary.

He nodded at Susan. It was the right move for her to come.

When they had filled their four remaining bottles, Lee, Juan, and Nate put theirs into their packs. Susan slid hers into her large coat pocket. She watched the skies, not believing they were safe.

"Let's go," Lee said. Another jet flew overhead in the dark clouds. Lightning flashed, and a crack of thunder echoed. They went to the helicopter ruins. Somewhere in the smoldering machinery were the pilots who had come to help. Two lives were lost. If they hadn't come, they'd still be alive. But Susan guessed right when she called in the missing persons.

Tahoe's owners, car thieves or not, didn't deserve to be killed by this dragon. Maybe they could have been reformed. *Maybe we should all be reformed when this is said and done.*

Maybe redeemed was the better word, Lee thought.

They stepped around the boulder and came to a ledge, the spot where they had to help each other up. They were not a team then. They were becoming one now.

A missile fell from above and hit the southern cliff. An explosion of rocks and debris and dust exploded from the rock wall. The concussion from the explosion knocked Lee back. He put his hands on his ear. Susan and Nate were on the ground next to him. Juan was behind him. Lee's ears rang from the impact. Rocks fell and thudded on the canyon floor. The wall was caving in.

"Get up. Run!" Lee climbed to his feet. He grabbed Susan's arm and lifted her.

The walls crumbled like a steep avalanche. Dust fell on them. Another jet flew overhead, and a stream of fire shot perpendicular across the sky. There was another explosion.

"To the cave!" Lee shouted. Then he stopped and turned around. The southern canyon wall collapsed onto the trail. Dust and debris rumbled onto the canyon floor, leaving a tall mound of boulders, rocks, rubble, and dust. The dust swirled through the air, becoming mud and sticking to the wet rocks and the snow.

Lee fell backward.

Another jet flew past, its rocket sounds whizzing in the clouds above. When the rumbles ended, the crumbled cliff wall covered the trail, leaving an avalanche of rocks that dammed the base of Ice Box Canyon and rose halfway up the southern cliff wall.

"We're blocked!"

Lee climbed back to his feet. The dragon screamed above him as the battle waged. He then heard another sound.

Juan stopped. "Captain!"

Lee stopped as well. It was the rotor of a helicopter.

"We have aerial support!"

Lee watched the clouds.

The helicopter sound grew closer.

Another jet echoed past.

An explosion rocked the mountainside.

"Nate, Susan. Wait!" Juan shouted.

Lee waited. They might get rescued after all.

A black machine fell out of the dark clouds as if it was thrown from right to left. It burned and flames surrounded the dark metal. It was the helicopter, a military one, their rescue. Its blades swung perpendicular to the wall and stopped as it hit the rocks. A burning person fell from the helicopter before it exploded into the cliff wall. The flames lit the canyon in a dancing orange glow.

# REVELATION

"Duck!" Lee shouted. Lee ducked behind a boulder as the helicopter hit the cliff wall, exploding into shrapnel. Light and heat hit the canyon.

He waited for shrapnel. Burning pieces rained upon them, hitting rocks and boulders.

After a few seconds, Lee checked himself. He had no injuries. He stood up.

Juan and Susan were on the ground.

Nate rolled on his side as Tahoe tugged on his leash to get to safety. No one was hit by shrapnel.

The ringing was still in Lee's ears.

Another explosion rocked the mountain.

The dragon roared.

"Get up!" Lee shouted.

They got to their feet and raced past the demolished rescue chopper. The white snow fell upon them.

"To the cave!"

Lee splashed in the slush and streams. Nate and Tahoe ran up the slope and ducked left into the cave.

Juan jumped in next.

Susan fell on the slope.

Lee grabbed her upper arm and pulled. She held onto her Rosary as he tugged her up the slope. The ringing in his ears stopped, and he heard the rockets fly past the canyon.

Lee pushed Susan into the cave, then dived in himself. His head hit the blanket they had left behind.

Juan and Nate pressed back against the far wall.

Susan held her Rosary.

Tahoe barked and panted, his eyes wild. Nate held his leash.

A loud explosion rocked a nearby mountainside. Dust and ash drifted over the snow-covered canyon floor.

"We're trapped," Juan shouted.

"I know!" Lee pushed everyone to the back of the cave. Tahoe panted, his tongue sticking out and dripping with saliva.

"What do we do?"

"I'm thinking!" Lee watched outside. Jets and explosions echoed. Rocks and debris fell over the cave entrance. The water fountain still gushed.

"How's everybody's water?" Lee said.

"I don't have any left," Juan said.

"I've got one," Nate said.

Susan tapped her coat. "Here."

Lee bit his lip. If we could get more water, Lee thought.

The dragon's tail hung from the rim. The dragon perched on the top of the southern cliff wall.

Two jets flew past, their engines roaring and their guns ablaze.

The dragon breathed its fire. One of the fighter jets exploded in the clouds. The dragon's wings spread. Lightning streaked through the storm. Thunder rocked the canyon. A barrage of missiles hit the dragon. A jet flew past.

*The last jet?*

The missiles exploded in a barrage of heat and fire and flames. Rocks fell into the canyon, collapsing upon the fountain in the level below. The smoke from the explosion wafted into the canyon. There was still the stench of soot and sulfur.

Then the jet engine disappeared into the distance.

# REVELATION

And the noise returned to that of falling snow, trickling water, and burning debris.

They waited.

"Captain?" Juan said.

"Shhh." Lee held up his hand.

Tahoe's panting echoed in the cave.

"Do you hear anything?"

"Shhh, I said!"

Nate put his hand on Tahoe's mouth, trying to muzzle him. "Quiet, boy."

The snow fell upon the canyon. There was no more sound of the fountain water gushing from the opposite cliff.

But there was no dragon, either.

"Did we get him?"

"I'm waiting. Last sound I heard was one of ours." Lee stuck his head out of the cave.

Juan leaned to the cave entrance. "We got him."

Susan remained quiet, holding her Rosary. She leaned forward.

From inside the cave, Lee stuck his head out and watched the skies.

The clouds rolled past. The snow fell.

The water trickled.

The wood burned.

All was quiet.

.

# CHAPTER 42

The smoke filled the air. The rocks had fallen and landed in their new place, but the scent of jet fuel and missile smoke covered the canyon.

There were no more explosions.

"Captain, we got him." Juan stepped hard to exit the cave, but Lee put his strong arm up against Juan's chest.

"Hold it."

Juan stopped.

Tahoe barked.

"Keep that dog quiet."

Nate lowered his eyes, and then he put his arms around Tahoe.

Susan held her Rosary. She was praying.

Across the canyon, near the opposite cliff, a pile of red and white boulders covered up the fountain. The water was buried. So was their protection. Lee hoped that the dragon was vaporized.

Lee said, "Let me go first." He held Juan back, then he stepped outside. The snow fell on him, and the smell of fuel became strong. A mist of smoke floated on the air like the angel of death in The Ten Commandments. A rumble of thunder rolled above. The falling snow landed upon his hair and his clothes. "Susan, your fountain. It's buried."

"What?"

Lee motioned for them to come out, but he held his finger to his lips reminding them to stay quiet.

Juan was the first outside. He stood tall.

Tahoe barked as Nate brought the Australian Shepherd out, leading him by his leash.

Susan ran past Lee, splashing in the pool and slipping down the slope. "No!" she said. She ran to the rocks that buried the fountain, and lifted a rock and threw it down the trail toward the smoking remains of the rescue helicopter. She picked up another and threw it again, working hard to uncover the water.

"Cap'n, we need to check on the other chopper," Juan said.

Lee nodded. The smoldering craft was fifty yards beyond the remains of the rescue helicopter. Smoke rolled out of its ashes. Flames jumped several feet above the wreckage.

Juan adjusted his rescue pack. "Think anybody survived?"

"We need to find out." Lee turned around. "Nate, are you up for checking out that chopper with Juan?"

Nate stood on the upper slope, holding the dog by its leash. "What do you want me to do with him?"

"Susan, would you take the dog?"

Susan picked up rocks and threw them.

She'll never uncover it, Lee thought. He looked at the base of the pile, and he saw no water leak through. Snow began to cover the pile.

"Susan?"

"We need to uncover this. He's not gone."

Juan shook his head. He whispered, "I know she's been right about a lot, but come on. Nothing could withstand all that firepower."

"She's not coming," Lee said, shaking his head. "Nate, you might as well stay here and hold that dog. Juan, let's go."

Nate saluted, holding Tahoe's leash.

Lee and Juan walked to the second wreckage. Smoke burned Lee's eyes. But there was no sulfur or soot, and he felt relieved.

Before they saw the helicopter, the remains of the avalanche stood before them. A tall pile of rocks and boulders leaned against the southern cliffs. It covered the base of Ice Box Canyon.

"Geez, Cap'n. Have you ever seen anything like that?"

"It's blocking our way out."

"Can we climb it?"

"We'll have to."

They approached the helicopter. Flames spread around the crash area.

It was military, designed to rescue foot soldiers in combat.

The charred remains of a soldier lay on the ground, the body a smoldering corpse, the helmet and gear melted from the intense heat.

Lee's legs weakened. He put his hand on a nearby boulder and caught his breath.

"Son of a…" Juan said. "That monster. I'm so glad he's dead."

Lee's lungs stung. Smoke was all around him. Flames emitted from the burning fuel. Nothing else moved. "You see anyone?"

"No."

"We need to get back."

# REVELATION

"Shouldn't they come down here?" Juan said, referring to Nate, Susan, and Tahoe.

"We need to drag Susan away from that pile. Then we can go."

"Captain, it's dead. We saw those missiles blow it up. You saw it, didn't you?"

"I did."

"Then let's go with it and get the hell out of here."

Lee pointed up the canyon. "She won't come."

Juan scratched his head. "I just want to get out of here."

Lee nodded. "I know. Me too. But remember: four in, four out."

"I'll get her," Juan said. He motioned up the canyon.

"No. I'll go. She'll listen to me." Lee took two steps. "Take a look at the wreckage. Let me know if you see anything we'll have to report when we get back to the truck."

Juan nodded, and Lee left him.

Lee walked past the rescue helicopter wreckage and over the wet rocks to the pile of rubble.

Susan was sweating while Nate and Tahoe stood by.

A chill entered the air as the cold weather turned worse.

Susan threw rocks.

Nate was talking with her, holding Tahoe's leash.

As the sleet fell upon her, she bent down and picked up a large rock with both hands and heaved it several feet down the cliff wall until it rested near a burning bush.

Lee joined them and said, "It's time to go. There's an avalanche down the canyon. We'll have to climb it. We need to get out of this canyon. Better start now before the snow gets too thick."

"We won't make it. We have to get the water back," Susan said.

Nate raised his eyebrows. He shrugged his shoulders.

Lee put his hand on the back of his neck. Why is nothing ever easy, he thought. "No need. That thing is dead."

"I don't think so." She hurled another rock, which splashed as it rolled on the ground. "If we don't find it, we won't make it out of here."

"Susan-"

"I've been right so far, haven't I?"

Lee lowered his head. If he was going to control this situation, he had to find another way. "Okay. What do you suppose we do?"

Nate's eyes widened, surprised at Lee's new tactic.

"You could help me." She rolled a heavy oblong piece off the mound, which splashed and almost hit Lee's foot.

"There's too many rocks. We could be out here all night?"

"We could die up here, too." She grabbed another rock. The snow fell heavier now. She tossed the rock where it crashed into a boulder and rolled. "Help me."

Nate held the dog. Tahoe sat down. The dog didn't act nervous. He had warned them of danger before, but now he seemed calm.

Juan hiked up the trail, in their direction. While he was still thirty yards away, they heard a jet engine in the distance. The dark clouds screened their view. "They're coming back!"

# REVELATION

Tahoe stood up and barked. Lee's hairs stiffened on his arms. *A warning?*

Tahoe tried to run. Nate tugged on the leash.

"Back in the cave!" Lee said.

Nate didn't hesitate. He tugged Tahoe's leash. The dog sprinted past Nate, pulling him up the slope.

Susan dropped the rock she held and said, "I agree."

She ran toward the slope. She slipped on the wet rock; her hands fell onto the snow-covered ground. She regained her footing and hurried up the slope.

The jet noise grew louder.

Nate stopped Tahoe at the top of the slope. "Captain?" Nate said.

"Go!" Lee pointed, running and slipping up the slope.

Nate made it to the cave entrance. He let go of Tahoe's leash and the dog ran inside, while he waited outside to help. Susan reached Nate and turned around.

Juan stood by the burning helicopter, watching for the noise. "He's coming from the east."

Lee reached the top of the slope and stopped. "Juan, get up here!"

Juan opened his rescue pack and pulled out his flare gun. He lifted the gun, pointed at the clouds, and fired. "Maybe he'll send help!"

The jet engine sound became unbearable.

The bright flare shot up into the falling snow and the storm, leaving a red glow in the clouds.

"He'll see where we are now!"

The clouds opened up. A fighter jet engine spun in circles like a Chinese star, its wing missing, but its engine roaring. The cockpit had been destroyed in orange and red flames. The multi-million dollar piece of equipment hurled at them like a fast-pitch baseball.

Lee's eyes widened.

Juan was in its path.

"Take cover!"

Lee pushed Susan and Nate into the cave.

The jet hit the ground and exploded. Fire and fuel and vapors rocked the canyon. The earth rumbled. The noise echoed in the cave. Lee covered Susan's and Nate's heads as shrapnel hit the cave entrance and ricocheted off of it. They trembled from the explosion and the impact.

Tahoe yelped at the rear of the cave.

Rocks fell from the roof and hit Lee in the kidney. Dust and dirt fell on his back and head.

The noise died down. Several seconds went by, and all they heard was a rumble from fire and a clap of occasional thunder.

Lee said, "You two okay?"

"Yeah," Nate said.

Susan nodded. "I'm okay."

"Juan?" *Where was Juan?*

Lee got on all fours.

Juan wasn't in the cave.

Lee scrambled to the cave entrance. Metal and fire and smoke covered the snow. Heat spread through the air. The fighter jet wreckage had hit the lower level. A fire burned near the pile that covered the fountain.

REVELATION

Juan had been standing down there.

Lee left the cave. The smoke and the heat burned his lungs and skin. "Juan!"

Nate climbed out of the cave and put his hands over his eyes. The heat hit him, too. "Captain? Where is he?"

Lee didn't hear him. He yelled again. "Juan!"

The canyon looked like a war zone.

Fire and burning fuel crackled over the running water.

Machine parts blazed and glowed with orange flames.

Snow fell in thick flurries and melted when it reached the smoldering wreckage. Distant thunder rumbled.

Lee yelled again, longer and deeper.

"Juaaaannnn!"

There was no answer.

# CHAPTER 43

The smoke seeped into the air like a low-hanging smog. The fire's heat burned Lee's skin and dried his clothes. Lee covered his mouth. He observed the destruction all around him.

The back of Ice Box Canyon was now a war zone. Fuel and flames and jet machine parts spread all over, melting the falling snow. Water trickled through, under, and in-between the flames. Burning fuel drifted with the water, carrying bright orange and yellow flames as it poured over the rocks and through the cracks.

"Juan!" Lee yelled, his voice drowned out by the burning trees and the crackling fire. "Juan!" His voice cracked as the hope in him faded.

Nate said, "Any sign?"

Lee scanned the area again, hoping there would be some movement, some chance. He imagined Juan's emergency pack at a spot on the lower level, near the place Juan fired the flare gun. But the flames rose, covering the area with smoke. He wanted to hope, to say he was there, but he could not. "It's too dangerous out here," Lee said. "Get back inside."

"Cap'n, you should come in, too."

# REVELATION

Lee's neck veins bulged. "Did you not hear what I said? Get inside!"

Nate stepped backward, then crawled inside the cave.

Susan peeked her head out, her brow deep with worry. She searched the scene with her eyes and lowered them. Then she retreated into the cave.

Lee stumbled to his left.

The flames were everywhere, permeating the canyon with their flickering orange glow.

The machine parts were black, silhouetting the ground and the rocks amidst the flame-burning water.

Juan did not appear. Lee hoped that maybe, just maybe, Juan was still in the area he had last seen him, down the slope several yards away.

And Lee could not get there.

He imagined Juan, somewhere in the flames, still alive. What if he was hurt? What if there was a chance to pull him out. What if Lee didn't get to him to save him? What more could Lee do?

Lee took a step on the slope. His rescue pack shifted with his weight.

There was a fire at the base of the slope. It burned black the pieces of wreckage.

The flames were hot. He couldn't go that way. At the rock pile, shrapnel covered the rubble. There was no way to get to the fountain. They had been cut off.

His gut was wrenched. Despair welled up within him.

Nate's head peeked out of the canyon. "Sir, can we help?"

"Get the hell inside!" Lee yelled.

Nate was shocked at the response. He jerked his head.

"Get in!"

Nate's head retreated into the protection of the cave.

Lee backed up, and his shoulders hit the wall. The disaster scene outside was too much. The lives lost. The hopelessness at losing his own man.

The despair was filling.

His abdomen tightened.

The dragon was still alive and winning.

He tried to hold back the tears. He put his head to the rock. He lifted his fist and pounded the rock, hurting his hand, but he didn't care. There was a large crack in the wall, large enough he could bury his face in it. He put both hands on the wall and lowered his head between the cracks. The heat penetrated his wet clothes and his skin grew hot.

He wanted to shout at God. If he was there, then why did he let this happen?

He pounded the wall with his palm. Then the tears flowed, and he bent down and wept.

# CHAPTER 44

The explosion of a fuel container at the far wall brought Lee back to the present. He did not flinch. He wiped his eyes. The orange glow illuminated the canyon. The flames sent sparks that went up and were caught by the swirling clouds.

The rubble still covered the fountain. There was no sign of Juan, or anyone living. But there was the cave. Nate, Susan, and, yes, Tahoe were all in the cave. The cave entrance was dark.

Lee stood. His pack jiggled behind him.

His clothes had dried somewhat from the heat. They had a musty odor to them that he smelled despite the smoke.

The clouds pushed past the canyon rims. The image of the flipping jet aircraft stuck in his mind. Only the dragon could have done that. It was still alive.

He did not run. He leaned his back to the wall, keeping his body against it as he slid toward the cave. He expected the dragon to attack at any moment. He waited. The fires burned. The smoke spread and the snow fell. He slipped inside the cave.

Susan and Nate sat along the far wall. Nate was holding Tahoe's leash. The dog was still nervous, weary from a hard day. His eyes were wide open.

Lee didn't say anything at first. He observed them. Susan was holding her Rosary, but she wasn't praying. Her eyes were red, and her cheeks reflected orange light from the tear streaks. Nate's eyes were also red, his face stressed. He was trying to stay calm and in control, like Lee.

"I'm sorry," Lee said.

"Juan?" Nate asked. He looked like a worried family visitor at the emergency room.

Lee bit his lip, then shook his head, affirming the bad news. He could not bring himself to say it.

Nate rubbed his sleeve over his eyes as he held back a tear.

Susan just sat, her back against the wet cave wall, her hands holding her beads.

"Look, I've been wrong," Lee said. "There are some things I don't understand. But that doesn't mean we can't believe them."

Susan feinted a smile under her teary cheeks.

"I want to get us out of here alive, but we're going to need help."

Susan and Nate nodded. Tahoe pawed the ground.

Amidst the orange flickers outside the cave, a slow sinister laughter echoed.

Lee's heart sank.

It was the dragon.

And there they were, trapped like mice in a cat's playpen.

The dragon's voice rumbled.

Lee covered his ears.

"Your allegiance is misguided," the dragon said. "Your hope is in vain. I know the Almighty favors you, but he will not defend you. Your mortal weapons are powerless against me. Your holy objects did not save your friend. Join me, or you will suffer. Remain fools, and I will destroy your city. Remain fools, and I will ruin your families. Then I will return, and tear your limbs piece by piece, devouring them in my eternal fire. I will send your souls to judgment. I will relish your screams. Worship me, and I can give you power. Worship me, and I will make you kings. Choose not, and you will die. I decide who lives. I am Fury. I am the Dragon. I am the Revelation. I am now the god of this earth!"

The voice stopped. There was heavy breathing and a gurgling as air passed down the dragon's flaming neck into its lungs.

"Choose," Fury said. "Choose whom you will serve."

Then the breathing was gone.

Lee's heart beat hard.

Nate pressed against the wall.

Tahoe growled, ready to snap.

Susan held the Rosary to her chest.

Lee remained still. He pressed his lips together.

"What does he mean?" Nate said. "Susan, do you know?"

Susan shook her head. "I don't."

Tahoe growled. The dog backed into the rear of the small cave, his ears pinned back, his teeth showing. Nate held his leash. He was afraid to touch him and hold him steady.

Lee leaned his head back against the cold cave wall. His skull ached.

"Cap'n?" Nate said.

"I'm sorry," Susan said. "I did this."

"No, you didn't," Lee said.

"I called you here. I coaxed you into coming."

"You didn't know. You couldn't."

The three sat, silent. Tahoe licked his lips, nervous by the danger outside.

Lee had to choose what he would do. The dragon's power was alluring, enticing. The dragon planned to rule. He tempted Lee to walk outside, acknowledge the dragon's power, and yield.

"What do we do?" Nate said.

Lee lifted his head, clasping his cold open hands into fists. "First, Susan is going to teach us how to pray. Then, let's go get this son of a bitch!"

# CHAPTER 45

Fury raged.

He gave the three a choice. Worship him, or watch their families burn in his eternal fire.

He had waited on the mountains, expecting them to climb from the cave, beg his mercy, and grovel. He would let them live for a time, but only long enough to suit his purposes.

They chose not to worship him. Instead, they remained in the cave. A blue holy light shone from the cave, blinding him. It covered the orange flames and the burning wreckage. The three of them united in prayer and the light from the woman's holy item spread across the mountainside.

He dug his claws into the rocks, leaving giant trenches. He spread his wings, and lightning flashed across the sky. Thunder rumbled.

But the light from their prayer rose, extending to the heavens. Michael and his angels would be sure to come, launching an all-out attack.

He waited, readying his tail and his fire and his claws and his teeth.

But no attack came. There was only the light.

His scales sizzled.

He roared, and his roar rumbled across the mountain. He would make good on his threat.

He flapped his wings, and in an instant, he was off. Fury flew hidden in the clouds. He spread his great wings, and they soared through the turbulent air.

Thunder boomed as lightning flashed around him.

His red scales burned with fire. His long tail whipped through the air.

The mountains retreated behind him. The sun disappeared behind the mountains, casting great shadows that covered the eastern valley. There, he saw the city, its lights peppering the valley.

The lights adorned large, man-made buildings. They shone from the fronts of their wheeled carriages. They hung along the paved roads. They flashed from their airborne machines. They stood out like stars and galaxies within a shadow of black.

He knew now man's weapons were no match for him. The angels were still superior.

He was superior.

His strength increased.

As he flew, the hidden shadows underneath him bowed at his power. His allegiance was to the Prince, for he was greater. They had rebelled together. They would do so again.

The souls underneath him were gray, indifferent. Some were red and black, others blue, which angered him. But the blue souls were few. The rest would have to make their choice.

# REVELATION

As he soared above the city, he now knew why he had been freed. The Almighty respected the free will of his creatures. If they chose the Almighty as their God, he helped them.

If not, he respected their decision, leaving them to handle the consequences.

It was no different than the angels. When they rebelled, the Almighty did not invite them back. But Michael and his angels had thrown them from Heaven, scattering them upon the earth, or locking them up within it. The fallen had raged at the consequence.

As Fury circled above the city, the storm clouds flashed with lightning. The lightning spread like spider webs across the horizon.

He swung his massive head and dove toward the lights of a high tower. The sign on the building glowed with the words "Abo Hotel and Casino". Flashing kangaroos and koala bears and boomerangs adorned the structure, while palm trees decorated the clear fountains and pools outside, but Fury cared not for these things.

He watched the souls. Inside, there were some blue souls, but their aura was not bright enough to threaten him. None carried the same Holy objects as Susan and Juan had in the canyon.

Many of the souls were gray.

But there was one in the building he wanted.

He saw the man amidst the rest. He was dealing cards, aiding others with gambling. The man's soul was beyond black. It was beyond red. It was the color of the Prince.

Yes, this would be his priest.

# CHAPTER 46

Lee kept one eye open while Susan prayed the Our Father and Hail Marys. Nate had both eyes shut, his hands clasped on his and Susan's hands. Tahoe raised his eyebrows at Lee. Lee blushed when he was caught, but he kept his eye open. While Susan prayed he organized his thoughts.

A flame sputtered out of the wreckage and flew upward into the black clouds. The wind whipped down from the canyon and pushed a spark into the cave, which burned out upon landing on the wall. The heat from the wreckage was keeping them warm, for now.

In a few hours, however, they'd freeze from the cold winter wind.

"Lee," Susan said. "What are you thinking?"

"Huh?"

Susan was no longer praying. "Are you okay?"

"Yeah. Sorry."

"You look like your mind's running."

"It is."

"What now?" Nate said.

Lee nodded. "Remember your training. What do we know?"

"That thing is terrifying. That's what I know."

"Let's keep our heads."

"He's a demon," Susan said.

"I believe you," Lee said.

"What does that mean?" Nate said.

"He's a fallen angel," Susan said.

"Susan, nobody brought a bible. Please. Explain."

Susan nodded. "He rebelled against God. He sided with Lucifer, the angel of light. In their pride, they rejected God. Scripture says that Michael and his angels warred against the dragon, and they threw the dragon, and two-thirds of the angels, down to earth."

Nate shuddered. "Is that thing Lucifer?"

"It didn't call itself that," Lee said.

"It said its name was Fury," Susan said.

"Shocking."

"Maybe Fury's just another nickname?" Nate said.

Susan said, "I don't think it's Lucifer. It's one of the other angels. One of the higher ups. It may have taken a dragon form, like his master."

"But he said he's a god."

"Many demons pretend to be god," Susan said. "Ancient cultures were full of them."

"Okay," Lee said. "So we have some wannabe Babylonian god hanging out at Red Rock. We know his name. We know his intentions. We know the water from the fountain hurt him before it was buried. We also know he's blinded by the water."

"We know something else," Susan said.

"That he's going to destroy the city, our families, and eat us limb from limb?" Nate said. He shook against the wall, his worried face reappearing.

"Get a grip," Lee said.

"But-"

"Get a grip!" Lee turned his eyes to Susan. "What else?"

"He said the Almighty favors us."

"He did say that."

"But he said he won't defend us," Nate said.

"That's not true," Susan said. "Demons lie all the time."

"But what about Juan?" Nate said.

Tahoe circled and licked his lips.

"Focus on what we have," Lee said.

"What about our families in Vegas?"

A shudder of fear went through Lee's body. He did fear for Joan and Jenn. He wanted to protect them from ever seeing something so horrible, so hideous, so full of hate. The sight of the dragon would scar a man's memory, requiring years of help. What would his therapy bills cost if he made it out of Ice Box Canyon alive?

Lee said. "That's why we do what we do, to protect the ones we love."

Nate nodded.

Lee said. "We need to come up with an idea. Action is better than fear."

No one spoke for several moments. They heard the trickling water and the crackling fire and Tahoe's panting.

Nate gripped onto Tahoe's leash.

# REVELATION

The dog raised his ears. The dancing flames reflected in the dog's brown eyes.

Lee put his hands on his rescue pack. "Maybe there's something in here we can use."

"No," Susan said.

Lee lifted his eyes, raising his eyebrows. "You have an idea?"

"We need to uncover the fountain."

Nate put his hand on Tahoe's back and held the dog close. "What about the flames?"

"We can try," Susan said. She scooted to the cave entrance.

The flames lit the darkness, their light bouncing around the fighter jet scraps scattered across the canyon rocks.

"Look. The water and snow keep falling. The fire is dimming."

The bright orange light in the canyon had cooled to a dark burgundy. The sparks reflected off the snow and the trickling water. Was the dragon still there? He hadn't heard him in several minutes. But Susan was right. He knew the water could harm the dragon. Right now, it seemed the only weapon available.

"Alright," Lee said. "Let's do it, on one condition."

"What's that," Susan said.

"You keep good hold of those beads, and keep praying."

# CHAPTER 47

Fury ducked his head and flew toward the building. He spread his wings and opened his claws for landing. Hidden in the clouds, he hovered above the hotel. Then, he let gravity take hold and he fell, his claws crushing the roof. His weight shook the building, but it did not fall.

His tail swung in the air like a long coiled snake. He flexed his neck and spread his wings wide.

Lightning flashed across the valley in purple streaks. Thunder rumbled between the mountains.

He opened his mouth. The city lights reflected off his teeth and saliva on his long serpentine tongue.

A woman screamed.

The iron-supported roof broke under Fury's claws and the weight of his body. The sound of metal bending screeched like fingernails on a chalkboard.

Another woman screamed, and another. Car tires skid on black roadways as metal crashed upon metal. Drivers honked their horns as more people pointed, screamed, and ran.

# REVELATION

As the fear spread, many souls turned from gray to black. Their faithlessness now exposed, they would be helpless against him.

Fury opened his mouth. His eyes glowed red. As the people ran, he sucked in air, filling his lungs.

There was a second where all that sounded was the screaming, the screeching, the crashing, and the honking.

Then Fury released his torrent of fire, drowning out all the other sounds. His fire burned the cars on the road, the palm trees, the pavement, the other buildings. He incinerated many people. Others burned before they fell.

Upon their demise, the blue souls stood, wondering. Many blue streaks of light shot down through the clouds landing on the surface. The angels grabbed them, taking them up to their rest.

The black souls remained and stood in shock, wondering what happened. Then the shadows came. Thousands of them. The panicked screams of black souls filled Fury's ears, and he wanted more.

His tail whipped the building. It sliced through its side.

Shouts came from inside the building. Hundreds of souls ran outside, trying to avoid the fire and the clouds of smoke and the falling debris.

Sirens filled the air, growing closer. Then there were gunshots: first one, then many. Gray and blue souls ran through the crowd of fleeing people, yelling orders, aiding the injured, and firing their weapons at Fury.

Fury's scales burned a fiery red. He streamed fire in all directions, watching the souls, the angels, and the shadows.

The building creaked, and it broke under his weight. He flexed his wings with a mighty flap, and the wind from his wings blew the fire over the people, carpeting them with a half-mile of destruction and ruin.

The sounds of panic delighted and enraged him. He wanted more, though it could never fulfill him. He laughed, his voice carrying across the stormy valley.

The dark clouds swirled overhead, ominous and threatening.

He flexed his wings. Lightning formed in the clouds, and it streaked to all the corners of the horizon.

He sucked in more air, then spewed his flames in all directions. The flames spread, burning buildings and cars and freeways and people. A circular mile caught fire. People ran, but none escaped.

Sirens and gunshots and screams and fire filled the night. The bright orange of his eternal flames replaced the alluring glow of electric lights. The dark clouds reflected the bright flames, casting orange silhouettes across the valley.

Fury heard the now-familiar thumping of another flying machine.

It came from the north.

There was the rat-tat-tat of heavy guns.

The bullets and the tracers ricocheted off his red scales. He turned his head and launched his flames. The machine exploded in flight, and fell upon several parked cars, the souls landing on the ground in flames.

Fury had made his power known. In three minutes, hundreds of souls had learned their judgment. The Count increased. Terror filled the night.

# REVELATION

But there was one still in the building, his soul like the Prince.

Fury expected his priest at any moment. With him, Fury would rule. With him, Fury would conquer. With him, Fury would become their god.

.

# CHAPTER 48

Lee pulled up his red rescue pack as he leaned against the cave wall. There were black marks where fire singed the waterproof material. "How many water bottles do we have?"

Nate pulled out his plastic bottle and held it up. "Just this."

"I have mine," Susan said, patting her coat.

"That makes three, then." It wasn't much..

"I wish I came more prepared," Susan said.

"Don't I know it," Lee said. He shifted his weight. "The fire is dying down. Follow me." He exited the small cave. He thought his joints would be sore from crouching so long, but there was no stiffness in his knees or back. He felt he could run a marathon.

But he inhaled smoke from the jet. He coughed as the smoke stung his lungs.

Susan coughed also, as she exited after Lee. She recovered and studied the wreckage and the flames and the smoke. "Oh, Juan." She made a sign of the cross.

After Susan, Nate exited the cave. He tugged the leash pulling Tahoe outside.

Nate coughed and bent over. Tahoe pawed at the ground.

Lee said, "You going to be okay, kid?"

Nate, still hunched over, put his hand up. After a few seconds, he nodded. "Yes sir."

Susan said, "They'll never find him, will they."

Lee's eyes watered from the smoke, but he kept them open to study the wreckage. The night had closed overhead. The flames lit the sleet-covered canyon walls, their light bounced between them and cast shadows.

Lee reached into his rescue pack and pulled out a flashlight. He turned it on.

His heart ached for Juan. His friend was in the explosion.

But he had to take control.

"They will," Lee said. "And I'm going to make sure he's remembered."

Lee's flashlight beam hit the ground. Huge piles of black metal shrapnel, charred rocks, and smoldering ashes covered the canyon, mixed in with snow and water. He waved his flashlight, directing his beam left, then right. "There's just so much."

Nate said, "No one could have survived this."

Susan shook as the cold winter wind whipped down upon them. Nate stood tall. Tahoe waited, his paws in the snow, his eyes fixed on Lee, wanting to know Lee's next command.

"We need to get going," Susan said. "No telling when it'll be back."

Nate said, "Can we get around the wreckage?"

Lee shined his flashlight to the opposite canyon wall. Smoke drifted in the air, dulling the reflection of metal scraps and shrapnel. It was hard to see through the dark, misty haze of smoke and falling sleet. Red embers glowed on snow and wet rock and scrap metal. "This looks like a room in the house of Hell," Lee said.

The ground was black, staining the rocks. They'd have to go down the slope.

A piece of the fighter jet wing rested on the slope as red embers charred black splotches in the metal. It would have to be moved. But beyond it, if they stayed close to the rock cliff wall, they could maneuver down the slope to the lower level.

"Cap?" Nate said. "There's so much heat. Can we make it there?"

Lee stepped forward. His shoe touched an ember, and smoke arose from the sole of his foot. Lee swore, then he kicked his shoe against the rock several times, but the ember stuck. He scraped the ember on the wet rock, and it stuck to the stone, leaving a small black hole in his shoe.

"We have to get that water," Susan said. "It's the only thing that will protect us."

Lee said, "She's right. We're not going to make it out without protection." He studied the red embers through the smoke. A scrap of the wing blocked their path, and there was no way around it. He bent down to lift it, but the skin on his hand retreated from the heat emanating from the metal.

Nate said, "Captain, use this." He stretched both arms holding an elongated stone. It was heavy, but Lee could use it to move the scrap without the heat.

"Good thinking, kid." Lee reached past Susan and took the rock.

Tahoe whined again, the dog's eyes searching the sky.

"He sees something," Susan said.

# REVELATION

Lee didn't wait. He took his rock and shoved the scrap out of the way.

Red embers burned under the metal, revealing melted rock and steam.

Lee lifted the scrap and shoved it. The scrap clanged and rolled down a small incline, then hit a rock and made a clunking sound that echoed between the Ice Box Canyon walls.

The three of them ducked at the loud noise. "Did the dragon hear that?" Susan asked.

"I hope not," Lee said.

Tahoe scanned the skies, his tongue hanging out and dripping with saliva.

"Let's go." Lee moved forward, carrying the flat stone and watching the embers. He didn't want another hole in his boot. He stayed on his toes planting his feet where there was space, leaping where needed, and pointing the path to Susan and Nate. Tahoe also seemed to get the picture, and he was able to move his feet between the embers and not get burned.

After several careful steps, they rounded the wreckage and found the pile of rubble that buried the fountain. There was some burning debris where several large stones had fallen, but Lee determined that they'd move with some muscle. "Nate, come help me here." He braced his feet and swung the flat stone at the burning debris, knocking it off the rubble. Then he set it down and lifted a fifty-pound stone. He twisted and tossed the heavy rock. It crashed and rolled until it came to a stop.

Nate helped, picking up stones. Susan stood in front of the rubble for a few moments, then threw both hands at it, digging out small stones and dirt.

Lee and Nate threw more rocks. One was so heavy that the two had to move it together, using another longer oblong rock as leverage to get unstuck. It rolled past their feet and found the trail, knocking into other rocks and crushing them until it thudded down a small incline and crashed into the canyon wall opposite them.

"This place won't ever be the same," Nate said.

"None of us will." Lee answered. He picked up one more boulder. There was cool moisture on his fingertips. "We're there."

"Water?" Susan asked.

"Yeah." He pulled the rock, which was heavy. He lifted one end and, putting his weight into it, he shoved the rock. "Look out!" The rock fell and crashed down below. Water rolled down the remaining pile and onto the stone at their feet.

"Quick, get some!" Susan said. She bent down and filled up her water bottle.

Nate did as well, and Tahoe leaned forward to lap the water from the ground.

"Fill your bottles," Lee said.

They placed their three remaining open bottles in the flowing water.

Lee took a drink. As the cold water went down his throat, a strange sensation came over him. He had a vision of Las Vegas, of Las Vegas Boulevard, of fire and teeth and sirens and flames. People ran and pointed, screaming and crying. The dragon's large claws clutched the lighted stone roof of a hotel. Flashing kangaroos, koala bears, and boomerangs flickered and went dark.

The dragon's tail whipped out, then down. It rushed the side of the hotel, leaving a long burning vertical crack as broken glass shattered and shocked people fell from their rooms to the pavement.

The vision took him back to the dragon's eyes. Those eyes, burning yellow with growing hatred and power, noticed him. They flashed. The beast lifted its head and wings in one fluid motion. The dark clouds lit up with blue lightning streaks, and hundreds of purple bolts streaked across the valley sky in the dark swirling clouds, then bolts of lightning shot down from the clouds and struck the city in a torrent of electric currents.

A large explosion brought Lee back to his present state. Sparks and light spread like white veins along the canyon walls, up and down the crevices, lighting the area like fluorescent lights. Lee heard Nate yell, "Cap'n!" just as Susan screamed and Tahoe leaped onto the leftover pile of rubble.

Lee fell backward. Hundreds of blue and purple lightning streaked across the ground, reaching for him and his small team. His back against the rubble, water trickling down his backside and soaking his pants, he had no way to escape.

Susan's scream was loud in his ears.

Tahoe yelped.

The lightning rushed at them and then it stopped, unable to penetrate an invisible barrier that formed a semi-circle around their feet. They moved backward as the purple lightning shocked the ground around them.

Then the lightning disappeared. Orange darkness returned to the canyon, but the bright light blinded Lee as the streaks left their impressions on his retina.

"I can't see!" Nate yelled.

"Me either," said Susan.

It was so bright, but Lee blinked, believing the impressions would wear off. "Give it a moment," he said. Lee opened his eyes, and multiple flames and embers leaped and floated into the air, despite the cold rain and sleet. It seemed some of the rocks were on fire. How is that possible, he thought.

"Tahoe!" Nate said. Nate was righting himself after falling back against the rubble. Tahoe's leash had escaped Nate's grasp, and the dog was working his way through the fire, and up the slope. "Get back here!"

"Hold on," Lee said. "Don't chase."

"What happened?"

Susan sat up and reached over to Lee. "You okay? You spaced out there for a moment."

Lee nodded. After taking that drink, he had his vision. The dragon. The people. The destruction. The lightning. "He's destroying our city," Lee said.

"The dragon?"

"Yes. I saw him. This lightning. He did it. I saw him."

Susan drank some of the water.

Nate lifted his bottle and took a drink. He lowered it and wiped his lips with his wet coat sleeve.

Susan closed her eyes. Was she having a vision of her own? After a few moments, she opened her eyes, and bit her lip.

"You see anything?" Lee said.

"No," Susan said.

"Nate?"

"Uh-uh," he said, shaking his head. "But the water's good."

Tahoe reached the top of the slope and hid in the cave.

Nate didn't pay him any mind. "What next?"

Lee remembered the avalanche down the trail. The giant pile of rock leaned against the southern cliff wall of Ice Box Canyon. To get out, they'd have to climb the build-up that rested against the north wall. But If Lee climbed the highest point, he might see what was happening in the valley.

Lee said to Susan. "Tell me something. This thing talked to us. Can we talk back?"

"Yes," Susan said. "But, why?"

"Does prayer travel? I mean, when you're saying those words, God hears them, right?"

"Yes."

"And Mary. She hears them, right?"

"I believe so."

"But she's not God."

"No, but she hears."

"So, can other spirits hear us?"

"Yes. That's the Communion of Saints. You can ask a saint to pray for us, because he sees the face of God."

Lee nodded. "Okay."

"What are you going to do?"

Lee held up his bottle of water. "You still have those prayer beads?"

She reached into her pocket and pulled them out. They were wet from her cold damp pocket, and the crucifix shined in the firelight that floated around them. "Here."

"Hold onto them. We need to climb that avalanche. Then, Susan, pray as you make your way down the canyon. Nate, get that dog and go with her. I may have an idea."

"What's that?" Susan asked.
"I'm not sure, but I hope it works."

# CHAPTER 49

The explosions erupted around the city. The fire reached the heights of several stories as the entire valley caught fire from the lightning strikes.

Fury's claws crushed the iron beams inside the burning hotel. The hotel lost power.

Smoke billowed from the cracks and broken windows. Palm trees disintegrated by fire. Cars exploded as the heat scorched their gas tanks. Glass covered the asphalt and concrete.

Many people had lost their lives in the chaos. Others, too paralyzed by fear to do anything, froze in place until the chaos overtook them, whether by fire or smoke or falling debris.

Fury waited, sensing the souls. His target had moved from his position.

Then he saw him - the man with the black and red soul. He had escaped the fire, aided by several shadows who understood his worth. The man covered his mouth as the smoke flew past him. He made his way through the flames. His eyes were wide, his hair a mess. His clothes were those of a card dealer.

His name tag remained on his shirt: "Joe Belcher".

Joe paused amidst the chaos. He spun around.

Fury locked eyes with him.

While other souls fainted at the sight of Fury, Joe did not. He stood, knowing.

"I have waited for you," Fury said. "Your spirit has strength. With me, you can achieve power beyond your imagination. You can gain the strength of Assyria, and of Egypt, and of Babylon."

Joe kept his head up, but he went to his knees. A burning palm tree collapsed behind him, but Joe neither moved nor flinched. He stared into the dragon's eyes.

Fury's yellow pupils darkened. "Will you bow to me?"

Joe nodded, then he lowered his head and his torso, prostrating himself to the pavement.

Fury grinned. "Will you worship me?"

Joe nodded, then spoke. "I will, my lord."

Fury's lips grinned, exposing his sharp teeth. Flames sputtered from his mouth. He licked his tongue around his lips.

"Will you let me inside you?"

Joe raised his head, then lifted his body. He said, "Yes."

Fury raised his head and roared. His voice traveled across the valley. His wings spread, and a flurry of purple lightning spread across the clouds.

Then an explosion rocked the hotel building. Fire and smoke engulfed Fury. Another explosion, and another, and another. Their soundwaves spread the fire and the smoke across the valley.

The hotel crumpled under his claws, the iron skeleton giving way and collapsing to the ground.

Fury's weight brought the hotel down. As the building collapsed, debris and smoke and fire spread across the

# REVELATION

circumference of the hotel property, damaging nearby hotels and knocking down several buildings.

Fury clawed through the rubble. His man's corpse lay under a concrete slab. The man's red and black soul stood above the slab, shocked and bewildered.

Then the shadows came. Millions of them. They rushed him with their black pitchforks and swords. They grabbed the soul, and they tore at him. They ripped him into several pieces, but that didn't stop his screaming. He disappeared into the darkness among the flames, and then he was gone.

Fury spewed out fire from his mouth. His anger shot out in all directions. The fighter jets had attacked him as he was about to take possession of his priest and begin his rule.

But it was not the fighter jets that had stopped him.

It was Lee, Susan, and Nate. Their prayer had stopped him. Their prayer had made it happen.

As Fury stood among the crumbled ruins of the hotel, he launched fire in every direction.

Several swooshing sounds approached, and then the ground around Fury exploded into an inferno.

Fury rose his head from the smoke. His yellow eyes bore down on the fighter jets that whizzed past his head.

The jet guns shot his torso and wings with bullets and tracers, which fell to the ground.

Fury's eyes grew bright, their yellow becoming like the sun. He spread his wings.

The clouds turned a shade of burgundy. Flashes of purple erupted like a strobe light, gaining speed in their flashing.

Millions of purple bolts of lightning exploded from the clouds. They shot through the sky, hitting each jet. Many more charges left the swirling clouds and struck the ground.

In one instant, every fighter jet exploded, and they fell like fireballs out of the sky, landing in neighborhoods and parks throughout the metro area. Purple bolts crashed through the atmosphere, zig-zagging through the air and hitting trees, powerlines, cars, and homes. Flames scattered across the valley. Sparks rose through the sky, while smoke lifted and spread under the ceiling of the swirling clouds. Snow and sleet fell upon the city, but it evaporated upon contact with the heat of the city's flames.

Fury brought his wings down.

The people had no more weapons against him.

His eyes returned to their normal state. He opened his mouth, and he breathed a stream of his eternal fire at the four corners of the city.

The city burned. No one could deny the power of his might.

Still, Fury raged under the storm at the power of prayer.

# CHAPTER 50

At the fountain, Lee took several more swallows of the pouring water. It was warm and smooth as it went down his throat. He had no more visions, but his body seemed immune to the heat from the smoldering flames that burned the wreckage all around him.

When he finished drinking, he said, "There's an avalanche around the bend of the canyon. It caved in when a rocket hit it. Juan and I saw it. I need to get up there."

Lightning streaked across the swirling clouds, leaving hazy violet and blue zig-zagging streaks. They illuminated the canyon in purple and bluish hues, revealing shadows between the cracks and boulders. Trees and bushes burned with yellow flames, while hot embers floated upward and caught the wind, defying the cold mist that fell from the winter weather.

Another *crack!* echoed between the canyons.

Lee ducked.

Susan put her hands over her ears, while Nate flinched.

Tahoe had already hid in the cave.

"We need to find some cover," Nate said. "This doesn't look good."

"What about leaving?" Susan said.

"There's no cover down the trail," Nate said.

Lee knew this was all crazy. His heart hurt for Juan. But the vision of the beast destroying Las Vegas scared him all the more. What about Joan, or Jenn? What kind of danger were they in? We're they still alive? If the four of them ran out of the canyon, they might get to the city in time to catch the last few homes destroyed. And then what? Throw a water bottle at the creature? Lee held the bottle of fountain water in his hands. "I have a plan."

"From our training?" Nate said.

"There's no online training for this!" Lee shouted over the thunder.

Nate didn't laugh.

Susan clasped the Rosary beads with both hands and brought them up to her heart.

Lee pointed toward the cave. "Go up and get that dog. I want you three to hike out of here."

"But, Cap-"

"That's an order."

Nate stood for a second, then turned and went after Tahoe. Susan shivered as the cold fell upon her face and coat. She said, "You're going to need prayer."

"I'll need a lot more than that," Lee said.

"God will be with you."

Lee pointed at the storm clouds. "I don't need God up there. I need him here - with me - right now."

Susan touched his heart with the Rosary hand. "You have to let him in, first."

# REVELATION

Nate brought Tahoe out of the cave on his leash, and together they navigated the slope and the wreckage and the hot embers. Tahoe was nervous, but he trotted through the wreckage and the flames, like he knew he would leave the chaos behind.

Nate and Tahoe caught up with Lee and Susan, and the four of them worked their way through the smoldering wreckage.

Purple streaks colored the clouds overhead, and though one or two made a large thunderclap, many were silent; threatening, but always there.

"There's the first chopper that went down," Lee said. "We have to get around that. We're going to go slow." Lee said.

"Hail Mary, full of grace, the Lord is with you…" Susan said.

"Come on." Lee stepped forward, away from the rubble and the water. Strange charred streaks covered the stones where the lightning had reached for them. They left odd markings, like hieroglyphics from an ancient language.

Lee wandered at the streaks on a large rock, then he stepped on it, pressing his boot against the imprint.

They had distanced themselves from the fountain. If the dragon returned, there'd be no way to get to it before it cut them off.

He put his wet hand on the last bottle of water in his pack, just to know that it was there. He imagined many possibilities, but there were too many variables.

Susan placed her foot on the path past the rubble and on top of the lightning-struck rock.

Nate's shoulders relaxed. He and Tahoe moved forward.

They wound around the stones and the embers. Small pieces of rock glowed near the path. "Cap'n, is that rock melted?" Nate said.

"Wouldn't surprise me," Lee said. "Don't touch it. Keep that dog away, too."

Tahoe avoided the molten rock, following the dark shadows on the ground that Lee hoped turned into a path.

Lee passed the rocks and the wreckage. Water trickled downhill all around them. The darkness covered the terrain except for the flashes of lightning and the embers and flames. He put his hand on the stone wall to his left, and a strange sensation came over him. This was the ledge where the boulder had fallen from the sky and crushed Nate.

Nate was moving behind Susan. He guided Tahoe on the leash.

How in the world is he not dead, Lee thought. The kid should be gone, yet a miracle healed him, and there he was, standing tall and strong. Lee blinked several times. He didn't want the others to see a tear in his eyes. He looked up. *God, I need you here.*

They made their way slowly. Tahoe whined and jerked on his leash, pulling Nate off balance.

Lee's shoulders tensed. "Keep control of that dog."

Nate said, "I'm trying."

Lee glared. He almost issued a rebuke, but Susan stopped him.

They moved through steam and smoke. They placed their feet carefully around scrap and puddles of burning trees.

Lee pointed over the second helicopter wreckage to the avalanche where it peaked against the southern cliff. "There it is."

# REVELATION

Nate said, "That?"

"Yes." Lee searched for the best way up.

"It's too wet. You'll fall."

Susan grimaced. "That's not stable."

"Pray it is."

They arrived at the base of the avalanche. Mounds of rock dammed the canyon. The trickles of water filled into pools at the base of the boulders.

"Why?" Susan held her Rosary in her tight fist, her knuckles cold and white as the cross dangled in the air below her clenched fingers.

"It makes no sense, Captain." Nate said. "Let's just get out of this canyon."

A bolt of lightning streaked across the sky. Tahoe bolted and caught Nate off guard. He stumbled and almost fell into a pool of red embers, but he gathered the leash in his hands and controlled the dog.

Lee shouted over the rumble. "I know it's nuts. But this is what I have to do. We need to know what's happening."

Nate pressed his lips together. Susan nodded, understanding.

"You three wait," Lee said. He pointed to the height of the avalanche. "I'm going to go up there and see what I can. I'll let you know if there's a path over a low point of this avalanche."

"You'll be exposed," Nate said.

"We have to take that chance," Lee said. "Listen. If I say go, you three get over these rocks and run to the Skeeter. Get Susan to the emergency room right away to have her checked out. You should do the same."

"Yes, Sir."

"If I say, 'Run to the cave' and I point that way, you three book it back. You understand?"

Nate and Susan nodded.

"Good. I don't want you both stuck on rock unable to go one way or the other. Wait here. Watch for my direction."

Tahoe sniffed the ground and then raised his head.

"It'll be alright," Lee said.

Lee went to the avalanche. There were mounds of large boulders piled on each other. He found one he thought he could climb. He gripped the boulder's cold wet edges with his frozen hands. The stone stung as his fingers dug into its crevices. His boots slipped as he tried to gain traction. Where he got a hold, he pulled himself up. While his skin stung, he felt surprisingly good. His muscles were strong, stronger than when he woke up this morning.

He lifted his body up the boulder. He grabbed cracks with his hands and stepped on small indents and ledges with his boots. His knees burned with the strain, but like he was in high school again, exercising and testing his muscles. "It's not so hard," Lee said. He reached a high ledge, his chest rising and falling from the effort.

Susan, Nate, and Tahoe waited at the base. They covered their eyes from the falling sleet and snow.

"Dang, Cap'n," Nate said. "That's impressive."

Susan clasped the Rosary to her chin with both hands and closed her eyes.

From the ledge, Lee shouted. "Susan?"

Susan opened her eyes.

"Thanks."

## REVELATION

Susan nodded. She trusted her faith. The trust wasn't in him, however. She hoped in the God above the clouds.

He envied her.

He climbed over fallen rock and boulders. There was no order to the chaos. He made his way step by step, searching with his hands for jagged edges or clefts to grab on to. After several minutes, he reached a point where his height seemed extraordinary, halfway up the avalanche. He paused to gather his position.

To the east, the canyon opened up. The desert was dark, and the small mountains between Red Rock and Las Vegas silhouetted the horizon. Beyond them, an orange glow emanated into the night sky. The glow flickered across the dark clouds.

Lee's heart sank. This was not the glow of billions of fluorescent bulbs illuminating large hotels. It was the glow of fire, and it spread from north to south across the entire valley.

Las Vegas was burning!

Purple lightning bolts flashed above the valley. It did not let up. They began in one spot in the storm clouds, and they streaked across the valley, from Lake Mead, to Pahrump, to California, and above his head. Over and over again the lightning streaked. Loud *Cracks!* rumbled and echoed in the Ice Box Canyon walls.

And yet each bolt originated above one central point. Over and over again they spread from that one spot.

"He's there," Lee said. "The dragon is right there."

Lee held his water bottle in his hand. He felt the texture of the plastic, and shook it, listening to the sound of the water inside the bottle. "Okay. Here goes."

He filled his lungs, then yelled, "Hey Fury. Get your little lizard ass over here. You think you're so tough? I've got something for you. If you have any guts at all, come get me!"

Lee's chest heaved.

He flexed the muscles in his arms and legs. A twinge of apprehension ran through his veins. *Did I really just challenge a dragon?*

The fire's orange glow rose into the clouds.

The lightning bolts, which flashed above the central point in the distance, continued their barrage.

They streaked across the sky, leaving their purple residues in the swirling black clouds.

Then the lightning stopped. There was only the fire, and smoke.

And an eerie silence.

# CHAPTER 51

The silence penetrated the canyon. In the distance, the dark clouds swirled. Snow fell on Lee again, but he paid no attention. Why did the lightning stop? He waited. A cool breeze hit him in the face. A drop of water ran into his eye, and he blinked and wiped his face down with his damp arm.

Then a chill hit him, only it wasn't a physical chill. It was inside him like a cold had gone right through him.

The dragon was coming!

Susan, Nate, and Tahoe stood at the base of the avalanche awaiting Lee's instruction.

In the distance, their cars were still in the parking lot, two small dots in a sea of shadows, illuminated by a city on fire beyond the hills. They would never get to the cars in time. "Nate. Susan. Get to the cave!"

"Captain…"

"Now!" Lee swore, pointing to the rear of Ice Box Canyon.

Susan didn't move. "What's going on?"

"He's coming."

"How do you know?"

"I feel him!"

Nate grabbed Susan's arm while holding onto Tahoe with the other. They ran through the burning wreckage toward slope and the cave.

A rush of wind hit Lee before he climbed down. The clouds swirled above the ridge of the canyon wall. A flash of purple lightning streaked across the sky, illuminating the entire canyon.

"Hurry!"

It was too late.

A voice above the rim echoed. "What mortal fool dares challenge the god of the valley?"

Lee shuddered and slipped. He dropped his body onto the stone, keeping from sliding and falling forty feet to the canyon floor.

When the Nate, Susan, and Tahoe neared the slope, Tahoe jerked on the leash, pulling Nate. Nate lost his grasp of the leash, and Tahoe sprinted away from them, back down the canyon toward the avalanche, dodging boulders and burning trees and splashing through water. He reached the avalanche and jumped onto boulders, finding a makeshift path over the avalanche's low point to exit the canyon.

"Forget him!" Nate shouted. He pulled Susan the other way. Susan's water bottle fell from her coat and rolled into a ditch. They leaped over embers up the canyon toward the protection of the fountain and the cave.

Lee trembled. He had to get off the avalanche.

The voice seemed to be everywhere, and it was more powerful than before. Lee took his hand and found notches in the boulders to drop down. He worked to climb down the levels without falling and breaking his neck.

"Is the fool the one whose soul is gray, who has not accepted God, who is doomed to judgment in Hell upon his death?"

Hell? Lee thought. The word frightened him.

Before today, Hell wasn't real. He didn't like to think about it.

His lucky pen was gone, the one he tossed several hours earlier. He's right. I have been a fool, Lee thought. He clasped the water bottle in his hand, the only substance that had saved him today. While the water had helped, Lee knew there was more. His eyes lifted to the clouds, but his mind went beyond them. Somewhere up there was the source of his help. Somewhere up there was a God.

He stepped again, and his feet slipped. He dropped but clung to a boulder with his fingers. His weight shifted, and he was on the side of the boulder, his feet swung in the damp night air. The embers and rocks were thirty feet below him.

"Hang on!" he said. He swung his free hand to grab a notch in the rock, but his fingertips slipped and gravity took hold. He fell through the air to the rocky floor below.

He landed with a thud, and instant pain shot through his leg into his hip. He yelled. I broke something, he thought. Miraculously, the pain went away. He climbed to his feet, curious how nothing was broken.

The dragon's head peered over the edge of the canyon rim, its yellow eyes lighting the floor. A giant red claw reached over the edge and penetrated the cliff wall, slicing through the rock like a knife through butter.

The creature's neck glowed a hot red, releasing sparks and embers through the dark scales.

The other claw reached over the edge, and the neck arched downward. Soon, its large body slithered over the edge, its leathery wings outstretched. He had grown to the size of a large mansion.

The yellow eyes made Lee freeze. Flames leaped from the dragon's mouth as its gums receded, revealing sharp razor teeth.

Lee reached for his bottle of water. It was all he had.

The dragon climbed down the cliff wall above the avalanche like a cocky predator who had trapped its prey.

"What the hell are you?" Lee shouted. Purple lightning flashed in the sky, and a bolt hit the canyon floor thirty feet from where he stood. He flinched, stepping backward, but stayed upright.

"I am the new beginning," the dragon said. "I am also your end."

"The beginning of what?"

"Of power."

He held the water bottle behind his back, hoping that Mary was real, and had something to do with it. Mary, the mother of God? Lee squeezed the water bottle and the plastic crinkled in his grip.

"You are mortal," the dragon said. "Come with me, and I will make you immortal."

Lee felt a hole in his chest, a pull. The dragon was hideous and had immense power. Something inside him thought of his career, a fire captain on the Las Vegas outpost. He had struggled with his choices, and though he had done alright, he had never given his wife and daughter all he had hoped. It frustrated him.

## REVELATION

Was that why he argued with Jenn this morning? *Was all that just this morning?*

And Joan deserved so much more than a fireman's salary. She had married him and stayed supportive while he changed careers, taking a pay cut, and slowly moving up the ladder. She was always so positive, so wise. Why had he never been able to be more?

There was a twinge of agreement in Lee's mind. The dragon was unlike anything he had ever seen, and something about him was enticing. Was it asking him to join him? Imagine the power? Imagine the-

"You are wise to consider my offer," the dragon said.

Lee grimaced and remembered the water, and he remembered Mary. He had a strange awareness of his heart, a darkness. He couldn't explain it, but as he heard the dragon's offer, he felt a black, empty feeling deep in his chest.

The dragon moved closer, its yellow eyes alluring Lee with the power in its eyes, the fiery glow of the eternal heat seeping through its membranes and its shield-like scales. The beast's neck glowed with fire waiting to escape through its mouth and fangs. "Join me, mortal. Join me, and you will be a king." The dragon stepped forward one more time, grinning like a salesman who had delivered a perfect pitch.

Lee's emptiness grew. He clenched the bottle, and an image of Susan's Rosary entered his mind. The Rosary beads were gentle, but they glowed. He closed his eyes and held onto that image. Somehow, the darkness in his chest lessened.

The earth shuddered as the dragon took a forceful step forward. Lee stepped back and opened his eyes.

The dragon's eyes glowed hot. Its lips trembled. Its eyebrows narrowed in anger. "Don't be a fool," he said. "Your soul has no place here. I control your soul. I create kings. I send people to judgment!"

The dragon's force and heat burned Lee's skin. But he remembered the Rosary. In his mind, the more he remembered the beads and the crucifix, the more they seemed to glow, and the more the darkness lessened.

He felt hope.

If he had any divine help, it was somewhere above the clouds. He said, "Mary, I need your Son's help. Please pray for me."

The dragon leaned forward. "What did you say?" Its breath stank.

Lee ignored the dragon.

He gripped the bottle, crinkling the plastic.

His eyes remained focused above the beast. "Mary, please pray for me. What can I do?"

The dragon reared his head back and extended its wings. "Mortal, bow down and worship me!"

Lee felt his heart grow, like a radiant light had replaced the dark void and filled his chest with something powerful. The black, empty feeling in his chest retreated, then it disappeared.

He was connected to a power beyond his comprehension, but it was a power that had with it peace, hope, and love. This power fell upon him and inside him. Lee knew then that God was real, and that God was wanting to offer his love, if he asked him.

Lee gripped the water bottle in his hand, crinkling the plastic.

Fury's large eyes squinted. His red scaly face gave the hint of concern amidst his great arrogance. Lee noticed the dragon looked not at him, but at his hand. He did not like the contents of the bottle.

Lee took a step forward and raised the bottle.

The dragon stepped back and then laughed. "You amuse me, mortal."

Lee took another step forward, the water in his hand. "You don't like this, do you?"

The dragon's head flinched. "You are doomed. I could make you like a god, but you choose weakness over strength."

Lee moved forward again. The snow fell in sheets, but it evaporated as it fell on the dragon, leaving steam in the air that stank of sulfur. His clothes, already heavy, clung to his wet skin. But Lee took three steps forward, and the dragon's heat warmed his face.

The dragon snapped and roared. The echo of the roar rumbled between the canyon walls, and stones fell around him. Lightning flashed above them; the thunder echoed. The dragon took a step back, its eyes no longer showing arrogance, but focused on the water held inside the plastic bottle in Lee's hand.

"What happens if you swallow this?" Lee asked. "Would it make you sick?"

The dragon backed against the cliff. Its left arm swung up and dug into rocks, a move to climb up the wall. "I will incinerate you," the dragon said.

"So why don't you?"

The dragon pulled himself up, clinging to the wall like a giant lizard climbing up a tree. It glared at top of the canyon, back near the cave, and then it smiled.

Lee followed the dragon's glance.

The cave!

Fury's eyes glowed bright yellow. "You will watch your friends die, first!" The dragon laughed a slow, dark guttural laugh, then clamored along the wall with strong purposeful steps, its tail and wings scraping along the rocks, toward Nate and Susan.

Holding the bottle, Lee sprinted through the burning wreckage toward the cave.

# CHAPTER 52

Lee raced through the scattered flames and shrapnel, his eyes watching as the dragon slithered atop the canyon rim, climbing sideways as each large claw pierced the rock like ice picks in a glacier. Lee ran, leaping over the smoldering embers, the rocks, and the metal scraps. Snowflakes hit his eyes, but he kept watch as the dragon glowed between its scales and gained ground on his friends.

The dragon went vertical, its large tail leaving a gash in the rock wall as it swung. It moved up, higher to the top of the canyon, and then it went over the edge, a yellowish glow remained as it reflected off the mist and the clouds.

Lee's foot hit something sharp, and he flew face-first into molten rock. He put his hands in front to brace his fall, and as he fell, he knew it was his end. Fire and burned skin awaited him.

He landed hard. There was immediate pain. His face, arms, chest, and hips burned. His clothes caught fire. He yelled, but his will said not to give up. He somehow held onto his water bottle, clung it tight to his chest, and rolled off the embers. His wet clothes caught fire and went out. Lee rolled onto the wet dirt trail and rocked back and forth as a man possessed. He had to put the fire out.

He imagined the burned skin falling from his body. But something strange happened.

He felt no pain.

His training told him third-degree burns destroyed nerve endings, but this wasn't it. He stopped. His skin was there, and he still held the bottle of water.

He touched his face.

Nothing. There were no cuts or bumps or scratches, just his stubble from his five-o'clock shadow.

He sat up. His clothes had holes where they had burned, but he was intact. "What the hell?"

The glow where the dragon had disappeared was now gone. The dark clouds swirled overhead. He stood on his feet. He was at the wreckage where the first chopper had gone down. Ahead was the plane wreckage where Juan had died. The rubble that covered the fountain was thirty yards ahead on his right.

Above that was the slope that led to the cave. He did not see Nate or Susan. He did not hear Tahoe.

*Has the dragon already struck?* He didn't think so. He had to get up there to warn them to stay in the cave.

He gripped his water as he ran. Holding it gave him some hope. There was more water pouring from the fountain, but he didn't know how he could collect it in time.

He jumped over a large metal scrap. The slope was close. "Nate, get in the cave!" he yelled.

There was no response.

REVELATION

He ran past the burning jet remains. He tried not to think of Juan.

"Captain!"

It was Nate. Thank God! "Get in the Cave!"

Nate's shadow emerged at the top of the slope. "You're alive!"

"Get in the cave. He's coming!"

"Where?"

A glow appeared above the canyon rim. It grew brighter.

Before Lee could shout, a bright light blinded him, and fire and flames spewed on top of Nate.

Nate's shadow moved, but Lee fell, unable to watch. He heard the rush of fire as it flew through the air and covered the canyon where Nate had stood. Then, the flames were gone, and the canyon returned to cold damp darkness.

Nate was gone. Was he incinerated? Lee's heart sank.

Where was Susan?

He gathered himself and he sprinted past the remaining wreckage. He jumped the burning embers until he reached the slope. He leaped up the slope with ease like he was eighteen. Was it the adrenaline? How did he move so effortlessly? Nate's last water bottle lay at the top of the slope, melted.

The cave was ten feet to his left. "Nate!"

He rushed to the cave. "Nate!" Lee moved left.

A rush of air came at him, and before he saw inside the cave, a large solid mass crashed onto the stone floor.

Lee fell sideways.

Rock and dirt fell all around him and on top of him. He covered his face.

The shaking stopped. He lifted his head.

A giant boulder blocked the cave entrance.

Lee got to his feet and rushed to the boulder. "Nate. Nate!"

There was a soft sound. He felt around the boulder.

"Captain!" It was Susan.

"Tell me Nate's with you!"

"He is!"

"Is he okay?"

Before she could answer, a second giant rock crashed into the ground next to Lee. The earth rumbled.

He fell and landed on his back. The large rock crunched the ground next to him. He rolled down the slope, his head and elbows and knees hitting and scraping rocks and fire and embers until his momentum stopped. He opened his eyes. He was at the bottom of the slope. At the canyon rim, the yellow glow of the dragon radiated.

Lee reached for his water bottle. It was gone. Where was it? He got to his knees. The bottle of water wasn't near him. "Where'd it go?"

The dragon's head appeared over the rim. Its eyes glowed with hatred behind the pouring snow.

They squinted, studying Lee's position.

The dragon's lips curled. Its teeth showed as it laughed and flames sputtered from its mouth and nostrils.

Lee scrambled to find the water. He must have lost it at the top of the slope. He started to climb the slope, but the dragon went over the edge of the cliff and raced down the rock wall.

Lee stopped and backed up. He was powerless.

# REVELATION

The dragon laughed, its wings spread, its fire in its gut glowing hot with hatred.

Lee stood paralyzed, trying to think.

# CHAPTER 53

The large red dragon made its way down the canyon walls. Lee worked to get an idea. Anything.

Would the dragon pass the cave and his friends inside it? They were trapped. The dragon could move the stone, exposing his friends.

Lee had to help.

His legs were still. Something was happening.

He watched.

The dragon's yellow eyes glared at him, penetrating his soul. He wanted the bottle of water to throw it at the beast, but it was nowhere to be found.

He heard the rush of wind first, then the light grew intense. Lee dodged to his right and rolled as a large stream of fire escaped the dragon's mouth and flew into the north wall. Lee rolled. The fire stopped, but he continued. The wreckage was in his way, and he rolled over embers and melted rock.

The dragon breathed with the intent of fire. The heat from the embers didn't affect him. Why? It had to be the water. It had to be-

Another flame spewed at him. Lee jumped from his low position to his right again and splashed into the water.

# REVELATION

The fire stopped.

He stepped in a small stream.

Lee's soot-covered clothes were wet again.

He lifted his chest..

The pile of rubble! The fountain water was trickling down from its place in the wall.

The dragon stepped down the slope. Fury's eyes squinted. The dragon was fighting pain.

*It has to be the water. It has to be!*

Lee rose to his knees. "Hey. I'm over here. What's the matter, too bright for you!"

The dragon snarled. "The Almighty has favored you, but your sins will send you to judgment."

"So be it."

The dragon closed its eyes. Then, in a fit of rage, the dragon lifted its head and spewed fire straight up into the dark swirling clouds. Purple lightning flashed across the sky, and several bolts shot straight down into the canyon.

Lee kept his ground. The dragon was more terrifying than any beast he had ever imagined, but the fountain stream kept him safe.

Susan was right. This fountain was holy.

The dragon lowered his head. It groaned in several heavy breaths. In a flash, it closed its eyes, flared its nostrils, and launched a rush of fire at Lee. Lee dove into the stream, his back still exposed. The fire flew all around him. He covered his head with his hands. This had to be it, he thought.

There was no heat. He noticed the stench of sulfur.

But there was another smell - roses. *Roses?*

He opened his eyes. Yellow and orange flames covered him, but he was not burning. His clothes, which should have caught fire, did not burn. What was going on?

Then the fire stopped. Lee stayed motionless. The dragon did not move, but its eyes remained closed. Could it see him?

The dragon stood in its place, its ribs expanding and collapsing with large breaths, its wings raised ready to leap. Its tail extended up the slope. But the dragon's eyes were closed.

Lee made no noise. He got to his knees but stayed silent. His hand was in the stream, and the cool water soothed as it went around his fingers. His hand moved and he touched a stone. It was wet, but he grabbed it and lifted it, making no sound.

The dragon waited. He snorted and chuckled.

Its head moved toward the slope.

Lee wasted no time. He took the wet stone and hurled it at the beast. It flew through the air, holy water spinning in the air with each rotation of the stone.

The dragon gasped, its eyes blinded by the rock as it came upon him. The stone hit the dragon in the chest below the neck, and a flash of bright light exploded. One of the dragon's scales disintegrated.

The dragon reared back and screamed in pain. Red fire spewed out of its chest.

Lee looked at his hand, and then at the water. Several more rocks had been soaked in the holy stream, covered by the water. Then it occurred to him - *these wet rocks were weapons!*

Lee reached down and grabbed another rock. He threw it at the dragon. He flung it through the air. It spun droplets as it flew through the falling snow.

# REVELATION

It hit the dragon on its right shoulder. There was a second explosion of light and flame. More screaming, the loudest demonic scream Lee imagined. He picked up another rock.

"I will hunt down your woman and child," the dragon said. "I will eat them slowly and tell them how you cried for your mother while you died a slow death in my stomach."

Lee squeezed the rock. The dragon's words were cruel, but Lee stood strong.

The dragon's eyes searched for Lee, but they did not find him. The water where he stood was blinding the beast.

The dragon reared his head back and sucked in the air. This was it, Lee thought. He waited, and when the dragon lowered its jaw, Lee threw a strike into the dragon's throat.

A huge explosion erupted from the dragon's mouth. Light and fire and flames flew in several directions.

Lee shut his eyes and covered his face with his arms. He fell back against the stones and landed on his rear, splashing in the creek.

The dragon screamed what sounded like a death scream, and in an explosion of light and flames and wings and claws, the dragon disappeared.

Darkness covered the canyon, except for the orange glow reflecting from the embers.

Lee lowered his arm. Where was the dragon? It was not in front of him, and he did not see it fly away or climb out.

A cold rush of air hit him. It rumbled and rushed through the canyon. Lee's insides felt a chill, and he folded his arms across his chest to keep warm. The wind swirled in a vortex. Lee thought he heard screeching, and the wind went up into the clouds like a tornado, and it was gone.

Lee lifted his eyes.

The dragon was gone!

# CHAPTER 54

The snow fell from the clouds. There was a quiet peace. No lightning flashed, though the clouds remained, darkening the canyon except for the molten embers that remained along the canyon floor.

Many plants still burned, though not many of them remained.

There was still a high heat in the canyon. It should have affected him more, but it did not.

The sulfur and the soot hung in the air. Lee thought about those lives lost nearby, of Juan. He thought about the citizens in the valley, and what destruction had happened there. He worried about Joan and Jenn. He had to reach them.

But the dragon was gone. Lee's throw, the spinning rock, was a direct hit. Susan was right. The water was holy.

Lee sprinted over the embers and up the slope. He'd rescue Nate and Susan. Perhaps they'd find Tahoe waiting for them at the Skeeter. Once home, he'd take Joan and Jenn to church. It had been so long. He wouldn't know what to do.

But that didn't matter. He clamored up the wet slope. To his left was the giant boulder, now blocking the entrance to the cave.

"Susan!"

"Captain!" Susan's voice was muffled by the boulder. It left a tiny gap between the boulder and the rock cliff. "In here!"

Lee reached through the darkness with his hands. "Where?"

"Here!"

Lee followed her sound and found the gap, a space he could slide his hand in. He put his hand through it, only his fingers would fit inside.

Susan clasped his fingers. "We're trapped!"

It was good to know they were alive. "How's Nate?"

"Hurt bad. He needs water. The fire got to his legs and he's going back into shock."

"That kid's been through enough already."

"Can you get some water?"

Lee said, "I lost the water bottle. But the fountain is coming out again."

"Get some!"

Lee patted his emergency pack. *Think!*

Tahoe barked, but not from the cave. The bark came from down the canyon, surprising Lee.

Susan said, "Hurry!".

Lee tried to think of a solution..

"And here…" Susan said. "Take this."

Lee went back to the gap. He saw light pale fingers sticking out through the darkness. He touched her fingers and felt the shape of plastic beads. Her Rosary. "These are yours," Lee said.

"Just in case."

"The dragon is gone."

"Please. Take it until you get us out of here."

# REVELATION

Lee grasped the beads and held them. "Okay." He put them in his pocket.

"Hurry!"

Lee turned and ran down the slope, splashing slush as he went. He stumbled and landed at the bottom.

The embers showed the way to the fountain. He cupped his hand, and the water filled it. It wouldn't work. He dropped his hands, and the water splashed at his feet.

"Come on. Think!" he said.

He examined several rocks from the pile, most of them were oval-shaped with small indentations that wouldn't do. He found some that were too flat, limestone flakes that had fallen from the cliffs. Then he found one, about the size of a football, and flat like an oval plate. "Maybe." He dipped it in the water that poured from the fountain. It held some water, but it would spill if he didn't balance it. He tossed the rock.

He then had another idea - his pack. His pack was designed to be water-resistant. Maybe he could open its pockets, fill them up with water, and bring it to the cave entrance. He took off his pack and opened the zippers, took out the first aid kits, and he put the empty pack into the water. The pack filled quickly. He lifted it, and water dripped through the pack. He hoisted it in one hand and he hurried past the embers, up the slope, and to the cave.

"Susan!"

Her fingers stuck through the gap. "Here!"

He got on his knees and stuffed the pack into the hole.

Susan grabbed it and pulled.

The pack became stuck in the hole. The water spilled.

"It's not working," she said.

"Let me try this." Lee brought up the pack as water seeped through the material. "There might be enough here." He twisted the pack into a long bulky cylinder. He gave one end to Susan, who grabbed it. The edges drug over the rocks. He shoved the pack through the gap, and Susan tugged at it from the other side.

"Water's spilling everywhere," Susan said.

"Get it through. I've zipped up the pockets. Maybe there'll be enough in them that you can get it on Nate."

Lee squeezed the pack through the gap.

"It's coming," Susan said. The pack slipped through into the darkness. He waited, hearing the faint sound of zippers opening.

"There's nothing in here."

"Nothing?" Lee leaned closer to the gap.

"They're wet, but they're empty."

"Can you wring out the pack? Maybe some water is still in the material."

"I'll try, but I can't see."

Lee put his hand on his forehead. "Can Nate talk?"

"No," Susan said. "He's not answering me."

He's going into shock, Lee thought. *Quick. What to do?* He stepped back. If only he found a cup. Some sort of...

He leaned into the gap. "I have an idea. Hold on. I'll be right back."

"There's no water coming out. It must have all spilled out."

"Hang on," Lee said. He ran down the slope and went to the embers.

Metal scraps were all around. Many still glowed with embers despite the falling snow. The scraps, though, were man-made. Something among them had to have the shape of a cup. Something small enough to pour water into it and get it through that gap. He lifted his first piece of scrap and dropped it. The metal was still hot.

And then he remembered - Juan. He was under here somewhere. The last thing he wanted to do was pull up a piece of metal and see Juan's lifeless eyes. *Would Juan even be in one piece?* No, Lee thought. *And no telling how many pieces.*

The thought of it made him step back. Was he able to do this?

Nate was in trouble.

Susan was trapped.

He had to get them out. He was not going to move the boulder that blocked the cave. If the water performed another miracle on Nate, at least they could survive until he found the help to get them out.

Lee stepped away from the wreckage. His boot stepped on a burned twig, and Lee got an idea. He found a solid wet branch. He picked the branch up and returned to the wreckage. Using its tip, he turned over a piece of scrap metal. There were small embers under it, having not been doused by the falling mist. Among them were other scraps of small shapes, some flat, all of them black with soot. And hot. He poked at them, and then one caught his eye - a silver piece of metal about the size of a shot glass. He poked at it, and it moved. One end was open, the other solid.

It would do.

He shoved it with his stick, pushing aside embers.

Not wanting to burn his hand, he dropped the branch and took off his coat. His coat reminded him of a wet used car towel.

He held the coat in his hand and bent down. He picked up the metal piece. He examined it once more. "Perfect." He ran around the embers to the pile of rubble. The stream still flowed from the fountain.

Lee put the metal piece in the water. He heard a slight sizzle as the metal cooled. Water poured into it. He lifted the metal, now filled with water, and carried it up the slope to the cave.

"Susan!"

Susan put her fingers in the gap.

As Lee reached the gap, there was a loud *crack!* The canyon flashed in purple as a lightning bolt flew across the sky. A strong wind rushed through the canyon, and a loud screech echoed with the wind.

"He's back!" Susan shouted.

Lee put the coat carrying the water in her hand but steadied her fingers. "Careful. This will fit, but it's filled with water."

She gently put her fingers around the coat and clasped the metal piece.

"Careful with the metal. I tried to cool it in the water."

She pulled the coat and the water inside. "Hide!"

There was a rumble, followed by several large cracks. He wanted to get inside the cave with Nate and Susan, but the boulder blocked him. Was the dragon back? The wind rushed, and the mist hit his chest from the side.

The rumble grew louder. It came from down the canyon.

Cracks and breaking rocks echoed in the canyon. Lightning flashed above him in a strobe of lights. Amidst the flashes, he watched in horror as the canyon walls collapsed inward in a second avalanche. They caved in on each other, burying the first helicopter wreckage, sending clouds of dust that filled the canyon.

# REVELATION

Lee ducked, and then opened his eyes. The new avalanche had filled the canyon with giant boulders and mounds of rock, trapping them inside. The earth shook as giant rocks fell on one another, the rumble echoing in his head as the sound bounced between the remaining standing walls of Ice Box Canyon.

Lee stepped away from the cave. The exit was blocked like a dam. They would have to climb an avalanche wall of stone rubble made of huge boulders, a pile several hundred feet high.

The wind stopped. The lightning above him flashed, but there was no thunder. It gave him a strange, ominous feeling.

He waited.

Then there was the faint yellow glow. It came from beyond the dam of boulders of the avalanche.

His heart missed a beat when the eyes appeared. The dragon was not dead. The head lifted, looking bigger than before. Its giant claws tore into the top of the rock dam, grabbing the stones like a hawk perched on a large limb. Its wings spread covering the canyon from wall to wall. Fire seethed through his scales, this time raging like hell burned inside him.

Lee stood.

This was it.

His fists were empty.

He rushed toward the fountain, but the dragon launched fire at the slope before him, blocking Lee's path. He stopped at the top of the slope. He could not get to the water.

The dragon went at Lee, spewing its fire from its gaping jaws.

Lee backed up and moved away from the cave. If the dragon got him, maybe there was a chance it would miss his friends.

Then perhaps Nate and Susan would be rescued.

The heat from the fire was extreme, hotter than the burning buildings he had trained in as a fireman. He thought of Joan and Jenn. He would stand strong-

The dragon was now at the jet wreckage, crunching the scraps of metal with its large claws. It stopped its fire, keeping its face away from the water that somehow blinded him.

Lee was trapped. The back of Ice Box Canyon was behind him, a circular eroded wall of stone made in the distant past. His chest heaved. The dragon reached the slope, the stench of death hitting Lee's nostrils like a corpse.

The dragon's head leaned in close, its eyes fiery with hate, its nostrils opening and closing with rage, its lips curled like a cobra, its fangs white like a lion.

"You are no saint," the dragon said. "You are no hero. I see your soul, and it has not the light of the Holy One."

The sulfur made it hard to breathe. "Why don't you just kill me?"

The dragon waited, its head unmoving. Its raging hatred penetrated its blood-red scales.

Lee clenched his fists. "Well!"

"Why does the Almighty favor you? You are not written in the Book of Life."

Lee didn't like the way that sounded. He stood there, silent.

The dragon cocked his head. "Now, here you are, defenseless, weak. You do not know the power of the spirit. You lean on your own understanding, on the material. You are unable to reach your hope, the water behind me, and yet you know not the source of its power."

# REVELATION

Lee backed up a few steps. He studied the pile of rubble flanking the dragon on the left. He thought he might be able to run to the water, but the dragon was too close, blocking the way.

Tahoe's bark came from the canyon behind the dragon. The dragon's eyes moved in that direction but went back to Lee. "Your friends have no escape. The canyon is blocked. You cannot help them."

A blackness entered Lee. The dragon's eyes sucked hope from him.

No! He could not lose hope. He removed his eyes from the dragon, and he focused on the clouds. Somewhere up there was the answer. Not the water, but up there. He remembered how Susan prayed to Mary, asking for protection. He remembered Susan's Rosary in his pocket. He quietly said, "Mary, I need your prayers."

The dragon smirked. "She cannot help you anymore. Where are the angels? They are absent."

Lee said nothing.

The dragon smirked. "I will thirst on the blood of your family," it said. "Then I'll be back to thirst on you."

Lee stepped forward. "The hell you will!"

Lee didn't see the tail. It whipped around, snapping as it smacked Lee on his left side. The air went out of his lungs and stars swirled in his head as he flew in the air. His body thudded against the stone wall next to the cave. He thought he heard the bark of a dog, but his insides turned to jelly as his ribs shattered. His skull fractured, and he knew he would be dead.

He bounced off the stone and landed face-first onto the canyon floor. He somehow managed to pray for Joan and Jenn as blackness overcame him, and he experienced death.

# CHAPTER 55

Susan leaned into the rock, her hand covering her mouth. After she gave Nate the water, he woke up. But the noise outside captured her attention. She left Nate and watched through the gap.

Lee lay motionless on the stone floor next to the cliff. She prayed he'd move, maybe an arm or a leg. Anything. Did his chest move? Was there blood? The darkness made it impossible to see except for the lightning that flashed, the constant purple lightning.

She wished that her Rosary had protected Lee.

Nate sat up. "What's happening?"

Her heart leaped seeing Nate's silhouette in the dark cave. Her eyes had adjusted. "Shhh. I don't see the dragon."

"Where's the Captain?"

Susan hesitated. "He's out there."

"Where's the monster?"

"Shhh," she said again. She whispered, "I don't know."

Outside, the orange flickered from the burning trees and wreckage. Lee lay unmoving, crumpled on the stone floor near the opposite cliff wall.

Nate shuffled closer. "Let me see?"

Susan whispered, "Hold on." Then she looked back outside.

The monster's yellow demon eye peered back at her.

Susan screamed and fell backward, tripping over Nate's legs. Her shoulders slammed into the cave wall, and she scraped her head until she was on the ground, her focus on the yellow eye peering in at them.

Nate moved to a crouch, his head just under the rock ceiling.

The yellow eye remained, its black pupil focusing on them.

The boulder moved, its surface grinding on the rock walls. Giant clawed fingers pulled the boulder away.

Susan and Nate scooted back, pressing their backs to the wet stone rear of the cave. They brought their legs up to their chests. There wasn't much room.

The boulder rolled away, and the hot scales of the dragon revealed red and orange membranes. Its face was too large, it could not fit through the cave entrance. The dragon glared at them.

Susan's insides grew dark. The dragon's eyes sucked the life out of her. She shut her eyes and said a Hail Mary.

The dragon laughed, a slow maniacal laugh that mocked her words. "You have no power. You are far away from the water, and your friend lies still in the canyon. Your holy object was defenseless to protect him."

"Leave us alone!" Nate shouted.

"I will for a time," the beast said. "Your judgment will come when I return."

The dragon's head retreated from the cave entrance. It picked up the boulder and blocked the cave.

"Is Lee dead?" Nate asked.

"I think so."

Nate dropped his head and hunched over. "We're trapped."

# REVELATION

"Here," Susan said.

"What?"

"Take my hand."

After a few seconds, Nate's warm hands covered Susan's, a warm respite from the cold and fear. She was glad to hold his hand.

"Now what?" he said.

She closed her eyes. "Hail Mary, full of grace, the Lord is with thee…"

Nate didn't speak with her, but he squeezed her hand as she prayed.

Silently, Susan asked for a miracle for Lee.

# CHAPTER 56

There was darkness. Lee saw nothing. He heard nothing. But there was pain. Pain all over: his head, his back, his legs, his neck. He had to be dead, and yet he felt pain. Would he feel pain if he were dead? Is that what happened, people felt pain.

Yet he felt. Even though the pain was excruciating, and he wanted to scream, the fact that he felt meant he had to be alive. Would he be alive much longer?

Something told him, "Yes." Then he heard the dragon's voice, muffled like he was under water.

His leg moved. He thought he heard a crunch. There was a burning sensation in his neck, back, and head. The sharp pain had reduced to a headache.

He opened his eyes. His vision was blurred.

The snow fell. His cheek was pressed against ice.

His left pupil caught a blurry flash of purple.

There was a red fire. It moved.

The voice came from that direction. His vision improved, and the pain lessened. He moved his eyes down. His leg was fractured, but something was happening. A strange heat flourished in his bones. Then, as though an invisible doctor was resetting his leg, it snapped in place. And the skin, broken and bleeding, conformed together. His mouth opened, astonished that his leg was like new except for the holes and bloodstains on his pants.

His vision was clear again, and there was the dragon. It spoke at the cave. Its voice was loud and rumbling.

The entrance was small. The dragon moved the boulder and lunged his head inside, but his head was too big. He could have breathed fire upon Lee's friends in the cave, but he did not. After his words, he returned the stone to its place.

The dragon's eye slanted toward where Lee lay. Lee lay still, keeping his eyes open, but pretending to be dead.

The dragon huffed. It stepped onto the slope toward the burning wreckage and moved a few steps through the canyon over the flames and embers.

Lee now had no pain. After pretending to be dead, he assumed a cat-like pose.

What to do? If he let his friends out of the cave, the dragon might kill them all. He had to keep them quiet. They probably thought he was dead.

*Does the dragon think I'm dead, too?*

There was no telling.

What he did have, though, was surprise. His leg had healed. His hands and skin had also healed. His headache was gone. Yet, all around him was blood - his blood. How was he still alive?

*It has to be the water!*

When that thought went through him, so did a twinge of weakness..

No, he mouthed. There's something to this. Is this the faith that Susan kept talking about?

The dragon stepped away again. It stretched its wings and raised its head, ready to launch into the sky.

Lee said he was ready. He was going to have faith. *This whole thing's a choice, isn't it? Faith is just a choice!*

He felt strong again. His nausea went away.

That's it. He glanced one last time at the entrance to the cave. His friends would have to stay there for now.

Then there was barking. It came from in front of the dragon, near the avalanche.

Around the bend, Tahoe ran, ears back and teeth bared. Tahoe rushed at the dragon, stopped twenty feet from him, and barked.

The dragon fixated on Tahoe. Its claws stepped toward the dog, positioning for a strike. Lee saw an opening. While the dragon was distracted, if there was ever a moment, it had to be now. Lee sprinted at the dragon.

The dragon took a step forward at Tahoe, lunging with his mouth.

Tahoe moved, but the dragon was too quick. The barking stopped.

The dragon lifted its head and swallowed.

Lee's footsteps splashed in the puddle, and he lept off the slope.

The dragon, in all its heat and power and evil, spread its wings to fly.

It did not see Lee run at it from behind.

# CHAPTER 57

The dragon's tail stiffened. Lee ran past it, noticing the scales and the spikes that ran along the vertebrae. Lee knew it was going to be hot. He had to trust that whoever was helping him, be it God or Mary or Susan's prayers, would protect his body. He had survived the dragon's blow. Somehow he was still alive. The heat would be excruciating. No matter. He had to have faith!

Lee pressed his boot down onto a rock and leaped. He flew through the air, grasping one of the spikes near the base of the tail, and flung himself onto the dragon's backside.

A great chill ran through Lee's body.

A dark, hopeless, depressing cold swelled inside him.

He stumbled on the moving scales.

The dragon shrieked and twisted its neck. Its yellow eyes narrowed. The dragon shifted left and right, working to make Lee fall.

Lee kept climbing, holding onto the cold spikes. The emptiness enveloped him. He expected heat, yet his spirit chilled with cold. It was the kind of emptiness Lee would feel if he came to an emergency call and the victim was already deceased, except a hundred times worse.

Between the dragon's wings was a space on the back. Lee grasped each cold spike and clamored on all fours to the space. The cold, empty scales sent despair into his chest. Lee thought of God, and Mary, and faith. He had to hold on!

The yellow flames inside groaned in agony, weeping and gnashing. The despair was everywhere with the dragon. Touching it sucked the life out of him.

So this is Hell, Lee thought. It was despair in physical form, death, hatred, and everything evil in the world all combined into one monster.

The dragon breathed fire, but the fire did not hit Lee. The wings flapped hard, raking the canyon walls, and rocks and debris fell to the floor.

And he remembered the Rosary in his pocket.

Purple lightning filled the sky. The dragon launched fire. There was heat with the fire, but the body of this creature was cold to the touch.

The tail swung at Lee, but it did not reach him. Lee had found a place where the fire did not reach him.

The dragon screeched. In a single move, it extended its wings and launched into the sky.

Lee's stomach turned at the speed of the liftoff. He imagined the feeling astronauts had as their rocket lifted them off into space.

He held onto the large spike in front of him. The canyon retreated below them. They broke through the ceiling of the storm clouds. Purple lightning flashed all around him. The wind blew into his face and raged in his ears. Lee held on.

## REVELATION

The creature moved like it didn't need the wings. It seemed to know every efficiency of how air operated. He flew through it like a shark through water.

The dragon's scales moved above the skin, leaving small spaces. A few feet in front of him was a missing scale. Was this where his first bottle of water hit him?

Then he noticed a second missing scale, a larger open wound. It had the remnants of a scar as though it had been sliced through.

The membrane where the scales were missing was transparent, and inside it was fire, like lava moving underneath a volcano.

Holding onto a spike, Lee reached forward and put his hand inside the scale. A dark chill seeped into his fingers and up his arm. He had a sudden need to doubt his faith. He would never survive this.

Then the nausea came back. The darkness went into his chest like a plague. It gripped his heart, and his spirit decayed inside him.

"No!" he shouted. "Not today. Today, you're mine!"

The nausea dissipated.

He held.

The dragon darted through the sky.

Mountains and clouds and lightning whizzed past him.

The dragon blew fire as it flew. Some of the heat burned as it went into the air.

How he would survive this, he did not know. But Lee held on. For his family in Vegas, for Juan, for Susan and Nate and Tahoe - hell, he didn't even like dogs - he would hang on. And that's all he could do. As the wind blew his hair and the chilling blackness of the dragon's spirit infected him, Lee held on.

Something protected him.

Lee hung on with everything he had.

# CHAPTER 58

High above the flames and the smoke, high above the storm clouds that rumbled with purple thunder, high in the atmosphere where it seemed they were heading to the stars, the dragon stopped flying. It hovered in mid-air.

The milky way shone brilliantly like a sash across the night sky. The moon was clear, its craters visible as it reflected the sun's light. Together they kept the night from total darkness.

Living in Las Vegas, Lee rarely saw the stars. The city lights had blocked them, replacing them with the artificial glow of luminescent bulbs.

Up here there was no artificial light. Up here, the light was beautiful.

Someone good had created these lights. Someone powerful, someone amazing, someone with a plan.

Someone who loved.

*And it sure as hell wasn't this dragon I'm on!*

How had he let his faith falter? Why did he become lukewarm?

A shudder jolted him to the present. Lee gripped the spike and the scale with his hands while squeezing his thighs around the dragon's back. The chilled blackness kept trying to enter into his soul like a plague. It told him to doubt, to forget God, to hate him. He imagined millions of demonic voices screeching at him.

"No. I will not!" Lee said.

The clouds erupted below them in a web of purple lightning. To the west, an orange glow melted through the black clouds. The orange danced, like the flames of a bonfire. Smoke seeped through the clouds.

The dragon tilted its head, leaned its wings, and darted through the wind toward the burning clouds. Lee squinted, the smokey air burned his eyes. He held on, the wind pressing him, the blackness infecting him.

But he held on.

The dragon spun like a missile, and the flashing clouds rushed at him. They fell faster than gravity, and Lee's stomach was in his throat. His fingers slipped, but by divine providence, they held on.

Inside, the voices infecting him shouted "Doubt. Doubt!"

"No! No! No!" Lee shouted. He had to win, to keep his faith. It was all a matter of will.

They zipped through the clouds, and there was Las Vegas, his home. Fires raged from east to west, and north to south. There was chaos everywhere, cars and people and flames in every direction.

The dragon stopped in flight again. "Do you see that?" he said.

Lee gripped tightly. The sight of the city hurt him. The chilling blackness seemed to wrap around his legs. It wanted to pierce Lee's heart, but he would not let him, so long as he didn't doubt.

REVELATION

But the scene of chaos, of blood, of hurt, of pain tempted him.

"Do you?" the dragon said again.

"Yes."

"These are your people. Look at them, how they relish power and violence when chaos strikes. They see chaos as an opportunity. It's humorous. They are created in the image of God, yet they destroy themselves when left alone."

"You did this," Lee shouted. "You're the one that's evil!"

"Am I?" The dragon smirked. "Look again. They made their choices. My presence exposed what's in their hearts. They do not love God. They love me. Their hearts are awed by me, the fact that spirits like me exist. Many of them want my power. More are willing to join me in eternal fire for a taste of my power, to know what it feels like to rebel against the Almighty. To resist his power is to defeat his power!"

The blackness was inside Lee's chest. His heart beat, like a sacrifice about to be offered to an Aztec god.

"Join me?" the dragon said. "Join me, and I will share my power with you."

The offer tempted Lee. It surrounded his heart like an infection.

His fingers loosened their grip.

"Join me, and we will rule together. Join me and I will make you a king, with my eternal spirit guiding you, causing all people on the earth to fear you. Your family will be revered. Your wealth will be uncountable. Your kingdom will last beyond your life. All you must do is say you will serve me."

The blackness was seeping into Lee. He mouthed "No." But it was weak. His temptation was real. He had wanted power, control, all his life. He would have it.

But at what cost. "No." He mouthed again.

The dragon's pupils narrowed again, showing a slant of desire, a desire to possess.

Lee felt fear. Possess what? Me?

A blackness crept inside Lee, and he let go of the scale. His left hand held onto the spike. Then he knew. The dragon wanted to possess a man, to defile him, to corrupt the image of God within him. The beast wanted to possess him.

Lee's eyes flashed. "Oh, no. The hell you will!"

The dragon's eyes flashed with rage.

Lee remembered Susan's Rosary that was in his pocket. The missing scale, where he had hit it with the water bottle, and the soft membrane behind the wing.

As the dragon raised its wings, Lee, with his right hand, searched in his pocket for the Rosary.

The dragon's sudden movement caused him to slip, but he held onto the spike.

The wind rushed into Lee's face.

He pulled out the Rosary and held it tight.

The Rosary glowed a bright blue, warm light. The light contained a peace about it.

He no longer doubted.

"Jesus, help me!" Lee shouted.

The infection left him in an instant. Lee felt strong again, but the strength was not his own. It came from another source, one he knew was there.

# REVELATION

It was never about Lee's ability to control. This is what Susan had been saying.

Lee needed Faith.

That was the answer.

With the Rosary in his fist, the cross flailing in the wind, and the blue light shining, Lee shouted, "For God!" Then he leaned forward into the wind, and he punched the glowing Rosary through the dragon's membrane behind the wing, and he pressed his arm deep into the dragon's back.

# CHAPTER 59

The explosion burned his spirit like a bright light exposing all his nerves. The Rosary in Lee's hand burned like fire. The dragon's skin and body writhed in immediate agony.

The dragon shot through the sky like a meteor. Wind and fire swirled around Lee as he held onto the spine with his left hand, and pressed his arm into the dragon with his right.

The dragon screamed such a scream, Lee thought his ears would burst. Except the sound was not a normal sound. He heard it inside his soul.

The chilling blackness that tried to enter his body and pierce his heart left him. He held on, but the speed of the flight to God-knew-where caused his thighs to lose their grip. He held on with his hands, the left gripping the spine, the right pressed into the monster.

If he let go, he would fall thousands of feet to his death. He had to hang on.

Lava flowed from the gaping hole, but the light from the Rosary seemed to deflect it. His hand should have melted, but it did not. The scream was full of death, rage, hatred, evil, and revenge. Lee pressed the Rosary further into the flesh.

# REVELATION

And then the dragon changed - into a man, a large man with wings, a beautiful man dressed in a tunic and carrying a sword and two feathery wings.

He was the most beautiful creature Lee had ever seen, but his face was that of a man in complete anguish, in pain, in torture. The large winged man flashed back to the dragon, but like a strobe light, he went to the man, then the dragon, to the man, to the dragon - back and forth, back and forth.

Then a pull sucked Lee's soul from his body. In an instant, everything was quiet and peaceful. He was in a place high up. An incredible light shone in the distance, a light that surrounded a being so large and so great and so wonderful and so loving that Lee had a complete urge to run to it, to be near it.

But Lee was far away.

Surrounding the light were millions of angels who wore tunics and carried swords and held books. On their backs were magnificent feathery wings. These beings were the most powerful beings he had ever seen. They stood in a long row, in front of the great light.

Then there was a gap, a chasm of space, a blackness. On the other side of the chasm were millions more men and women angels, about one-third the number on the other side of the chasm. These angels also carried swords, but their posture was one of boasting and rage. Their wings raised as if on the attack.

One of these stood out, an angel so great and so full of light he outdid all the other angels, his light inferior to the great light in the distance. This great angel stepped forward. His wings and his face twisted.

It terrified Lee.

The angel said, "We will not consent. We will not lower ourselves to a creature!"

A voice came from the distant light. It was loving and kind, yet powerful and just. It was the voice of God. It said, "It is my plan. Man requires saving. They have their free will, as do you. But I will not leave them orphaned. My Son will be born of a woman, and through Him I will save them from their sins."

"Mankind," said the arrogant one. "They are weak. They are mortal. They have no standing next to us." As he said this, the angel changed its form. His head became elongated. His wings became leathery. His back crowed, and his sword forked. His features went from white to red.

The other angels followed. They twisted into hideous beings, creatures with leathery wings and yellow eyes, with clawed feet and fingers. Many became ogres, some snakes, some dragons like the one he rode only a moment ago. They screamed and raged at the great light and at the angels who remained loyal to him.

"We reject your image!" the prideful creature said. "We are immortal, and we will rule in your stead!"

Lee shuddered. The contrast was so great. The light of God was completely holy. The arrogance of the angel of light was completely evil.

He felt sick. "What have we done?" Lee said. "How could we entertain these creatures, and give them an opening?"

At that, a mighty angel stepped forward and faced the brood of demons. He stood tall, his wings wide. He held his sword like a gladiator. His face showed power, but it was the power granted by God. His light reflected that of God, as though the two were one.

# REVELATION

The mighty angel, his chest out, his arms flexed, stepped one foot forward and pointed his sword at the arrogant angel who was the brightest of them all. In a statement firm with truth and courage, the mighty angel said, "Who is like unto God?"

At this, the demons across the chasm raged and held their swords.

The arrogant angel raised his sword, and a mighty yell echoed in eternity as all the beings rushed at each other. A large battle ensued. It was like men charging on a battlefield, except this one was faster, mightier, bloodier, and more ferocious. The creatures in red had tails and claws. They bit and they chewed and they ripped off their wings.

The angels of God sliced and cut, chopping off wings and limbs and legs. Slain angels disappeared, their light shooting up in a blue beam. Slain demons shot down likewise in a beam of red.

Lee looked below, and far underneath him was a small blue ball. "Earth!" he said. He saw red light after red light fall to the small blue planet. Each defeated demon fell to Earth, millions upon millions of them.

Lee brought his eyes back up to the battle.

The angels defeated the demons, except the arrogant one, the angel of light. Lee shuddered at how the angel of light rejected God, who was infinitely more beautiful and powerful than anything he ever imagined.

"Lucifer, you are defeated!" said the mighty angel.

"Michael, you are nothing without God."

"Neither are you," Michael said. He took his sword and thrust it into Lucifer. Shrieking in pain and anger, the demon fell from his place. His fiery red beam fell to Earth. When the beam hit the small planet, there was a shadow of red. It covered the sphere for a moment, and then it was gone.

"And that is what happened," said a woman's voice behind him.

Lee spun. Next to him was a woman, a blue gown around her, and a white veil above her head. She held a set of beads in her hand. Rosary beads. They shined like stars as they hung from her open hand. She was the purest woman Lee ever laid eyes on.

"Who are you?"

"I am the Immaculate Conception. I am Mary, the mother of Jesus."

"I don't understand."

"You've witnessed the first pride, the one that rejected God. One-third if the angels refused to submit to God's plan, that He would be born of a woman to save his people from their sins. They refused to humble themselves. Upon hearing God's plan, the one-third rebelled."

Lee's heart swelled with love. The great light that shone in the distance, he wanted nothing other than to run to it, to be with it. "What should I do?".

"Pray. Follow my Son. He is the way, the truth, and the life. And bring your family to him."

Lee wanted to stay, to ask many questions. But before Lee spoke there was a pull. Lee's soul fell fast to the planet. He saw the comet that was the dragon that flashed between forms. He saw his body hanging, with his arm inside the membrane.

And from the Rosary was a beautiful light, exploding beams through the dragon's body that shot outward in all directions.

# REVELATION

Lee was back in his body. He pressed his arm within the dragon. The dragon flew like a meteor over a mountain, then down. For a brief second dark earth rushed up at Lee. Then there was a crash, an explosion of fire and light and dirt and rock and spirit and flesh and lava.

And Lee's arm unlatched from the dragon. He fell, pulling the Rosary from the serpent's flesh upon the impact.

Lee rolled on the hard desert sand over rocks and pebbles until he fell into a ditch next to a sagebrush bush.

# CHAPTER 60

Lee groaned. He spat dirt from his mouth. Small rocks pressed against his stomach. Dirt scraped his cheek.

One eye was closed.

His body was broken but, as before, it healed quickly. He moved his head. He lied next to a sagebrush, It stuck its pointed branches into his side.

He brought his knee forward, making a move to get up.

He lifted his head. He was in the middle of the desert. Black mountain silhouettes surrounded him, lit by the dim reflection from the moon. The tops of sagebrush dotted the landscape, ebbing and flowing with the mounds and the dunes of the desert.

The storm clouds were not above him. There was only the night sky. A cold night desert wind blew over him.

Lee had no idea where he was.

Then the earth rumbled. A second rumble came. Lee shifted his position, and there was a fire.

The dragon writhed on the ground. Lava and magma poured from its open wounds where the Rosary's light burst through him.

# REVELATION

If any living creature had sustained such injury, it would not have lived.

But the dragon lived. Its wounds closed. Its membranes reconnected. Fire and lava poured from its body but soon stopped as membranes sealed the openings.

The dragon no longer strobed back and forth to the anguished angel. The dragon healed and regained its strength right in front of Lee.

Lee gripped the Rosary beads in his hand. Their light still glowed in the night.

The dragon regained its stature. It stood on all fours, its torn wings healed, leaving jagged scars where it was wounded.

Its eyes went from black to yellow. They glowed.

Then they turned toward Lee, and its pupils raged.

Lee backed up, but there was nowhere to run.

The dragon pressed forward, limping, grinding its teeth and flicking its tongue while flames emitted from its mouth and smoke came from its nostrils.

Lee had no water. He had no help.

Except there was the Rosary.

The dragon opened its mouth and roared, its breath knocking Lee back. Lee rolled until he was helpless on the ground.

He dropped the Rosary. It lay on the ground several feet away.

The dragon took a step forward.

Lee got his legs under him and jumped for the Rosary.

The dragon took two powerful steps.

Lee hugged the Rosary, and in his vulnerability shouted, "Have mercy on me, Lord, a sinner!"

The dragon took two fast steps, its jaws gaping open, its flames seeping from its mouth, its sulfur pouring from its nostrils, its claws puncturing the desert sand.

Lee closed his eyes. It was over. He was done.

A strange white glow came from above.

The dragon noticed it and roared.

Like a shooting star hitting the earth, a giant winged angel crashed into the back of the dragon. His feathered wings spread fifty yards from tip to tip. He wore golden sandals on his pale feet. His curly blond hair crowned a handsome face. His white tunic was wrapped in a golden sash. He held a shield in his left arm. The shield was made of a metal Lee had never seen before. The shield's face showed a scene he had never imagined. Three crosses stood high on a hill beneath a stormy sky. Three men hung from the crosses. The one in the middle was the most bloodied man he had ever witnessed. On his head was a crown of thorns. The thorns stuck into the man's skull.

In the winged man's right hand was a brilliant sword that glinted with the starlight. The blade held an image of a place more beautiful than Lee had ever seen. The place had colors and plants and animals he never imagined. It was so peaceful and so exciting at the same time.

The dragon's jaws snapped at the angel. He shouted, "Michael!" and he spewed fire, but missed.

The man's wings flapped as he lifted his shield.

The dragon swiped at the shield, but its teeth skidded off the metal. Before the dragon could move its head, the winged man swung his sword faster than a lightning bolt, thrusting it into the dragon's spine.

# REVELATION

The dragon flung its head back. The most horrible roar Lee had ever heard turned into a scream.

Lee covered his ears. The sound pierced his soul.

Flames poured from the wound and out of the dragon's mouth. Then other openings poured more flames.

The angel held his sword firm into the torso of the beast.

The beast's wings flapped and it clawed his weak claws at the angel, but swiped air.

Flames engulfed the dragon. Its flesh fell to ashes, its wings blew away with the dust, and it was no more.

The giant angel put its sword back into its sheath.

Lee fell to his knees. The Rosary beads glowed on the sharp desert sand.

The angel stood up and walked to Lee. He bent down and opened his hand.

Lee did not know what to do. He put the Rosary beads into the angel's large hand.

The angel grinned. He lifted the glowing beads, kissed them, and placed them in Lee's hand. The angel put his finger to his lips. "Shhh," he said. Then he smiled and winked.

The angel shot straight up in a beam of blue light like the shooting star he arrived in. He went into the Milky Way. A bright star flashed where the angel disappeared into the starry sky. Then it was gone.

The night sky remained dark blue as the moonlight shone and the stars twinkled.

The Rosary in Lee's hand glowed. It spun in his palm.

The earth spun.

He thought he heard a dog bark.

He leaned forward.

His face hit the sand, and everything went dark.

# CHAPTER 61

Something moist touched Lee's face. It was wet and warm. Then the cold air left a chill on his face.

Lee opened his eyes. He saw sand and sun.

Black paws under gray, black, and brown legs stood inches from his face. He lifted his chin. "Tahoe?"

Tahoe pawed Lee's arm, then licked Lee's face again.

"What are you doing here?"

Tahoe nudged Lee with his nose.

Lee reached up and rubbed Tahoe's head. He tried to understand. They had drunk the fountain water with their bottles, but Tahoe lapped it up from the ground. Somehow, it must have protected the dog, even when it seemed all was lost. "That's right. You drank the water, didn't you?"

Tahoe wagged his tail.

"You know, I was wrong about you."

Tahoe pawed Lee with his foot.

"Where are we?"

The winter wind whipped past Lee's face. He shuddered, and he noticed aches and pains return to his body. He brought his knees up and he knelt on the ground and covered his face. Susan's

Rosary was still in his hand. It no longer glowed but remained in one piece, its beads pink in the morning light.

Lee struggled to understand everything: first the ordeal, and second the miracle. It was all a miracle, the event, the battle, his life.

Everything.

His thoughts raced in circles.

Tahoe barked.

"I know, boy. Let's find a way home." Lee wanted to see Joan and Jenn. He wanted to hold them tight. He had to get home.

Lee stood, his legs wobbly. Black mountains surrounded the desert landscape under the morning sun, and between him and them were sagebrush moistened by the winter rain. Above the mountains were white clouds and a blue sky. The black clouds and the purple lightning were gone.

Above the southern mountains, though, black smoke rose. Vegas. It had to lay fifty or more miles from where he stood. The bright blue sky spread across the horizon. "God? I never prayed before. Not like I should."

Lee paused. No one was near to hear him, except for Tahoe. He fingered the Rosary. The beads rubbed against his fingers. He wished someone was near. No one was around for miles. "I'm not sure how this works. I need to get back. I have to be there for my family. I have to help Nate and Susan get out of that cave. How do I get home?"

A gust of wind blew.

Lee crossed his arms.

He shivered. He had left his coat in the cave with Susan.

He studied the mountains. Off to the right, he noticed a flat stretch of desert. "If there's a road, that's where it is."

He took his first step, his boot crunching the desert sand, and he walked across the winter desert.

Tahoe walked next to Lee. The landscape was barren. To the east, the morning sunlight brought some warmth. Lee welcomed the warm rays of the sun. His moving helped him keep from freezing, but he knew he needed warmth soon, or else he wouldn't make it. Hypothermia can hit in the desert as much as anywhere, he thought. God wouldn't want to have him go through all he did, only to have him die in the desert, would he?

He pressed on, choosing not to doubt. He thought of Susan and her faith. She believed, but she also chose to believe when things didn't make sense. How he had thought poorly of her, and he was sorry he had.

Morning clouds disappeared against the rays of sun. "God," he said. "I need some help here."

Tahoe trotted, his paws working the desert sand like an expert.

Another gust of wind blew, and Lee saw a sagebrush roll in the sand. He thought of doubting, but no, he wouldn't.

Then he heard a crunch. An engine? There was a dirt road to his left. A red truck, headlights on, came in his direction. He was fifty yards from the dirt road. Lee and Tahoe ran to the road as the truck neared, and he waved his arms.

The truck slowed and rolled down the passenger window. A large bearded man in his sixties, wearing jeans, suspenders, a plaid shirt, and a cowboy hat kept one hand on the steering wheel. His other hand held a pistol as a precaution. "You look like you don't belong here."

Lee nodded. "I'm no threat. I'm with the Clark County Fire Department. How far are we from Vegas?"

"Fifty-nine miles as the crow flies in that direction." He pointed over the southern mountain. "Before I ask what in God's name you're doing out here, I take it you need a lift?"

"I'd be grateful."

The cowboy unlocked the door and motioned for Lee to climb in. He held onto the pistol.

"What about the dog?" Lee said.

"There's room in the back seat," the cowboy said. "My name's Lloyd. It's your lucky day. I was just out exploring. What, if you don't mind my asking, were you doing out here all alone, in the desert, in winter, dressed like that?"

Lee pressed his lips. "I don't really know."

"Well, from what I heard on the radio, a lot of strange things went on last night. The city's on fire, which I'm sorry I missed. But there was this comet that came over the mountain. Saw it while I was camping, and had to see what it was. When I got there, there was a crater, but not much else. Some strange holes in the dirt, though. Kind of like T-Rex claws. I did see a man's footprints in the middle of it, though. Strangest thing." Lloyd leaned over and studied Lee's boots. They were covered in dirt and soot. One boot had a hole in it.

Lloyd didn't comment. He drove his truck, and it bounced over the dirt road.

Tahoe turned in the back seat, lay down, and went to sleep.

The sun rose in the east over the mountains.

# REVELATION

Lee watched it rise in the passenger mirror. Sagebrush, rocks, and shadows stretched westward as the day began.

A new day.

The truck bounced on the dirt road.

Lee squinted at the sun in the mirror as they drove past the sagebrush.

# CHAPTER 62

It was Thursday. The day was cool, but the highs would get to a comfortable seventy degrees. Lee carried a notebook in his hand and a pen in his pocket. He walked into the small office building. It was one of the few left standing after the chaos from last week. The county offices were unfit for use, as were forty-five percent of the buildings in the valley. The city had been declared a disaster zone. Yet FEMA personnel and volunteers from cities all over the country came out in droves to assist Las Vegas valley residents.

He walked inside and went down the hall. He passed the sign for Partini and Jones, Attorneys at Law.

Lee opened the door. He bumped a wastebasket next to the door with his foot.

There was an executive desk. Battalion Chief Sawvel sat on the right.

Two other men, one large and heavy, the other small and graying, sat at the table on the left. They did not look happy.

"Captain Tommen?" said the small, graying man.

Sawvel did not get up to greet him. He shifted his eyes to the man, indicating to Lee that Sawvel did not have authority here.

# REVELATION

"Yes."

The man did not get up to shake Lee's hand. Instead, he gestured to have a seat.

Lee took the hint. He put his notebook on the table, pulled a chair, and sat down.

"We reviewed your report-"

"Excuse me," Lee said. "Who are you?"

"I'm Agent Morris with the FBI."

The large heavy man in the middle spoke up. "The name's Lucas. John Lucas, Chief of Staff for the Fulton County Commissioner."

"Go on," Lee said.

"As I was saying," Morris said. "Your report was very detailed."

"Best I knew to do under the circumstances." Lee said.

"But, Captain Tommen, I'm afraid the Federal government does not want you to release this report."

"It's all true."

Morris laughed. "Come on-"

"All of it."

"A dragon-?"

Lucas leaned forward. "If I may?"

Lee leaned back. Sawvel gave him no encouragement. He raised an eyebrow, hinting that Lee had better listen.

"Captain Tommen. There's no doubt that the entire city has experienced a recent traumatic event. Many of our citizens perished, as did several of our first responders-"

"And Air Force personnel," said Morris.

"Please," Lucas said. "Captain Tommen. The city and the nation are trying to get a grip on what happened here. People are suffering. Many lost loved ones."

"I know," Lee said. He was grateful that he had found Joan and Jenn alive, though their neighborhood had several burnt homes. They had offered to put up several of their neighbors in their spare bedrooms, as did others whose homes managed to stay standing.

Volunteer crews rescued Nate and Susan twenty-four hours after Lloyd dropped him off in Vegas. The city was in such chaos Lee had to convince some volunteers to go and rescue them. The trouble was convincing them. If Lee hadn't known about the missing helicopters and fighter jets in Ice Box Canyon, they would not have believed him.

But some did, and the volunteers climbed through the debris, used leverage to move the boulder, and rescue Nate and Susan. They were dehydrated, bruised, and bloodied, but they were alright.

Juan, on the other hand, was gone. Lee had to tell Juan's family and girlfriend what had happened, and the fire department planned funeral services but delayed them because of the local chaos.

"But, Captain Tommen, wouldn't it be dangerous, even insulting, to insist that the cause of all this was some mythological creature?"

"No. That's what happened."

Morris said, "Bull-"

"If I may continue," Lucas said. "No offense, but since the event, scientists around the world are concluding that what happened here was an anomaly, caused by climate change."

Lee leaned forward. "Am I hearing that right?"

"Yes. Dr. Patel with the National Environmental Committee said they were picking up strange weather patterns off the Pacific two days before any of this happened."

Lee leaned back and laughed. "You've got to be kidding me."

"Weather patterns in the Pacific, brought about by magnetic reversals in the earth's atmosphere-"

"Unbelievable!"

"Captain Tommen-"

Lee leaned over to Sawvel. "Can you believe this? Climate change?"

"Captain Tommen, I'm speaking."

Lee ignored Lucas. "Chief, what did you see out there?"

Sawvel paused.

Lucas leaned forward, but Lee held up his hand. "Hey, let him speak."

Sawvel rubbed his face with his hand. "I've been a fireman for over thirty years. I've never seen a catastrophe like I saw last week in all that time. I'm not trained to tell you what caused it. I can tell you I hope to God I never see anything like that again."

"Chief, you saw it."

Lucas interjected. "Captain Tommen. I don't care what you believe. The issue is we can't release that report to the public."

"What do you mean? It's the truth."

"Scientists say otherwise, Captain Tommen."

Lee stood up. "I don't give a flip about what scientists say. I have multiple witnesses and one dead fireman. I'm not going to let their testimony go up in smoke because some scientist wants to promote his agenda."

"It's not just the scientists," Lucas said.

"Then who?"

Morris didn't answer.

"The commissioners? The county?"

Lucas said, "And the Las Vegas Mayor-"

"And the President," Morris said.

"The President?" Lee said.

"That's right."

Lee sat back down in his chair.

"Okay. So you don't like my report. What are you going to do about it?"

Lucas pulled up a briefcase and pulled out a manilla folder. He flipped it open and slid a formal letter across the table to Lee. "We have talking points. We want you to relay these to the press," Lucas said.

Lee rubbed his neck with his hand before grabbing the paper. He noticed a few words right off: climate change, weather, lightning, sparks, wind, mechanical malfunction.

There was no mention of the dragon.

"Can't do it," Lee said.

"Captain Tommen, this has been corroborated among scientists-"

"Doesn't matter. It's not true."

Morris said to Sawvel, "Maybe he got hit in the head."

## REVELATION

Lee said, "I don't care what agency you're with. If you saw what I saw, you'd be crying to your mother right about now."

"Captain!" Lucas said. "I can appreciate your reservation. But the fact is the press wants to talk with you. They want to see this report. It's been all we could do to keep them from getting to Nate and that lady, what's her name, Susan."

"They saw it, too."

"We interviewed them. We know what they said. But we also know they suffered severe trauma up on the mountain, caused by lightning."

"Now you're making stuff up."

"Scientists confirmed multiple lightning strikes in the canyon, and we believe they are suffering from electrocution trauma. It's a wonder they're alive."

"It is a wonder. But what they say is true."

"That Susan is a dingbat," Lucas said.

"You don't know her," Lee said.

"She lost multiple jobs before last week, and was facing financial ruin. Her history is suspect, Captain."

"You don't know her," Lee said again. "Up there, she was the one who knew what was going on. I wish I had listened to her earlier."

"It doesn't matter," Lucas said. "The fact is the county is commanding you to state these points to the press."

"Commanding?" Lee turned to Sawvel.

Sawvel's eyes went down.

"I see," Lee said.

"You need to join us at a press conference in two hours. Learn these lines-"

"And what if I refuse?"

"Excuse me?"

"You heard me."

"Then I'm afraid you will face immediate termination. We'll reveal your acts prior to the storm as insubordination. You disobeyed orders when you entered the canyon. Your work with the County, and in the Country, will be over."

Lee raised his chin. "I see.".

Sawvel didn't look up.

Lee stood up. He grabbed the paper in his hand.

Lucas stood as well. "Great. Now Captain, we're holding a press conference in two hours in front of what's left of the Fulton County Government Building."

Lee crumpled the talking points in his hand and threw them in the wastebasket. "Do what you will. I resign."

"Captain Tommen, may I remind you-"

"You're the one that needs reminding," Lee interrupted. "If you need me, you'll find me at church."

Lee grabbed his notebook and left the room.

# CHAPTER 63

Lee drove through the charred neighborhood, passing frantic and shocked people. One mother ran to hug a teenager, crying and saying how grateful he was alive. Another loaded belongings into the back of his S.U.V. Others scurried to find help since their vehicles had been destroyed by fire, or lightning, or both.

His home stood at the end of the cul-de-sac. The Jones's home next door had been cut in two by a lightning bolt during the storm and badly burned. Cathy Jones carried a pile of shirts out of the front door and loaded them into her car.

In any other circumstance, the authorities would have condemned their home as hazardous and plastered tape out front to keep people out, but there was not enough personnel to handle the destruction throughout the city.

The city and county put all personnel to work to help the citizens of the Las Vegas valley.

Still, Lee resigned, and his superiors accepted it.

Lee pulled into the driveway. The garage door was open, and Joan's car was inside. He walked in, and the sound of the local news report echoed in the kitchen. Tahoe walked up to Lee. "Hey, boy," Lee said.

When Lloyd had brought Lee and Tahoe into Vegas, he drove them both through the damaged neighborhoods until they had found Lee's home. When Lee got out of the truck, he had brought Tahoe with him. Joan and Jenn had been so upset, but they were safe. Also, the dog seemed to make things better. That was it, Lee thought. Tahoe stays. He bent down and patted his head.

Joan was bustling around the home, giving orders. Robert Jones was in the living room on Lee's recliner, half watching the news and half on his cell phone. He was asking someone on the phone about insurance.

"Oh, I'm glad you're home," Joan said. She grabbed a bag of clothes from the hallway. "I put some of the things you never wear in a bag for goodwill. Could you take it there? The news says lots of people are without shelter and enough warm clothing."

Lee nodded. He was glad to see Joan so kind, so helpful to others in need. "I need to let you know something."

From down the hall, Jenn called, "Mom. Can you help? I'm not sure what I should give?"

"Ok!" Joan answered back. She shrugged, keeping her eyes on Lee. "Please give me a sec." She rushed down the hall.

Robert still had the cell phone in his ear. He nodded at Lee and gave a small wave, then he returned to his call.

The TV reporter, a handsome Hispanic male, said, "And, this just in. The Clark County Commissioner's Office has announced they will be giving a press conference in a few moments."

# REVELATION

The other reporter, a pretty blonde, added, "Yes, and they sent us a copy of what they are going to say. They have issued a statement saying the following:

"We grieve with so many who are suffering in Clark County. We want to let all our residents know we are doing everything we can to assist those who need aid, but we ask people to be patient. We're doing the best we can. As for the cause of the storm, scientists around the world have concurred that this was the effect of dramatic climate change. They have determined atmospheric abnormalities brought about a congruence of severe weather patterns. State and Federal officials are recommending multiple policy initiatives to prevent this scenario of destruction from ever happening again."

"Unbelievable," Lee said. He bit his lip, trying not to swear.

There was a knock on the door.

Tahoe barked.

"Lee, would you get that?" Joan said from down the hall.

"Sure." He opened the front door. Nate stood on the porch. "Nate?"

"Hi Captain."

Tahoe walked up to Nate, wagging his tail.

"Hey, boy," Nate said.

"Come in," Lee said.

"I can't. I'm sorry, but my apartment is burned to the ground. I'm leaving, and I wanted to say goodbye."

Tahoe tilted his head, studying Nate.

"Where are you going?" Lee said.

Behind him, Jenn called, "Tahoe?" She hurried down the stairs holding a leash. He hugged Tahoe and put the leash on his harness. "We're going for a walk."

"Be careful!" Joan shouted.

Jenn and Tahoe went out into the subdivision, moving around cars and people.

"St. George," Nate said. "I have some family up there."

Lee said, "So, what are you going to do?"

"I don't know. I'll attend Juan's funeral, whenever they decide to hold it. After that, I don't know if I can go back. They didn't want me to release my report."

"Me, too."

"Climate change?" Nate said.

"Yeah."

"You going back?"

"No. I resigned."

"Resigned?"

"Well, yeah. I won't lie for them."

"Me either."

"Good for you," Lee said. "I'm proud of you."

"Will you go work for a fire department somewhere else?" Nate said.

"Maybe. I'm thinking about starting a ministry."

"Really, Cap'n? What kind?"

"Not sure."

Joan's voice came from down the hall. "Lee, can you come help me?"

"I'd better get going," Lee said.

# REVELATION

Nate stuck out his hand. "Captain, thanks for everything. You taught me more than you'll ever know."

Lee said, "You'll go far, kid. I have a feeling you will."

Nate saluted Lee, then he climbed into his car and drove away.

Several houses away, past loaded up vehicles and neighbors helping neighbors, Jenn was walking Tahoe. She followed the sidewalk and turned left around the corner.

Lee shut the front door and wiped away a tear.

Susan sat in her car in a parking space across from her apartment. Smoke billowed from burned wood and ashes. The whole thing was a pile of black and charred rubble; everything was destroyed. All her belongings, her papers, everything. She didn't have much, but what she had was either in her car or buried under the smoldering apartment rubble.

She remembered Roger, her apartment neighbor who had invited her over to watch the Knights. He was nowhere in sight. Was he okay? He seemed like a nice man.

How things could have been different.

She had liked Juan. She tried not to think about him.

A group of people argued down the street. There were about twenty of them. A woman screamed, and a gunshot went off. Susan ducked as people scattered. Another gunshot, and another. Susan put her car in gear and drove away, fast. There were more gunshots, and she heard one whiz past the roof of her car. She stepped on the gas and turned right.

As she drove, she tried to piece the events together in her mind. She followed I-215 and headed east, going around the stalled cars and charred asphalt. She thought of Arizona. Her gas tank was three-quarters full. "I can make it," she said.

She followed the freeway into Henderson, and then around the bend toward Boulder City. Smoke rose in her rearview mirror as buildings burned throughout the valley. She went around the bend and the mountain blocked her view of the city. Smoke floated across the valley sky.

She focused on the road in front of her, now more open with fewer stalls and charred areas. Arizona was on the other side of the Colorado River. Kingman sounded good, but what about Flagstaff, or the White Mountains? She liked the idea of the mountains, somewhere small, and quiet. She didn't know. She'd decide once she stopped for gas along I-40.

The flames burned around Fury. He would welcome the flames, except that he was tied by the neck, arms, and legs with chains, tied to posts that reflected the holy light of God. The angels, Galamiel and Joran, stood at the entrance.

Fury pulled and tugged at the chains, but they would not break. He screeched and roared, but he would not escape. The holy light burned him. In his anguish, he strobed between his dragon form and his angelic form, back and forth, back and forth. God created him. Now he was punished for having rejected God.

He clawed at the chains.

He ripped at the clamps.

He lunged at the posts.

He breathed fire upon them.

The chains would not break.

# REVELATION

He screamed obscenities at the angels. He clawed himself, leaving gaping wounds that poured lava and fire from his membranes. Then he jerked at the chains, which would not budge.

Joran reached to unsheathe his sword.

Galamiel put his hand on Joran's shoulder. "Let him be."

"But-"

"He's not to see the surface again, unless man turns his face from God."

Joran sheathed his sword.

Fury raged as the flames around him grew hotter, and hotter, and hotter.

THE END

# ACKNOWLEDGEMENTS

There are many to thank for the creation of this novel. The people who helped me most either inspired me to push through when things got tough, or they educated me on techniques and tactics in order to create the finished product.

To those who gave me the fuel of inspiration, I thank first those I have spoken with personally. Fellow authors Carolyn Aspenson, Karen White, Emily Giffin, David Frizzell, Linda Sands, Marsha Roush Cornelius, and Haywood Smith each contributed nuggets of wisdom either in person or through phone calls. With their encouragement, whether it was one word of hope or an hour conversation of strategy, they inspired me to push through.

For those who were not authors, but recognized some ability in me to write, especially Father Matthew and Father Patrick from St. Brendan's Catholic Church in Cumming, GA, I thank them. They set me on a path of study that has been invaluable. Their wisdom about story and human nature raises our spirits in ways that expose us to the deeper meanings of life.

For those authors who have written so much about writing, thank you. I've read about thirty books on the subject, and each of you contributed in some way to my growth. But I want to thank especially James Scott Bell, Robert McKee, Larry Brooks, and Rayne Hall. Yours were the books I referenced the most. This project would not be complete without your advice.

Thanks to technology. I saved a whole lot of pictures on Pinterest that helped me with my ideas over the last two years. I discovered the value of Google Docs so I could revise my work on the go from my phone, Thanks to Canva.com for helping me with my cover. Thanks to the 20Booksto50K Facebook group for all their ideas and support. And thanks to my wife RaDonna for getting me a steering wheel desk to work in the silence of my car at the local park. These things helped tremendously!

And thanks to my Beta Readers: Eric Bruggink, Wayne Boston, Dottie Marlan, and Robert Rosner. Your comments helped me to strive to be a better writer, to know what I was good at, and to know where I needed work. Your time was invaluable to me, and I'll never forget it.

Finally, thank you to my wonderful wife, RaDonna, who has been so supportive of the time I've spent on this book. Your hope drives me forward!

And thank you to God, and his Son Jesus Christ, for sending me divine help when everything seemed so insurmountable. I know you laughed every time I told you my plans. There definitely is a God, and I'm not him!

# ABOUT THE AUTHOR

**Matt Kunz** is all about the adventure. He has climbed mountains, competed for sports championships, ran for office, and helped lead a city. An Eagle Scout and former walk-on football player at the University of Notre Dame, he spent years contributing to his community as a city councilman and non-profit president in the city of Milton, GA. He learned several insights into team building and human nature during his exploits, many of which can be found inside his books. Whether you pick up a fiction or non-fiction book, you'll find yourself pulled inside the stories, joining with a cast of characters as they experience life's lessons through conflict and suspense. So, don't just sit there. Your journey awaits. Come along, and enjoy the adventure!

https://www.subscribepage.com/mattkunzwrites

# OTHER FICTION BOOKS BY MATT KUNZ

LOCH NESS
FIGHTING HANDS

Coming Soon
ONE NIGHT IN NASSAU

For all of Matt Kunz's links, visit:
www.mattkunzwrites.com/linktree

**Follow Matt on Facebook at www.facebook.com/mattkunzauthor**, and **sign up for his email list** using the following link and get a free copy of FIGHTING HANDS:
https://www.subscribepage.com/mattkunzwrites

See all of Matt Kunz's books at
www.mattkunzwrites.com

Made in the USA
Columbia, SC
20 June 2024

37293041R00240